LIGHT
IN THE
DARKNESS

RICHARD E. VALDEZ

iUniverse LLC
Bloomington

LIGHT IN THE DARKNESS

iUniverse books may be ordered through booksellers or by contacting:

iUniverse
1663 Liberty Drive
Bloomington, IN 47403
www.iuniverse.com
1-800-Authors (1-800-288-4677)

ISBN: 978-1-4917-3664-7 (sc)
ISBN: 978-1-4917-3665-4 (e)

Library of Congress Control Number: 2014911452

Printed in the United States of America.

iUniverse rev. date: 8/5/2014

Dedicated to my wife, Dallas, whose unwavering support and encouragement made fulfilling a dream possible.

CONTENTS

PROLOGUE

As the young man, Honaw, sat in his night camp with his people all around him, he could see the beacon of light glowing in the distance. For many nights, they had used the beacon to show them the way north. Honaw did not know what awaited them when they reached the beacon. He only knew that the old man had instructed him to lead his people to the light in the darkness.

The San Juan Basin of northern New Mexico and southern Colorado is a windswept desert that lies in a shallow bowl 125 miles in diameter. It is surrounded by mountains and rivers on all sides. Sandstone mesas rise from the surrounding land covered with saltbush, greasewood, and a variety of cacti and yucca. It is cut by washes that can be torrents after a thunderstorm or dry streambeds when rain is scarce. It has searing heat in the summer and is bitterly cold in the winter.

In the year AD 1055, the basin was inhabited by a people called the Hisatsinom. They were the ancient ancestors of the Hopi, Zuni, Tewa, and other tribes who had lived in the American southwest for thousands of years. They were a highly spiritual and ritualistic people. Their world was filled with symbols and mysticism. Their cultural, political, and economic ideology was born out of, and maintained through, symbolism and ritual. They inhabited the whole of the San Juan Basin, but the center of their world was the mysterious and beautiful city of White House. This is a story of the people of White House.

PART ONE

CHU'A VILLAGE,
AUTUMN AD 1055

CHAPTER 1

❖

THE RABBIT HUNT

The sky above the basin was a hazy blue, and although the day was young, it was already hot. Sweat dripped from Honaw's nose as he squatted in the saltbush that grew along the wash. He hid in the central portion of the basin, called Chu'a Wash. It had been cut by water that came rushing down from the mountains after a thunderstorm. Rainfall in the basin was unpredictable, and droughts were common. The rain that did fall developed from spring and summer thunderstorms that boiled up over the surrounding mountains. These storms began with black mushroom clouds that darkened the sky. Lightning flashed from the clouds, and the rumble of thunder warned of a coming storm. To the people of the basin, these thunderheads were gifts from the gods and evidence that their prayers had been answered. There had been very few thunderstorms this autumn, so the wash was almost dry.

Honaw's legs ached, but he dared not move until he heard the signal. He held a piece of deerskin in one hand and a sharpened stick in the other. He was prepared to spring to his feet and run down the wash, yelling and waving the deerskin. He had waited eagerly for weeks for his grandfather, the Soyala Moiety of the village, to announce that it was time for the hunt.

Not far from him, other children of the village also waited in the brush. They strained to hear the whistle that would signal them to start their dash down the wash. The day before, Honaw's father and other men of the village had strung a net made from yucca and human hair between two rocks across the wash. Honaw could see dozens of jackrabbits nibbling on the grass between him and the net. The animals were oblivious to the children waiting in the brush. The anticipation was almost more than Honaw could bear.

When will Grandfather give the signal? What is he waiting for? Honaw thought.

Suddenly he heard Grandfather's whistle, and before the sound could fade, there was an explosion of boys and girls leaping from their hiding places and racing down the wash, yelling and waving deerskins and sticks. The confused jackrabbits dodged and weaved but were driven inexorably toward the net. A rabbit darted out in front of Honaw, and he jabbed his stick at it. It was a perfect thrust and struck the rabbit through the neck. He quickly grabbed it and threw it to the top of the embankment. As he moved closer to the net, he repeated this action again and again. The other children around him were doing the same. Many rabbits lay lifeless on the embankment, and many more fled frantically but became entangled in the net. Men of the village clubbed them as they thrashed about.

Before the children reached the net, women of the village were already gathering, gutting, and skinning their prey. Later they would cook the meat over hot ash. Some of the meat would be eaten at a feast to celebrate a successful hunt; most of it would be dried for later use.

As Honaw reached the net, his grandfather proudly smiled and said, "It has been a good hunt!"

The people of the basin had been hunting jackrabbits in this way for centuries. It was just one of countless ways the people stayed connected to their past, which was an integral part of the Hisatsinom ideology. Sitting around campfires and under ramadas, the elders told stories that kept Hisatsinom ancestry alive. They spoke about how, in the beginning, the people roamed the land gathering pine nuts and hunting the deer and the sheep with rounded horns that lived atop the mesas. They said life was hard and the people struggled to survive. Then one day, strange visitors from far to the south came to the basin. They brought with them beans, squash, and corn and taught the people how to plant the seeds. This changed the lives of the people. Although they continued to hunt and gather, their main source of food became corn.

The elders told how clans stopped roaming the land and became farmers growing their crops along the washes of the basin where there was water. Their lives improved, but they had been hunters and gatherers for a long time and did not understand how to grow strong crops; survival remained difficult with starvation a constant threat. The farming was extremely hard work. They learned that everyone needed to work together in the crop fields and share the food that grew. At first, they carried water to their thirsty crop fields in pottery jars. Then they realized the fields needed a better supply of water to prosper. They learned to dam the washes so that they could catch more of the spring runoff and water from the thunderstorms on the mesas. They began to dig canals from the small ponds behind the dams to irrigate their fields.

In this way, the people were able to grow more food, but the planting, cultivating, and harvesting remained strenuous work. It took many hands to sustain a successful crop every year. Soon the clans of the basin began to join together to share the workload. It was then that the first villages appeared along the washes.

The elders always ended these stories with a warning. They said that even now, after all the people had learned, they had to work hard and share. They had to strive to live the right way so that Sun Father would continue to bring the rain to the mesas and snow to the mountains. They said if the people turned away from Sun Father and the ancestors, they would suffer starvation, and many would die.

CHAPTER 2

❖

THE VILLAGE

Honaw and his family were members of the Spider Clan and lived in the great house of Chu'a Village. Honaw was eleven growing seasons old in the autumn of 1055. Small in stature, he showed the effects of being undernourished. He had no body fat, and his ribs protruded slightly through his dark skin. He was often hungry, but he did not see this as a hardship because he had just as much to eat as his sisters and the other children of the village. He had jet-black hair that hung loosely around his shoulders, and he wore a deerskin loincloth and sandals woven from the yucca plant. He lived with his grandfather, Kwahu; his father, Tocho; his mother, Nova; and his two older sisters, Sihu and Kele. Old Kwahu was honored to be the Soyala Moiety of the village, which allowed the family to live in the small eastern wing of the great house, instead of a house in the village like his friends.

During the Time of Soyala, Old Kwahu gathered the children of Chu'a Village around campfires—or in the pit house when it was cold—and told them stories about their ancestors, stories handed down through the generations. He told how a small group of the

Spider Clan had come from somewhere far to the north to settle along the banks of Chu'a Wash and how the Bear Clan came later and joined with the Spider Clan. Together the two clans cultivated the fields, built Chu'a Village, and lived together in peace.

One of the children's favorite stories was about a holy man who visited Chu'a Village long ago. Old Kwahu said this holy man told of a sacred city nestled in a beautiful canyon in the north. The canyon had magnificent gardens filled with colorful flowers and trees. The city had immense great houses built to honor Sun Father and all the ancestor gods. Magical ceremonies celebrating the Time of Soyala and the Time of Niman were held in giant pit houses large enough to hold hundreds of people. The sacred city was called White House.

The story of how White House came to be and the story of how Chu'a Village came to be were similar. The first people who came to White House built their homes along the wash and in places where water ran off the mesa. This land was fertile, and they grew abundant crops. Their crop yield was so great that they found they could store a portion of it for times when the rain was scarce and crops failed. The people who came later had to take land farther from the wash. That land was very dry, and their crop yield was meager. They struggled just to feed their families and were not able to store food for the dry years.

Kwahu told of the time when Sun Father became angry and withheld the rain. For two growing seasons the crops failed. The wealthy landowners of White House had stored enough food to survive the drought, but the poor went hungry, and some died from starvation. The starving people went to the wealthy landowners and asked for a share of the food to sustain them until the rains returned. The wealthy landowners did help them, but for a price. They started to trade food for labor. They gave the people food when they worked in their fields and built the great houses where they lived. Each of the wealthy landowners wanted the biggest and most beautiful great house to show his strong relationship with the gods. The poor people began to believe that because the families of the great houses had such wealth and power, Sun Father had chosen them to rule White House.

The patriarchs of the wealthy families became the first Moieties of White House. The Moieties were the overseers of the crop fields and directed the building of great houses. But most important, the Moieties were the spiritual leaders of White House. They imitated and expanded on rituals passed down from the old ones. Out of these rituals, the ceremonies of Soyala and Niman were born. There were certain days of the year that were extremely important to the balance and order of the lives of the people. The Soyala Ceremony came in midwinter and started on the day Sun Father showed his face for the shortest amount of time. The people believed that during the Time of Soyala, the ancestor gods emerged from the sipapu in the ceremonial pit house and joined in the ceremonies. The Soyala Celebration lasted for sixteen days. It was marked by singing, dancing, and the exchanging of gifts. Old Kwahu performed sacred rituals and recited prayers in the pit house in hopes of bringing Sun Father back to his summer path and establishing life anew for all the world.

The rituals brought the rain for the crops and the deer to the mountains. Above all, they kept the world in balance. Only the Moieties knew how and when to conduct the sacred rituals, so they and their descendants became very powerful.

One Moiety at White House was so favored by the gods that Sun Father appointed him the first Tiyamunyi, the most holy and powerful of all the Moieties. He and his descendants ruled White House and dwelled in the largest, most beautiful of all the great houses.

Working on the great houses eventually became more than a means to barter for food. It became a way for the people to worship the gods. They labored to honor Sun Father and all the ancestor gods.

Over time, the act of building became part of the sacred rituals, and clans from all around came to work on the great houses of White House. White House prospered and grew into a beautiful city with many different clans. These included the clans of the Rabbit, the Eagle, the Young Corn, and many others.

At the Mount of the Dagger of Light that towered high above White House, the Tiyamunyi and his Moieties learned to mark time by watching the movement of the shadow cast by the Great Butte. They climbed the mount to watch the Dagger of Sun Father pierce the rings of the Sacred Circle. By these observations, they marked the sacred times of Soyala and Niman.

The holy man taught the first patriarchs of the Spider Clan and Bear Clan in Chu'a Village about the sacred times of Soyala and Niman. Together they climbed the mesa, and he showed them Tuwa Mountain, which rose southwest of Chu'a Wash. Gods and ancestors of the people lived on the sacred mountain, and the shadows of the mountain marked the times of Soyala and Niman. The holy man taught them the prayers and rituals of Soyala and Niman so that forevermore their crops would grow strong and there would be plenty of rabbits, deer, and sheep for hunting. He taught them that White House was the center of all things and that all the people were spiritually tied to White House. Kwahu said that through the holy man's instruction, his grandfather of three generations past, the first patriarch of the Spider Clan became the first Soyala Moiety, and the first patriarch of the Bear Clan became the first Niman Moiety of Chu'a Village.

Under the guidance of the holy man, the people built Chu'a Village to mirror White House. They built a great house that was smaller and far less grand than the great houses of White House, but the holy man said Sun Father would be pleased.

The great house of Chu'a Village was a one-story, L-shaped structure built around a plaza. It had twenty rooms, but only a few of those rooms were occupied by the Moieties and their families. Most of the rooms were used to store crops and the sacred prayer sticks used by the Moieties during the Soyala and Niman Ceremonies. Other rooms in the complex were used to store the goods to be traded with visitors who sometimes came to the village. Still others were used as guest rooms to accommodate those visitors. There were two rooms set aside to be burial chambers.

In the center of the plaza was the ceremonial pit house where Old Kwahu told his stories. Along the sides of the plaza, sheltered work areas extended out from the ground-floor rooms of the great house. Under these ramadas were large storage bins that held wild grain, seeds, and piñon nuts gathered by the people. Other bins held the life-giving corn, squash, and beans from the last harvest. Some of the crops were to be consumed, and some were saved as seed for the next planting season. These sandstone bins were lined with clay and tightly sealed so that the precious seeds would not germinate before they were ready to be planted. The bins were filled each harvest by the people of the village, who had to pay a tithe to the Moieties who ruled the village. The tithe consisted of a portion of the crops harvested by each family and would be redistributed to the people in times of need.

Moieties were both spiritual and secular leaders of the village. They held authority to rule through their knowledge of rituals and by their social standing. They also acted as arbitrators when disputes arose among the people. They heard both sides of an argument and tried to find a compromise that could be agreed to by all concerned. Sometimes they were able to broker agreements, and other times they ruled in favor of one party or the other. In these cases, their decision was binding and the dispute could not be brought before them again.

Old Kwahu ruled during the Time of Soyala. The people considered his rulings good and fair. He was not power hungry and did not hold with the practice of trading food for labor. He and his family worked in the fields side by side with the people of the village. Over the years, his family contributed more to the communal bins than any family in the village. When there was construction to be done, he did his share and more. He cared only for the people. He was loved and respected by all.

CHAPTER 3

SPIDER GRANDMOTHER

The people were a matriarchal society. The position of Moiety was handed down to the eldest son of the female line. If there was no male or the eldest son was not of age to assume the position, it was filled through a marriage arrangement. Honaw was next in line to become Soyala Moiety of Chu'a Village. It was Old Kwahu's responsibility to teach him the prayers, rituals, and skills he would need to know to assume the role of spiritual leader during the Time of Soyala.

The instruction began on summer evenings when Kwahu and Honaw walked to the top of the mesa. There Kwahu told Honaw stories about the creation of the sky and the earth. He told him how in the beginning there was a great nothingness, only blackness without space or time. Then Sun Father created all the stars of the universe. He created Earth Mother, and so she would not be alone, he reached deep inside her and planted the insect creatures. Sun Father created the mockingbird and instructed him to give the ants, beetles, and all the things that crawled in the First World the laws they were to live by. But the insect creatures did not understand how Sun Father wanted them to live. They began to fight and quarrel among themselves. This angered Sun Father, so he sent Spider Grandmother to show the insect creatures how to live as he wanted.

Spider Grandmother showed the insect creatures the path from inside Earth Mother to a Second World on her surface. When they reached this new world, their bodies began to change and they became the wolves, bears, rabbits, deer, and all the other animals that lived on Earth Mother. But still they did not understand how Sun Father wanted them to live, and they began to fight and kill each other. Again, Sun Father sent Spider Grandmother to them. This time she led the animals to the Third World just below the surface of Earth Mother. In this world some of the animals became men and Spider Grandmother taught them how to live in peace and to worship Sun Father and the ancestor gods.

For a time all was good and Sun Father was pleased, but there were some evil men among the people. These evil ones tempted the people away from the way Sun Father wanted them to live. Some people began to steal, fight, and kill each other. They forgot about their crop fields, about their hunting, and did not worship the gods. A few people refused to follow the evil ones. These people remembered to hunt, to tend their fields, to make prayer sticks, and to live peacefully with each other.

When Sun Father saw what was happening, he became angry with the evil people. For a third time he sent Spider Grandmother to them. She led the good people through a hollow reed that was a passageway to the surface of Earth Mother, and she revealed to them the light and warmth of Sun Father. The people who emerged from the hole are the people of the present world, the Fourth World. The Fourth World is known to the people as the Daylight World.

On another walk to the top of the mesa, Grandfather Kwahu told Honaw how Sun Father lived in the heavens and Earth Mother lived with the people and animals on the surface. He also told him about the underworld and how it was not to be feared. He reminded Honaw about the Creation Story, and how the people believed that the most sacred of all places was the spot where the first people of the Daylight World climbed up the hollow reed to the surface of Earth Mother. All people emerged from the underworld and would return to the underworld when they died. He told him how the dead needed to be respected, revered, and never forgotten, because they had joined the world of the ancestor gods. Sun Father controlled the heavens, Earth Mother controlled the earth, and the ancestor gods controlled the underworld. But just as the people had obligations to help each other and share with each other, the gods were also required to help and share with the people. That was why, even though the ancestors were gone from sight, they were still part of the family.

He spoke of the importance of thinking and acting in the right way to maintain balance in all things of the universe. Thinking and acting incorrectly would disrupt the balance of the universe and displease the gods. The right way included joyfully sharing in the work of planting and harvesting, and helping with the building of houses so that everyone would be warm in the winter. Sharing food with the hungry was one of the most important aspects of living the right way. If the people practiced thinking and acting in the right way and maintained the balance, the gods would provide them with all they would need to live. Most important, the gods would provide the rain that watered the corn, squash, and beans so that they would grow strong. If the people did not think and act in the right way, the balance would be disrupted and the gods would punish them by stopping the rain from falling. Hunger and illness would then come and many would die.

When the sun began to set, Kwahu and Honaw would start back down the mesa and Kwahu would always finish with the same instructions.

"Remember the words I have spoken, Honaw, so that one day when you become Moiety, you can repeat them and the people will know the way Sun Father wants them to live."

Honaw loved his grandfather very much and cherished his time with him. He vowed to himself to learn the lessons well, so that one day he could lead his people the way his grandfather did, with fairness and kindness. He would teach them how to live the right way and keep all things in balance.

A man named Istaga was the patriarch of the Bear Clan and the Niman Moiety in Chu'a Village. He and his son lived in the great house in the large rooms on the western side of the plaza. He ruled the village during the harvest. He was responsible for planning and organizing the ceremonies that honored the gods of fertility and rain. Only the Moieties knew the exact time to hold the sacred ceremonies and only they possessed the prayer sticks needed to perform the rituals. During the Time of Niman, Istaga was the most powerful man in the village.

Since he was a small boy Istaga listened to the stories of White House. He imagined what it looked like with its beautiful gardens and immense great houses. He dreamed of becoming not just a Moiety, but a Tiyamunyi, who would rule the village throughout the year.

When he became the Niman Moiety, he tried to emulate the Tiyamunyi he had heard about in the old stories. He wore beautiful robes and aprons made from magnificent bird feathers brought up from the cities in the south. His robes and aprons were inlaid with the precious bluish-green stones that shone brightly in the sun. He strutted through the village and fields barking orders at the people. He considered himself to be royalty and the people mere peasants.

He knew the Tiyamunyi of the White House did not work the fields, and being an important Moiety, he also refused to work the fields, nor did his son. He felt that sort of labor was beneath their station in life. He felt no obligation to contribute to the food bins. All the crops from his fields were stored in his bins, and no other. He had his own gatherers and hunters. He and his son wanted for nothing. He relished the feeling of power, and he hated relinquishing it to Kwahu, the Soyala Moiety, during the winter. He believed the Niman Moiety was much more important than the Soyala Moiety. After all, his skill brought the rain. Without the rain, the village would surely perish; crops would fail, there will be no nuts or seeds to gather, and game would disappear.

Istaga was biased in his arbitrations. He ruled in favor of people he liked or when he stood to make a profit. He often ruled in favor of a person in exchange for his support when decisions were made at council. Some of the people held him in high regard and others mistrusted him, but no one could deny his power.

He really wanted to eliminate the Soyala Moiety. He yearned to be a Tiyamunyi and rule throughout the whole year. There had never been a Tiyamunyi in Chu'a Village, but because of his inflated image of himself, he believed he could be the first. Kwahu and Honaw stood in his way.

Istaga had one son, Chuchip, who was in line to become the next Niman Moiety. He was sixteen growing seasons old. He was a stocky young man with natural strength. Chuchip's mother died giving birth to him, and Istaga had very little to do with him as a boy. The servants in his father's house raised him. The servants spoiled him and at a very early age, he learned to use intimidation to get his way. With no guidance, he grew into a lazy, self-centered young man. Being the son of a Moiety, he did not gather pine nuts, work in the fields, or labor with construction. Not surprisingly, the other young men of the village disliked him because of his arrogance.

He had approached some of the young women of the village, but they either ignored him or were afraid of him. They saw him as a braggart and a bully. When he came of age, Istaga attempted to instruct him in the rituals and prayers performed during the Time of Niman, but Chuchip found many reasons to avoid the lessons. Istaga sensed his son was an unhappy, angry young man but did not care to help him.

When Honaw was not up on the mesa with his grandfather, he spent his days working the crop fields. He labored at the never-ending job of weeding, or dug irrigation canals from the pond at the dam to the fields. The days were long and the work was hard, but he remembered what Kwahu told him about the right way. He never complained and he always tried to maintain the balance. He did not want to be the one to cause the gods to stop the rain from coming. Besides, he was not alone in his work. Almost the whole village toiled in the crop fields.

There was one job that Honaw truly enjoyed. He loved protecting the field from the black ravens that came to steal the corn. Late in the day after the fields had been weeded and the canals maintained, he and the other boys would gather stones and pile them under the juniper trees next to the field. They had learned to make slings using pieces of deerskin securely tied to thongs made from deer sinew. They would sit in the shade and wait for the ravens to settle in the field to eat the corn. Then they would load their slings and fling stones at the birds. Some of the birds they were able to kill and others they would chase away. It was great fun, and they devised a game with a reward going to the boy who killed the most birds each day.

The next day the best raven killer would sit in the shade of the trees and watch all the other boys gather stones and place them in a pile in front of him. He would scrutinize each stone and if it did not meet his standards, he would toss it aside and command the boy that brought it to find another that was more suitable. The boys would always complete the pile of stones for the previous day's best hunter before they started their own piles. It was an honor to be the best raven killer and Honaw proved to be a good shot with his sling. He won the honor many times, but when he did not, he dutifully gathered stones for that day's best hunter. He never complained when one of his stones was rejected. In this way the boys of the village honed their skills for the time when they would work together to hunt more than ravens.

CHAPTER 4

THE MOUNTAINS

Grandfather Kwahu enjoyed living with his daughter and her family, but the rooms were small and cramped. Kwahu could see that the family needed more room, and one night at the evening meal, he announced that they would add new rooms to the great house, large rooms that would provide space for a growing family.

Early that winter in 1055, before the cold winds blew from the northwest, Kwahu began the plans to build the new rooms for Nova and her family. Everyone helped in building one another's houses and in building the great house. The people were used to working together. It was important to do so in order to maintain the balance of the village.

The hauling of the material for the family's rooms was a laborious task. The spruce and pine logs needed to build the rooms had to be brought from the mountains southeast of the village. The three-day trek to the snowcapped peaks was difficult. The days would be hot and dry, and the night air would carry the chill of winter. To prepare for the trip, the men of the work party sharpened their tools and packed their tool kits. The women, including Nova, Kele, and

Sihu packed food and water in yucca baskets. On the return trip, the baskets would be filled with firewood for the cooking fires and pottery kilns. When all was ready, Kwahu started the work party toward the mountains.

At the evening camp, the women prepared piki bread, a mixture of ash and ground corn shaped into patties and fried in fat, served with dried rabbit meat. After the meal, they sat around the fire and the men told stories about hunting deer, or a time when they had seen the great bear. Honaw loved these stories and considered the whole trip a grand adventure. At night, to fend off the cold, everyone wrapped up tightly in blankets made from rabbit fur, turkey feathers, or hides from the mountain sheep.

For many years, the people of the basin had been coming to these mountains to cut logs to be used in building. Therefore, when this building party reached the mountains, they found a substantial stockpile of dried logs ready to be transported. They would take the dried logs because they were lighter and could be more easily carried back to the village. This did not mean that no trees would be felled on this trip. The party would have to replenish the stockpile to maintain the balance.

Kwahu climbed the hillsides, carefully inspecting the trees. Some trees he rejected as being too narrow and not strong enough, others were too crooked to be used. When he found a tree that was acceptable, he would tap it with his hand and Tocho or one of the other men would fell the tree using a stone ax.

Next, they would trim off the branches and throw them into piles. Young Honaw was allowed to participate in this part of the process. Kwahu instructed him in how to grip the ax and how to deliver precise blows so that the branch could be cut safely. Honaw relished the task and eagerly set to work under Kwahu's watchful eye. Later, Nova and the other women picked up the branches and loaded them into the yucca baskets to be transported back to the village.

By the end of the first day, they had cut and trimmed ten logs to be used for corner posts. Kwahu assigned twenty men to carry five of the dried logs from the old stockpile back to the village. The large logs were carried down to the village using a method that required a great deal of cooperation. It took four men to haul each log using stout branches as cross-members. Two men would position themselves toward the front of the log and two toward the end. Each two-man team would hold an end of a cross-member shoulder high and the log would be lifted onto it. In this way, the weight of the log was evenly distributed and the men could carry it down to the village.

As the rest of the men waited for them to return, they cut and trimmed the trees needed to replace the dried logs that they would take for the ceiling beams. They also cut the smaller white trees with the yellow leaves that they needed to support the doorway and windows of the new rooms.

Kele, Honaw's eldest sister, was fifteen growing seasons that autumn. She was a proud young woman and carried herself well. She was slender with beautiful black hair that hung almost to her waist. Most of the women of the people cut their hair very short because it was more practical, and because human hair was often used in weaving and making rope. Kele shunned this practice. She was proud of her hair. But everyone agreed that her most striking features were her violet eyes, which seemed to sparkle when she laughed. She had always been a happy girl and was considered to be helpful and a hard worker.

One afternoon in the mountains as Tocho was felling a tree and Nova and Kele were gathering branches, Tocho noticed that his firstborn had grown into a strong young woman.

"Kele is no longer a child. It is time for her to take a husband. She is strong and will make a good wife and mother," he said in surprise.

"It is about time you noticed, my husband. There are many young men in the village who have already taken notice." Nova laughed.

"Do not mock me, Nova. It is sometimes difficult for a father to see his daughters as other men see them. I am certain that Kwahu felt the same when I first looked at you. You must speak to her and tell her it is time for her to start her own family."

"I did not mean to mock you, my husband. I know it is hard to see her as a full-grown woman, but even though I have seen young men watching her, none have come to offer gifts for her. I am beginning to worry."

"I will bring this up at the next council. She is healthy and will give birth to strong children. I am sure I can arrange to find her a good husband."

Kele and Sihu had been watching the young men of the village for some time, measuring them to see who would make a good husband. Sihu was only twelve growing seasons old and not of age to marry yet, but Kele considered her sister to be her best friend. Sihu was a plain-looking girl, short and rather stocky, with short-cropped hair. Kele laughed with her sister when Sihu playfully chided her, saying, "If you spent as much time finding a husband as you do caring for your hair, you would be married by now." Sihu was a gentle, kindhearted girl.

In their judging of the young men of the village, both the girls agreed that one young man named Lansa was certainly the best prospect for Kele. He was seventeen growing seasons old and lived with his mother in one of the smaller houses in the village. He stood a little less than six feet, which was very tall compared to the other men of the village. He was lean and muscular from working many hours in the fields. He wore his hair in the traditional style of the people, separated into three sections, one on each side of his head, and one in the back. He wound each section into a tight bun tied with a thong. Almost all the men of the village wore their hair in this fashion.

The sisters considered him the most handsome man in the village. They also knew he was the best hunter, but what impressed them the most was his strength. They often talked about the day he walked into the village with a deer draped around his shoulders. They were amazed that he did not strain under the weight. It was then that Kele started thinking seriously about Lansa.

Most men of the village had certain skills that benefited the entire community. Lansa was a flint knapper. He had mastered the difficult skill of shaping arrow points and the stone axes the people used to cut down trees, trim branches, and chop firewood. He learned his skill from his father.

He made the arrow points and ax heads from the hard black stones found on the mesa and in the mountains. These items were very valuable to the people. The visitors who came to trade coveted them and were willing to trade for them with bracelets, necklaces, belts, and other objects made from the beautiful bluish-green stones.

Lansa lost his father in a woodcutting accident during the cold months before the last planting season. His father was using a stone ax he had made himself to trim branches off a tree. He was not careful with a blow to a branch, and the stone ax deflected off the wood and struck his leg below the knee. It was a terrible wound. The flesh was cut so deep that the bone was exposed. His father could not walk and was in great pain.

Kwahu made a poultice from medicine plants and wrapped the leg. He also prayed to Earth Mother to help with the healing. But Earth Mother, as she sometimes does, rejected his prayers. Lansa's father lay on his bed mat and cried out to the gods, asking them why they had forsaken him. Soon the fever came. Then his leg below the wound turned black. Six sunrises from when the accident happened, he passed to the underworld to be with the ancestors. They wrapped his body in a turkey feather blanket and buried it in the sacred mound along with a number of the arrowheads and axes he made. The women of the village sang the death song so that the ancestors would welcome him into the underworld.

Lansa remembered how many times his father had told him to be precise with every blow when cutting wood. *How could he have been so careless?* he wondered in great sorrow.

With his father's death, it became Lansa's responsibility to care for his mother. He loved his mother very much and took good care of her, but he was lonely. He felt it was time to find his woman and start a family.

CHAPTER 5

THE DRESS

Old Kwahu assigned Lansa to the logging crew for the construction project. It was his job to cut down and trim the big logs needed for the corner posts of the new rooms. One afternoon as he was trimming a tree he stopped to watch Kele as she moved to pick up branches. Her movements were graceful and strong. At one point, she caught him staring at her, and she smiled. He was struck by her beauty and the twinkle in her eye. He returned the smile and seriously began to consider her as a partner, but he had no fine gift to offer her mother, Nova. He had a sheepskin blanket and a turkey feather robe, but he did not consider them to be proper gifts for Kele. He had once seen his mother make a fine, white deerskin dress. He thought a dress like that would be a proper gift. He decided to hunt a deer and ask his mother to make another dress so that he would have something beautiful to offer for Kele.

Lansa knew it would take two sunrises for the first group of log bearers to return from Chu'a Village. He decided that now would be a good time to hunt the deer. He went out at sunrise with his bow and quiver. He was not satisfied with the arrows in his quiver. The shafts were strong, but the points had been used during the last deer hunt and they were not as sharp as he wanted. He needed to find the black stones to make new arrow points. He knew the stones could be found in the streams that ran through the mountains, and it did not take him long to find a small stream. There was little water in it because it was early winter and the streams ran shallow this time of year. But that was good, because the bed of the stream was exposed and he was able to find the black stones more easily. As he walked along, he saw many shiny, yellow stones in the streambed. He had examined these stones before and knew that they were too soft to make into arrowheads, but he thought his mother might be able to use them to make the dress more beautiful. He reached down and picked up a number of the yellow stones and put them in his pouch.

Before long, he found three of the black stones that were of the right size to make new arrowheads. He sat next to the stream and pulled his shaping tool from his pouch. The tool was made from a deer antler and had belonged to his father. It felt comfortable in his hand. He had made many arrow points with it. Because his father had taught him well, he knew exactly how to strike the stone so that it would flake off just the right size sliver of stone. If he hit too hard or took too much of the stone, it would be ruined, but he was too skilled for that. When he was finished, he had three perfect arrowheads. He held them up and thanked his father for giving him the skill to do such work. He fitted the new points into the notches at the end of the arrow shafts, and using sinew, he tightly secured them to the shafts.

Lansa had hunted deer many times and knew what signs to look for. He walked downstream looking for tracks left by the deer when they came down to the stream to water. It took him all afternoon to find the spot he was looking for. But he was patient and finally he came upon a small clearing and found the tracks. It looked like a good number of deer were using this spot to water. He followed the tracks away from the stream and found their sleeping place on a small rise covered with brush where updrafts would carry the smell of predators toward them. He knew that the deer would follow the same pattern of feeding, watering at the stream, and settling down on the rise for the night. He looked about and located the perfect spot to set up his ambush. Just downstream from the clearing stood a boulder field.

When he climbed onto the boulders, he found himself looking directly down on the clearing. He crouched down and waited. He was sure that the deer would follow the pattern and arrive at dusk. The deer behaved as he thought they would, and just as the sun was going down, a small herd cautiously walked into the clearing. There were six does and two bucks. One of the bucks was large and had six points on his antlers. The other was young with only four points on his antlers. Lansa decided to take the smaller buck because the larger one would be too big to carry and the meat would be wasted. He notched an arrow and took careful aim. The arrow flew straight and true. It struck the deer just behind the left shoulder and went clean through. It was a perfect kill shot. The buck dropped instantly. The rest of the small herd spooked, jumped the stream, and disappeared into the woods.

Lansa quickly climbed down to where the deer lay. The buck was still alive, but mortally wounded. He took the deer's muzzle in his hands, put his face against the deer's nostrils, and inhaling the deer's last breath, gave thanks for the kill. "Thank you, Sun Father, this day I have breathed in the sacred wind of your life."

It was almost dark by the time he cleaned the deer, so he hung it from a tree to drain and to keep it away from the small night scavengers. He would wait until morning to return to the work party.

The next morning a great excitement ran through the camp. The people stopped their work and watched as Lansa strode into camp with a buck draped about his shoulders. Kele was frying piki bread when Lansa arrived. She marveled at his power and smiled when he looked her way. Lansa, filled with joy, waved and returned her smile. He was anxious to prepare the buckskin into a gift he would be proud to offer Nova.

Many of the women volunteered to skin the deer, but Lansa was adamant. "This hide is special. I will skin the deer myself, but then you can have the meat to cook and to dry. We will all eat well tonight!"

He carefully skinned the buck and released the meat to the women so that they could prepare it to be cooked or dried. Drawing on a tanning technique that had been used by the people for hundreds of years, he started the process of turning the buckskin into a soft hide that his mother could easily work into the beautiful white dress he would present to Nova. He wanted the buckskin to be perfect so he put a great amount of time and effort into his work.

First, he leaned a stout log against a tree and laid the buckskin over the log. Using a bone scraper, he removed the remaining flesh and tallow. He turned the skin over and used the same method to remove the hair and grain. He was careful not to scrape a hole in the delicate skin. Next, he used his stone ax to remove the head cap of the deer and scooped out the brain. He mixed the brain matter with water and boiled it over the fire. He let the mixture cool until it was lukewarm and then mashed it into an oily liquid. He used a stone to buff up the skin and carefully applied the mixture. He gently rubbed it in by hand. Finally, he used a stone thumb scraper to stretch the skin. When he was satisfied with his work, he laid the buckskin on a boulder and covered it with a moist rabbit-skin blanket. He left it to dry overnight.

The next morning he repeated the process. After two applications he had a soft, pliable buckskin that his mother could work with. He did not smoke the skin because he wanted a white buckskin for the dress. He gently folded the buckskin and tied it with thongs so that he could carry it safely to his mother. Again, he thanked the gods and the buck for providing him with a skin that could be made into a proper gift to show Nova that he was serious about asking for Kele.

The men who hauled the first logs down to the village arrived back in camp the next afternoon, and that night everyone went to bed with a full stomach, thanks to Lansa. The next morning they started the trip out of the mountains and back to the village. Lansa and Tocho displayed their strength by just the two of them carrying a log by themselves. Lansa carried the buckskin strapped to his back and the log upon his shoulder. At the end of each day they were tired and their shoulders ached, but neither one complained.

The next morning Tocho and Lansa were the first in line to start the day's journey. Honaw was still too short to carry a log and Kwahu was too old, so they carried the smaller white trees. Honaw, wanting to show his strength, carried six trees. He proudly walked alongside his father, determined not to show the least bit of fatigue. But his mother noticed that he did not want to sit around the fire at night and listen to stories. By the time the stories began, he was wrapped up in his blanket, sleeping soundly. Kele, Sihu, and the other women also carried the smaller white trees, baskets of firewood, and the supplies they needed for the return trip. It took them three sunrises to reach the village.

As soon as Lansa returned, he brought the white deer hide to his mother and asked her about making a dress from it. "This will make a beautiful dress, my son. The hide is soft. It will be easy to work with. But why do you want such a dress?"

"Mother, it is time I take a wife. I have been watching Kele, daughter of Tocho and Nova. I intend to offer the dress for her. Do you think it will make a proper offering?"

Lansa was surprised to see tears start to well up in his mother's eyes. He thought she would be happy for him. "Mother, you are not pleased about this news?"

"I agree that it is time for you take a wife, and I do not want to stand in your way," replied his mother.

"What is it, then?"

"I am a selfish old woman. With your father gone to live with the ancestors, I have depended on you to bring me the deer meat I will need for the winter and the firewood for my pottery kiln. I am afraid that when you marry, you will have other responsibilities and I will be left to fend for myself. I am ashamed to tell you this. I am just a selfish old woman!" She started to cry.

Lansa wrapped his arms around his sobbing mother and held her close. "You never have to worry about such things, Mother. I will always be here to take care of you. You are my first love, and I could never see you suffer."

With that, she looked up at Lansa and smiled. "You have always been a good son. A mother could not ask for more. I am proud of you."

"Then you will make the dress?"

"I will make the most beautiful dress. It will be a fine offering for Kele!"

Lansa then reached into his pouch and pulled out the yellow stones he had found in the streambed. "I found these soft yellow stones in the mountains. They are not any good for making arrowheads, but I thought you could use them to make the dress more beautiful."

"I know just what to do with them," his mother answered.

CHAPTER 6

THE KILLING

Chu'a Village buzzed with excitement when the lumbering party returned. Kwahu quickly set about organizing another work party to bring the sandstone down from the mesa. He also set about organizing the women to mix mud from the wash with grass to make the mortar that would hold the sandstone walls in place. Finally, he assigned most of the men of the village to go on a deer hunt so that the village would have meat for the winter.

Being the best hunter, Lansa always led the deer hunting party, but this time, he asked Kwahu if he could stay in the village and help with the building of the new rooms. He attempted to explain his thinking by saying Tocho needed his strength to carry the sandstone and secure the walls. Lansa knew that Tocho, Honaw, and the girls could manage the construction, but he longed to be close to Kele and work with her family. He could tell by the way Old Kwahu smiled at him that he had seen through his ruse, but the old man was kind and gave his consent for him to stay and help with the construction.

It took two sunrises for the men of the village to bring down enough sandstone from the mesa to build the walls. When this task was completed, most of the men packed their supplies, made sure their arrows were sharp, and prepared for the deer hunt. Lansa helped with the arrowheads and gave counsel on where to find the deer and how to hunt them.

Finally, when the hunting party left the village, construction on the new rooms began. First, Tocho and Lansa dug holes to set the corner posts and stones were used to shim the posts securely in place. The stones for the rooms were carefully shaped by Tocho into tabular blocks that were fitted together to construct the walls. The stones were held together with mortar made from the mixture of clay mud and grass. Lansa and Honaw brought the stones to Tocho, while Kele and Sihu mixed and carried the mortar from the creek. Tocho carefully laid the stones, and then the rest of the family chinked the gaps using the mud. Finally, the logs for the ceiling beams were lashed together using thongs and set in place across the top. Again, gaps were filled using the same mortar that sealed the walls. A hole was left in the ceiling for smoke from the hearth to escape.

Lansa and Kele worked side by side and chatted happily while they labored. Everyone was excited about the new rooms, but they also knew there was another reason to be excited. The family was sure that when the rooms were completed, Lansa would offer Nova a gift and ask for Kele.

While Lansa was working with Kele and her family on the new rooms, his mother was working diligently on the white buckskin dress. One morning as Lansa was about to leave for another day's work, he said, "Mother, today we finish the roof on the new rooms, and it will be time for me to present Nova with the white dress."

"Then it is a good thing I finished it last night," she replied with a smile. With that, she brought out a soft bundle of rabbit fur tied with deer sinew. She untied the bundle and pulled forth the beautiful white dress. Lansa smiled when he saw it. It had a wide collar and was perfectly cross-stitched up the sides. The collar, sleeves, and hemlines were tasseled, and hanging from the tassels were small, yellow disks that made the dress shimmer like the yellow mountain trees on an autumn day.

"Mother, you should be proud of the work you have done! I have never seen a more beautiful dress. I see you found a use for the soft yellow stones I found in the creek bed."

"Yes, my son. I am proud. There is not another dress like it in the village. Is it good enough to offer to Nova for Kele?"

"Dear Mother, I cannot imagine anything better. It is a fine dress, and I will be proud to offer it to Nova. She will be pleased, and Kele will be my wife. I don't know how to thank you."

"The look in your eyes and the love in your heart are thanks enough for me," she replied.

"I will bring it to Nova tonight so that we can make the announcement of our wedding at the Soyala Ceremony. These are joyous times, Mother!"

To the people, the right way to live required a balance in all things, physically and spiritually. They believed there needed to be an order to their lives so that their universe would remain in balance. Sun Father and Earth Mother gave them that balance. The balance of their lives was maintained by observing the cycles of Sun Father. These cycles gave them day and night and told Earth Mother when to change the seasons of the year.

For generations, Moieties of Chu'a Village climbed the west mesa and observed the movement of Sun Father across the sky. They marked the passage of time by watching the shadow cast by Tuwa Mountain, the place where the gods of the southern sky lived. By tracking the shadow, they were able to determine when it was time to begin the

Soyala and Niman Ceremonies. Through the long centuries, this knowledge was passed down by the Moieties, and now it was time for Kwahu and Istaga to climb the mesa and determine the sacred day to start the Soyala Ceremonies.

The two Moieties started their climb up the mesa before sunrise. They needed to be atop the mesa at sunrise to observe the first rays of Sun Father stretch across the land. The sky was clear and they could see a great distance from the top of the mesa. They needed to stay atop the mesa all day and not come down until the last of Sun Father's rays disappeared in the western sky. They knew how the shadow of Tuwa Mountain would fall across the land, and that would tell them if the Time of Soyala had arrived.

Toward the top of the mesa the path narrowed and followed along an edge of a precipice. As they walked along, Istaga looked down into the precipice and thought, *If a person were to fall from this edge, it would be a long way down and the ground below is rocky.* He spoke aloud, "Watch where you step, Kwahu. It is a long way down from here."

"I appreciate your concern, Istaga, but you know I have made this climb many times. I know this path as well as you," Kwahu replied.

They spent the day atop the mesa. They laid out their prayer sticks and watched the shadow of Tuwa Mountain move across Earth Mother. They recited the holy prayers, thanking Sun Father and Earth Mother for the blessing they had bestowed upon the village during the past year, and asked them to smile on them in the coming year.

But Istaga's mind was not focused on his prayers. He kept thinking about how the people loved this old man and how he would never be able to take his rightful place as Tiyamunyi as long as Kwahu was alive. This thought angered him. He knew how to mark the shadows of Sun Father across the earth and he knew the prayers to be recited during the Soyala Ceremony as well as Kwahu. He felt Kwahu was an old man who had outlived his usefulness.

He was convinced that the only way the village would prosper was to have a Tiyamunyi with a keen mind and a strong hand. He felt because his lineage could be traced back to one of the first families of Chu'a Village, it was his right to be Tiyamunyi. He did not even consider how these thoughts were not the right way and how they could disrupt the balance of the village. The idea of one spiritual leader was in itself a disturbance to the balance of the village. The word "Moiety" means a separation, thus a Niman Moiety and a Soyala Moiety were necessary to keep the village in balance. The balance of the village was not what was on Istaga's mind on this cold day. He was already lost in his lust for power.

At dusk Kwahu and Istaga gathered their prayer sticks and prepared for the return trip down the mesa. Istaga said, "Kwahu, darkness comes quickly this time of year and you know the trail better than I. Would you mind leading the way back down?"

"I don't mind leading the way, but I doubt that I know the way better than you. You have been up here as many times as I have and made the trip in the dim light."

"My eyes are not what they used to be and I would feel safer following close behind you," Istaga insisted.

"As you wish," replied Kwahu.

Istaga did follow very close behind Kwahu, and when they reached the edge of the precipice, the only thing he could think of was how the change to the Time of Soyala would force him to relinquish his authority to this pathetic old man for half the year. Anger boiled up inside him and burned his soul. Blind with rage he suddenly kicked Kwahu's foot from beneath him and gave him a hard shove at the same time. Kwahu tried to right himself, but he lost his balance and fell headfirst off the cliff, landing hard on the rocks below.

Istaga peered down the cliff and saw Kwahu lying motionless on the rocks below. His head and neck were twisted at a strange angle, and Istaga thought Kwahu must be dead, but he needed to know for sure. He quickly ran down the path and came to a point where he could work his way down to where Kwahu lay battered on the rocks. When he reached Kwahu, he put his face up to the old man's mouth and was surprised to see that he was still breathing. He cursed the strength of the old man. He doubted that Kwahu would live much longer, but he was afraid that once it got completely dark, the people of the village would become worried and come up to look for them.

What if Kwahu could be revived enough to tell the people what I have done? He could not wait. He picked up a rock and struck Kwahu's head until he was sure that his skull was crushed and he was dead. He then took the rock covered in blood and buried it.

He returned to the path, and as he walked the rest of the way to the village, he formulated the next step of his plan to become the all-powerful Tiyamunyi of Chu'a Village. He knew Honaw was not of age to become the Soyala Moiety and there was no one to step into the position. If he could only arrange a marriage between Chuchip and Nova's oldest daughter Kele, Chuchip could then become the Soyala Moiety. He also knew Chuchip did not have the wisdom to be a Moiety and could be easily manipulated. Chuchip would have the title, but hold no real power. All the power would be in his hands. He was not yet Tiyamunyi, but it would be a good first step. Istaga could see that his dream was within his reach.

When he reached the village, he began to wail and moan very loudly so that the people would come to see what had happened. He stood in the plaza and called to the people, "Come, people, hear me! Something terrible has happened!" The villagers gathered quickly around him.

When Nova saw that Istaga was alone she ran to him. With her face veiled in fear, she screamed, "Where is Kwahu? Where is my father?"

"I am sorry, sweet Nova, but your father tripped on a stone and fell from the cliff at the top of the mesa. I fear that he is dead."

Nova fell to her knees and began to cry. She sang the death song through her tears. Kele and Sihu knelt beside their mother and cried with her. Honaw suddenly broke from the gathering and ran for the mesa. He did not want the village to see him cry. "Where are you going, Honaw?" Tocho called after him, but Honaw just kept running.

Lansa had been watching the awful scene, and he wanted to run to Kele and hold her, but he knew that it was not his place. Tocho was still calling to Honaw to come back. Lansa knew the pain that Honaw was feeling and softly said, "Let him go, Tocho. He will return when he is ready."

Then Lansa spoke to the crowd, "Do not sing the death song yet. Maybe he is only injured." Turning to Istaga he asked, "Are you sure he is dead?"

This caught Istaga by surprise. "I looked down from the cliff and did not see any movement. It is a long way down to the bottom of the cliff," he timidly answered.

"You did not go down and look for any sign of life from him?"

"I was too shaken and filled with sorrow. I did not think to go down to where he lay in the rocks. I came straight here to tell everyone what had happened."

"Then he still may be alive! Quick, bring us torches! Tocho, let us go to him! Istaga, show us where he fell!" he commanded.

With torches lighting the way, they ran back up the path. When they reached the place where the path followed the edge of the cliff, Istaga stopped and pointed down into the precipice. "This is where he fell. He lies down there on the rocks."

Holding the torches out over the edge of the cliff they peered down into the blackness. It was too dark to see anything at the bottom.

Istaga said, "It is too dark to see where he lies. I am sorry to say that I am sure he is with the ancestors. We should come back in the morning. It is dangerous up here in the dark."

"You give up too easily, Istaga!" Lansa argued. "I have hunted many times up here on this mesa. I know it well. Give me your torch, Tocho. I know a way down."

Istaga hesitated, "My eyes are weak in the darkness," he said. "I will wait for you here."

"What are you saying, Istaga?" Lansa snapped. "Quit acting like an old woman and show us where he lies!"

Lansa soon found the way down, and they worked their way over to where Kwahu laid broken and bloody on the rocks. Lansa put his face up to Kwahu's mouth and hoped he would still feel a faint breath, but when he felt Kwahu's lips against his face, they were already cold. There was no sign of life. He gently lifted the old man and said, "He has gone to live with ancestors. Let us bring him back to the village and place him in the burial chamber with the care and honor he deserves."

For the next few days, the sky over the basin darkened and a soft rain fell. It was as though Sun Father himself wept over the loss of Kwahu. Honaw returned but did not utter a word and would not eat. Tocho and Lansa tried to encourage him to eat, but he would have none of it. Nova and the girls prepared Kwahu's body for burial. They dressed him in a fine white shirt woven from the white fiber plant. The death song was heard throughout the village. Tocho dug a grave in the burial chamber next to Grandmother, and there they placed Kwahu in a sitting position facing north so that he could find his way home. They put a pair of new sandals in his grave so he could walk in comfort to the underworld. They also added his prayer sticks, his bow and quiver of arrows, and broken water jars. He would need these things in his life with the ancestors. Finally, they placed wooden planks over his body and sealed the room forever.

Lansa did not get the chance to go to Nova and offer the dress for Kele. It would not have been proper when the family was in mourning. His plans would have to wait. He could not understand how Kwahu could have fallen from a path that he had walked many times, day and night. He went back up to the spot where Kwahu fell and looked for tracks. His many years of hunting enabled him to read tracks very well. He did not see any stones on the path that Kwahu might have stumbled over. He did see scuff marks going right to the edge of the path, as if Kwahu had been trying to stop himself before he tumbled over the edge. This seemed strange if what Istaga was saying were true. Thinking back to the night Kwahu fell he remembered Istaga's strange reluctance to look for the body. He had never respected Istaga and he did not trust him, but he was powerful. His suspicions and the finding of these marks were not enough to confront him. He decided to keep quiet about what he found, at least for now.

The day after the burial, Istaga called the village together on the plaza. He was dressed in his finest robe and spoke with confidence and authority. "People, we all have suffered a great loss, but the future of the village is in peril. We are very close to the day we must start the Soyala Ceremony and we have no Soyala Moiety to conduct the rituals and recite the prayers. If we are late with the rituals, the gods will be displeased, and we will suffer in the coming year. I am calling a council tonight to discuss the situation and find a solution. Prepare the pit house!"

At dusk the men of the village began to descend the ladder into the pit house. A fire already burned in the hearth of the pit house, and smoke curled up from its opening. As Tocho prepared to descend into the pit house, he paused. He saw that his son had a troubled look in his eye.

"Honaw, I know your heart is heavy because of the loss of your grandfather, but is something else on your mind? I know you as only a father can know a son, and you look like you have something to say."

Honaw spoke clearly with a determination Tocho had never heard from his son. "I do, Father, I am next in line to be the Soyala Moiety. It is my right to attend the council tonight and take my rightful place."

Tocho knew how hard the loss of Kwahu had been on his son and he tried to be gentle. "Son," he answered, "you are right. You are next in line, but I am sorry you are not yet of age to attend a council, and you do not have the wisdom to be a Moiety. Your time will come, but not tonight."

"Grandfather taught me all about how to live the right way and how to instruct the people to keep the balance in the village. It is my right!" Honaw protested.

"Yes, Grandfather was a great Moiety and he taught you well, but he would not want you to take such an important position before you are ready. Have patience, my son."

"But, Father—"

"No, Honaw! The balance of the village has already been disrupted by a terrible tragedy. To make you a Moiety at such a young age would only make it worse. Now go and pray to Grandfather and the other ancestors to grant you the wisdom to understand." With that, Tocho climbed down into the pit house.

Honaw sat under the ramada listening to the foot drums and chants coming from the pit house. "Why did grandfather have to go live with the ancestors?" he said. He dropped his head and began to cry.

PART TWO

THE JOURNEY,
WINTER AD 1056

CHAPTER 7

❖

ISTAGA'S POWER

The only light in the pit house came from the fire in the hearth and a few burning torches. The men sitting on the stone bench that surrounded the inside of the pit house could barely be seen in the shadows. Tocho saw Istaga standing in his usual place, ready to lead the council, but this time he noticed his son, Chuchip, standing by his side. Both of them were dressed in elegant white robes with aprons of beautiful bird feathers. Although Chuchip had attended previous councils, he had never been permitted to stand in such a place of honor. This troubled Tocho.

Istaga led the prayers. "Most beloved ancestors and spirits of the four directions, we beseech you this night to grant us the wisdom to make decisions that will lead our troubled and sorrowful village out of the darkness." With that prayer, the men began the discussion that would determine the future of the village.

Istaga began. "The loss of Kwahu has left the village in grave peril. The balance has been disrupted and must be restored. Without a Soyala Moiety to preside over the ceremony, Sun Father will not return to his summer path. There will be much hardship in the coming year.

The harvest will be meager. We will have no food to last the winter season. I fear many will die. We need a Moiety for the Time of Soyala, and we need him soon. The first day of the Soyala Ceremony has already passed. It may already be too late. What say you?"

"I, Tocho, will speak. My son, Honaw, is next in line for Soyala Moiety, but he is not of age to be placed in such a responsible position."

Istaga quickly interrupted, not allowing Tocho to finish his statement. "I agree," he said. "The next Moiety must be determined through an arrangement of marriage."

Tocho did not trust Istaga. He knew him to be a clever man who always looked for ways to enhance his power. While the council discussed the possibility of an arranged marriage, Tocho watched Istaga, trying to discern what he was thinking. All agreed that a marriage arrangement was the correct course of action. When they reached consensus, Istaga revealed his devious plan.

"I have an arrangement in mind that will correct the problem and bring the village back in balance." He put his arm around Chuchip and announced. "I propose that my son, Chuchip, and Tocho's eldest daughter, Kele, be brought together as husband and wife. Chuchip should then be appointed Soyala Moiety. Kele is the granddaughter of the great Kwahu and daughter of Nova. The line of descent will remain in the Spider Clan, and the balance of the village will be restored. I propose that the marriage be arranged immediately so that Chuchip can preside over the Soyala Ceremony. I have already instructed him in the rituals and prayers."

Now it became dreadfully clear to Tocho why Chuchip stood next to his father dressed in his finest robe. He could also see by the shocked look on Chuchip's face that he had no inkling of his father's plan. When he did finally realize what his father was proposing, he could not hide his bloated ego. He stood tall next to his father, puffed out his chest, and sneered at the council. The thought of this arrogant boy marrying his beloved Kele was repulsive to Tocho. He was desperate to find a way to counter the proposal.

Thinking quickly, he immediately protested. "That is not possible! Kele is already spoken for! She is—"

Istaga again interrupted, not allowing Tocho to continue. "Who has spoken for her?"

From back in the shadows a voice called out, "I have."

"Who is that? Step forward into the light!" Istaga commanded.

Lansa defiantly stepped forward into the light. "It is me, Lansa! I have spoken for her. She is to be my wife!"

Istaga looked at Lansa indignantly. "Who are you to claim this woman?" he growled.

"I am a member of the Bear Clan, and I have made it known that she is to be my wife!" Lansa calmly replied.

"He is right, Istaga. He does have the right, and Nova intends to give Kele to Lansa," Tocho added.

Istaga's face turned red with anger. Tocho sensed his frustration as he fought to regain control of the situation. Then suddenly, the angry frown on Istaga's face turned to a shrewd smile. "Tell me, Lansa, have you offered a gift to Nova to show you are truly interested in Kele?" he asked.

With this question, Tocho knew the battle was lost. Lansa had not yet made the offer to Nova. Without that, he had no right to Kele. However, Lansa stood tall and was resolute in his answer. "I intended to offer a beautiful white deerskin dress for her at the opening of the Soyala Ceremony, but with the death of Kwahu I did not think it proper—"

"None of that matters!" Istaga interrupted. "If you have not made an offer to Nova, you have no claim to her, and you, Tocho, you must think beyond what is good for Kele and think about what is good for the village. Tomorrow Chuchip will offer a pouch full of the precious stones for Kele. That will make a better gift to Nova than a deerskin dress. It will make your family wealthy."

The council agreed that it was a generous offer and the marriage was necessary to restore the balance of the village. The arrangement was approved. Kele would be the wife of Chuchip.

Tocho was crestfallen. How was he going to tell this news to his family? His eldest daughter would be married to a man she did not love. His wife would be forced into an arrangement she did not want, and poor Honaw had lost his chance to be the Soyala Moiety. Tocho believed his main duty in life was to protect his family and to see to their health and happiness. He felt he had failed them.

When Tocho returned from the council, he found Honaw sleeping under the ramada. He covered him with a turkey feather blanket and sat down next to him. All was quiet in the house. He was sure everyone was sleeping. He pulled a blanket around his shoulders. It was a cold night, but he could not bring himself to go inside and face the questions Nova would ask of him. He could not understand how he had brought such pain to his family. First, to lose Kwahu, and then to fail his family was almost more than he could bear. He began to pray to the ancestors, asking their forgiveness for whatever it was he had done and imploring them to give him strength to comfort his family in the difficult time to come. He knew there would be no sleep for him on this night.

As dawn broke the next morning, Nova awoke to find that Tocho had not come to their bed and Honaw was not asleep on his mat. She became worried. Wrapping a blanket around her shoulders, she went outside and found her husband sitting next to her sleeping son.

"What are you doing sitting out here in the cold? Have you been here all night?" she asked.

Tocho slowly lifted his head and looked at her. She could tell by the sadness in his eyes that something was terribly wrong. "What is it, my husband? What is wrong?"

Tocho spoke slowly, his voice cracking, with tears running down his cheeks. "Oh, my sweet Nova, I have failed you. I have failed my whole family."

Nova knelt by his side and pulled his head to her breast. "Tell me, my husband, why do you speak such words? What is wrong?"

"At the council last night, Istaga made an arrangement of marriage that stuck a dagger into my heart. He proposed that Chuchip marry our Kele, so that Chuchip could become the next Soyala Moiety. He said that the village was not in balance since your father's death and we needed a Moiety to preside over the Soyala Ceremony. I tried to argue that Kele was already spoken for, that Lansa had asked for her hand and you had given it, but since Lansa had not yet brought you a gift, the council agreed that he had no claim to her. Chuchip will be bringing a pouch full of the precious stones to you this very morning. He will ask you for her hand."

Nova was stunned. "I will not accept his gift, and I will not allow Kele to marry him!"

"I am sorry, my wife. You must accept the gift. The council agreed to the arrangement. They said it was a very generous offering for Kele and that the village needs a Moiety for the Soyala Ceremony. The first day of the ceremony has already passed. They fear what will happen in the coming year if the prayers are not spoken. They believe this arrangement will restore balance to the village. It is done. Kele will become the wife of Chuchip, and he will be appointed Soyala Moiety. Now you see why I say I failed you and my children."

"Oh, Tocho, what have we done to so offend the gods that they have brought this upon our family? First we lose Father, and now this!" She, too, began to cry.

The decision of the council that night cut Lansa deeply. He had never been outwardly emotional, but when he heard the ruling, he could not hide his pain. He bolted from the pit house and ran to his house with tears of sadness and anger in his eyes. He was ashamed to cry, but his heart ached more than he thought possible. He had lost his Kele before he could even begin to love her. He burst through the door, startling his mother.

"Lansa, what has happened? Why do you weep?" his mother pleaded.

He could not find the words to answer her. He grabbed for his bow and quiver. He was about to leave when he saw the small bundle wrapped with rabbit fur. He picked it up and clutched it to his chest. He thought about Kele and how she would react to what had happened this terrible night. Then filled with pain and rage, he threw the bundle into the hearth.

"Lansa, what are you doing?" his mother screamed, but he was already out the door and running for the mesa.

The morning after the council meeting, Kele stirred from her sleep when she heard her mother and father under the ramada speaking in grave voices. She was standing just inside the doorway listening as her father described the terrible night in the pit house. Bursting into the ramada, she wailed, "I will not marry him! Lansa is to be my husband! I have prayed to the ancestors, and they have answered my prayers. They will surely not let this come to pass!"

Nova reached out, grasped her daughter's hand, and said, "It is done, my child. It is what is best for the village. We must all accept the decision of the council."

"No, no, no, I cannot accept it! What does Lansa have to say of this? I must go to him!"

"He spoke bravely for you at the council," Tocho explained. "But there was nothing he could do. The arrangement was made, and you must follow it."

"I must see Lansa!" She broke from her mother and ran for Lansa's house.

She did not care if the village saw her. She did not care what they thought. She was convinced that her Lansa would make this right. She burst into Lansa's house and found his mother sitting next to the hearth with tears in her eyes.

"Where is Lansa? I must speak with him!" Kele cried.

"He is gone, child," Lansa's mother answered. "Last night he took his bow and quiver and left without saying a word. It was the first time I ever saw him weep. He did not weep even when his father died."

The marriage ceremony of the people was a ritual that normally took a week to complete. It included many gift exchanges between the families, the grinding of corn, and making of piki bread. Then the week would end with a beautiful consummation ceremony in which the women of both families washed the hair of the bride and groom in a single basin. The hair of the bride and groom was then entwined to signify their lifelong union. With their hair still entwined they would walk to the top of the mesa at sunrise to pray to Sun Father. Nova and Tocho had been wed in this joyous way, and they had told their children about it many times, but it was not to be for Kele.

There had been very little joy and beauty in the village since the death of Kwahu. Chuchip had brought the pouch of precious stones to Nova as promised, and she reluctantly received them, but that was where the beautiful, weeklong wedding ceremony ended. Istaga declared that there was no time for the traditional vows because the Soyala Ceremony was upon them. He pronounced Chuchip and Kele husband and wife, and the council immediately appointed Chuchip the new Soyala Moiety.

The Soyala Ceremony was usually a happy celebration of feasting, singing, and dancing, but this time the ceremony was solemn. The men dutifully gathered in the pit house and Chuchip, supported by his father, stumbled through the prayers and rituals. No one sang. No one danced. Clearly the balance of the village had been disrupted. The people prayed to Sun Father and Earth Mother to restore the balance of their world and asked that the coming year be prosperous. They prayed that the crop fields would grow strong and the deer would be plentiful, but many silently feared the coming days.

It was the custom of the people that after a marriage, the husband went to live with his bride's family, but very little of this marriage was according to custom. Istaga announced that Chuchip and Kele would be living in the large rooms next to his in the great house. He insisted that Chuchip live close to him so that he could consult with him and quickly teach him the prayers and rituals he would need to be an effective Moiety. In reality, he wanted Chuchip to live close so that he, and no one else, could influence him.

Istaga was now a very powerful man. His plan had fallen perfectly into place. He told Chuchip that he was proud of him and that now they would rule the village together, but he never had any intention of ruling with his son. To him, Chuchip was but a figurehead, a puppet to be controlled. He alone managed all the surplus food. If individual families ran out in the coming year, they would need to come to him to negotiate for more. He did not yet hold the title of Tiyamunyi, but he held the power.

The council had sanctioned the marriage between Kele and Chuchip, and Kele was duty-bound to consummate the marriage, but from the beginning, she was determined to give Chuchip no pleasure. She would cook his meals and keep his house, but she would not lay with him. She shunned his advances again and again. She laid her sleeping mat at the far end of the spacious room they occupied. It was cold so far away from the hearth, but she would gladly bear the cold to stay away from Chuchip. The more she shunned him, the angrier he became.

Finally, one night as Kele again lay down on her mat on the far side of room, his anger boiled over. "Woman, I am your husband! It is time you perform your duty as a wife! I command you to come to me!" he screamed.

Kele was not shaken by his anger and calmly responded, "I was forced into this marriage by your father. I have no duty to perform. You are now a Moiety. You will have to be happy with that." She turned her face to the wall. Chuchip exploded with anger. Kele heard him race across the room, and she turned to face him. She was going to do her best to fight him off, but Chuchip was too quick and powerful.

"How dare you defy me? You are my wife and you will perform as I command!" With that, he grabbed her hair and roughly dragged her across the room to his bed. He threw her down and lay on her, ripping at her gown. Kele fought him. She kicked at him and scratched his face, but this only made him angrier. He had a menacing look in his eye and he slapped her hard across the face. The blow stunned her, and she almost lost consciousness. It felt as though she was looking through a fog. She could feel him tear her gown from her body, and she knew she was naked, and then there was the pain. She could feel his hot breath against her cheek and feel his weight upon her. She closed her eyes and remembered Lansa smiling at her as he did that day in the mountains. When Chuchip was done, she dragged herself back to her mat and turned her face to the wall.

Honaw was crushed by the decision of the council. All of his life he had been preparing to become the Soyala Moiety, but now he realized it would never happen. Tocho and Nova tried to encourage him. They told him that this was not the end and that his time to be Moiety would still come, but he knew in his heart that it was not to be. The thought of his beautiful sister being married to Chuchip was the worst of it. He had never liked Chuchip and certainly never had any respect for him, but now hatred was building inside him. Kwahu had taught him that to hate someone would surely disrupt the balance of the people, but he could not help himself. He could not see how the balance of his world could be disrupted anymore than it already was. He spent most of his days up on the mesa in the spot where Kwahu had taught him all about the right way.

The rest of the family went through the motions of life, but the joy of life was gone. Sihu sulked around and Honaw could hear her crying in the night. His father worked from sunrise to sunset cutting firewood or hauling large rocks to build up the dam on the wash. Honaw saw they already had plenty of wood and the dam was not in need of repair, but still his father worked until his hands bled and his body ached. It was as if he was punishing himself for failing his family. His mother baked her piki bread, fired her bowls in her kiln, but Honaw could see she no longer enjoyed the work. His family's world had come apart.

One very cold morning as Nova and Sihu were preparing their meal, they heard a soft voice from outside. "Please, Nova, may I enter?"

Nova went to the door and there, standing in the wind, was Lansa's mother. She had a dirty deerskin wrapped around her, and she looked worn and frail. "You may enter. Please come sit next to hearth and warm yourself," Nova replied.

The old woman shuffled to the hearth and stiffly sat down, shivering from the cold. "I am sorry to come to you this way," she said.

"You are always welcome here. Is there something we can help you with?"

"It is my Lansa. He has not returned, and it has been many sunrises. I am afraid something has happened to him. I am too old to climb the mesa and search for him. I do not know where he hunts. I understand that you have no reason to be concerned about Lansa, but I did not know where else to go. I am here to humbly ask for your help," she answered with tears in her eyes and in her voice.

Tocho was sitting on his mat listening to the old woman, and he could hear the fear in her words. He knew that Lansa was an experienced hunter and could survive on the mesa for many sunrises, but the love and concern of this old woman pulled at his heart.

"I know where he hunts. I can find him," he said.

"You and Nova are well respected in the village. Your kindness is well-known. I prayed that you would help find my son. When he ran away, he was so hurt that he could not even speak. I did not find out the reason for his pain until the next morning when Kele came to my door with the news of her marriage arrangement with Chuchip. It is not right that two young people who love each other so much should be kept apart. It is a hard sacrifice for them both. I hope the village appreciates what they have given. I do not know how to thank you for helping me. I need my Lansa home."

"We care very much for Lansa," Nova replied. "I know how much he loves Kele. We would have been proud to give Kele to such a fine man, but it was not to be. Now all of us must learn to live with what has come to pass."

"I will find him and bring him home," Tocho said. The old woman thanked them again and went back out into the cold.

Tocho started preparing for the trip as soon as the morning meal was eaten. "I will need food and water for two sunrises and I will need my sheepskin to fend off the cold. Lansa has hunting camps all along the top of mesa. I hope I can remember exactly where they are."

"Father, I will go also," Honaw said eagerly. "Together we can find Lansa and bring him home."

Tocho flashed an angry look at Honaw. "No, Honaw! You must stay here and bring in the wood and water for your mother. Your duty is here with your mother and sister!" Honaw began to cry and threw himself down on his mat, covering his eyes.

Tocho glanced at Nova and sensed her concern by the look in her eyes. He never spoke to Honaw in such a way. Since the morning Chuchip brought the stones for Kele, strutting about like a puffed-out turkey, Tocho had not been himself. Guilt and anger overwhelmed him. He knew he was hurting his family but could not see beyond the darkness in his heart.

"What of Kele, my husband? Should we tell her you go to look for Lansa?" Nova asked as she packed his pouch.

"Lansa is not her husband!" Tocho snapped. "I do this for that old woman." He slung his pouch over his shoulder and went out the door.

"Return safely, Father!" Sihu cried. But he did not answer. She and her mother watched him as he started up the path to the mesa. Honaw buried his face deeper in his arms.

"Oh, Mother, what is happening to our family?" Sihu asked through tearful sobs.

Nova held her and wiped away her tears. "Have faith in Earth Mother and the ancestors, my child. Pray to them, and they will help us find a way out of these dark days."

Tocho knew he should not start to look for Lansa until he reached the tree line. He knew Lansa would not hunt on the barren rock he now crossed. If he walked at a good pace he could reach the tree line before sunset. As he walked, he scowled, angry at himself for the way he had spoken to his family when he left the village. He knew he had crushed his son's spirit and mistreated Nova. He had not been living the right way since Kele was forced into this ugly marriage. He blamed himself but took his anger out on others. Now he had allowed his anger to cut even his family. He promised himself he would apologize to them as soon as he returned. He had to find a way to rid his heart of the blackness it carried since the morning he had to give his firstborn to Chuchip.

Chuchip is a man with no honor! he thought. *No, not a man, just a mere boy who is bloated up with his own image, as is his father. Neither knows the meaning of honor! How can the people learn to live the right way if the Moieties do not?*

Tocho hated Chuchip and he hated Istaga. But as he looked out across the land from the top of the mesa, he was reminded of Kwahu. He and Honaw had walked up here with Kwahu many times and he remembered the words of the wise old man. "You will never be able to live the right way and find balance in your life if you carry hatred and anger in your heart. That is not the way Sun Father wants his good people to live. All good, honorable men must fight against evil and live the way Sun Father has taught."

Tocho now realized that he had to turn his hatred away and find a way to restore balance to his family, to his village, to his world. He knew he would need the help of Kwahu and all the ancestors to accomplish this task. He was not on this journey just for the old woman. Bringing Lansa home was but the first small step to restoring balance to all things.

He reached the tree line late in the afternoon and quickly found one of Lansa's hunting camps. There was sign of a recent fire in the pit and the bones of rabbits were lying about. He knew Lansa had been there but was now gone. He found the track of his sandal moving north from the camp. He followed it a short distance, but then it disappeared. Lansa was at home in the trees. He would not leave tracks unless he wished to. Tocho was not sure where he would make his next camp, but the forest of scrubby trees continued north. It would be dark soon and the cold of the night would be upon him. He wrapped his sheepskin around his shoulders and kept walking north.

It was just beginning to get dark, and Tocho was thinking he would need to make camp and start fresh in the morning, when he smelled the smoke of a cooking fire. *It must be Lansa,* he thought.

He walked in the direction of the smoke and quickened his pace. He stopped in his tracks when he heard a voice from the shadows. "What do you want here? Go back from where you came. You are not wanted here."

"I recognize your voice, Lansa. Is this the way you greet a friend? Come out of the shadows so I may see you," Tocho answered.

Lansa stepped from behind a tree, but it was almost dark and Tocho could only see his silhouette. "I have no friends! Now go back to the village!"

"Ah, so you do recognize me. You may think you have no friends, but you do have a mother who needs you. I am cold and tired from walking all day. To stand in the dark like this is foolish. Let us go to your camp. I hope you have some warm food," Tocho said in a voice of calm reason.

"Come then," Lansa said, and led the way through the trees.

Soon Tocho could see the light of a cooking fire, and he saw that Lansa had made a lean-to between some trees. He had meat roasting on a spit and strips of meat drying next to the fire. When they stepped into the firelight, Tocho was surprised by the look of Lansa. He no longer had his hair bobbed in the traditional way. It hung loosely around his shoulders. He had a sheepskin cape on that was tied about his waist with a thong. Tocho stood by the fire to warm himself. "I feel a storm will soon be upon us. Do you plan to stay up here all winter?" he asked.

Lansa cut a piece of meat from the sizzling roast and threw it over to Tocho. "I have no reason to go anywhere. I am contented here," he answered tersely.

Tocho bit off a chunk of meat and savored the taste. "I have been walking all day. The only thing I have had to eat is piki bread. This is good!" He continued to warm himself next to the fire. "I remember when I was young. I could walk all day and night and not be bothered. I must be getting old. My bones ache from the walk today."

"Enough of your simple talk, Tocho." Lansa snapped. "Why have you come?"

"I have come to bring you home, Lansa."

"The trees are my home. I have no desire to go back to the village. There is nothing for me there, and I will not live under the foot of Istaga!" Tocho could hear the hatred in his voice.

"You are mistaken, my son. Your mother needs you badly. I saw her this morning. She does not look well. She is frail and her heart aches. She sent me up here to find you. Without you, she has no one to chop her firewood or bring her food. She will pass to the ancestors with no one to care for her," Tocho said.

The tone in Lansa's voice softened, and he said, "Then I ask you as a friend to care for her while she still lives."

"I am sorry, Lansa. I have my own family to care for. She is not my responsibility. The old woman needs her son. She is your responsibility. She is helpless, and it is your duty to take care of her, as she took care of you when you were helpless. There is another reason to return, Lansa. You may not think so, but the village also needs you. Ever since Kwahu died, darkness has hung over the village. The balance of all things has been disturbed. With your return we may be able to restore balance so that the people will not suffer."

Lansa cut another piece of meat and handed it to Tocho. He then cut one for himself. They stood in silence for a few moments and ate their meal. Tocho could see a great sorrow in Lansa's eyes. Staring into the fire, Lansa asked, "And what of Kele?"

"It pains me deeply, but she is married to Chuchip. They live together across the plaza in the rooms next to Istaga. He and Chuchip have made it difficult for Nova to see or speak to her. My wife is tormented by what has happened. She made me close up the doors and windows of the new rooms. We had planned to give the rooms to you and Kele as a wedding present, but now they sit empty," he answered sadly.

Lansa angrily threw what was left of his meal into the fire. "I hate Chuchip and I hate Istaga! How can I return to the village?" he yelled.

"I, too, hated them. I hated them so much that poison had overtaken my heart. I blamed myself for what happened to Kele, so I took my anger out on the people I hold most dear. The poison in my heart made me forget how to live the right way. On the way here I took the path that Honaw and I walked with Old Kwahu and it made me think about what he taught us. If you hold hatred in your heart, your life will never be in balance. Sun Father did not teach us to live this way. We must release the hate in our hearts, go back to the village, and do everything we can to restore balance and remind the people how to live the right way. This is more talking than I have done in many sunrises. I am tired. I need to rest." Tocho lay down next to the fire and was soon asleep.

Lansa lay awake most of the night. He stared up at the stars and thought about all of the things Tocho had said. He understood that his mother needed him, and he remembered that he had promised her he would always be there to take care of her. But he was not sure he could stand seeing Kele married to Chuchip. The thought of it still stabbed his heart and brought tears to his eyes. He also knew that staying here in the trees with hate filling his heart was not living in the right way, but he asked himself if going back to the village would bring balance back to his life. He did not know.

Next morning when Tocho awoke, Lansa was gone. His bow and quiver were also gone. Tocho ate what was left of his piki bread and a few strips of dried venison. He waited until midmorning, hoping Lansa would return, but he did not. Tocho wanted to get back to the village before dark, so he slung his pack over his shoulder and started the trek home. He doubted he had convinced Lansa to come home. If he had, Lansa would be walking with him now. *I have failed again,* he thought sadly.

By late afternoon Tocho reached the village. Sihu had been waiting for him to return, and when she saw him coming, she ran up the path to greet him. "Father, Father, you have returned!" she squealed happily.

"Of course I have returned. You know I cannot stay away from my family for long," he said as he hugged her close and stroked her hair. They walked hand in hand the rest of the way home.

When they reached the plaza, Sihu broke away and went running to their door, yelling, "Mother, Mother, Father has returned!"

Nova stepped out of the doorway and smiled when she saw her husband. Tocho threw his arms around her and held her close. "My sweet Nova, I am sorry for my actions when I left. I promise never to mistreat you like that again. My heart was filled with anger and hate, and I took it out on you. I found a way to rid my heart of the poison while walking those many miles. Please forgive me," he begged.

Nova held his face and softly kissed him. "I have already forgiven you, my husband. Let us not speak of it again. It is good to have you home. Did you find Lansa? Did he return with you?" she asked.

"I did find him. I spent the night in his camp. I tried to convince him to return, but this morning when I awoke he was gone. I waited for him, but he never returned to camp. I am afraid I failed," he answered.

"His mother will be heartbroken," Nova said.

"As will Kele," Tocho added. "Where is Honaw? I must speak with him."

"He is down by the pond. I worry about him, Tocho. He does his work, but he does not play with the other boys, and he has not eaten since you left. I fear he is in a very dark place."

"Do not worry, my wife. I will speak with him."

Tocho went to the pond where he found Honaw staring into the still water. "Greetings, my son, I have missed you." Honaw looked up but did not answer. He returned to staring into the water.

Tocho sat next to him and said, "You have every reason to be angry with me, son. I should have taken you with me. Your father is but a man and men make mistakes. I am sorry. What happened to your sister put poison in my heart, but as I was walking, your wise grandfather came and spoke to me. He told me I was not living the right way, that Sun Father did not teach his people to live with anger in their hearts. I know you feel you have been cheated, and I know the pain you feel when you think about your sister, but we must help each other to rid our hearts of anger and find our balance again. Will you help me?"

Honaw looked up at his father, his expression changing from frown to smile. "Did you see Grandfather? Did he appear to you in a vision?" he asked excitedly.

"You do not have to see the spirit of a person to know he is there and talking to you. As I walked along the path that you and I traveled with Old Kwahu, I heard his voice in my head. It was then he told me I must ask your forgiveness and seek your help to regain balance in my life. So will you help me?"

"I will help you, Father. I, too, have had that poison in my heart. I have been sick with self-pity, and I have been only thinking of myself. You are right. Grandfather did not teach me to live this way. I may not ever be a Moiety, but that does not mean I cannot teach others to live the right way. I owe that to Grandfather," Honaw answered.

Tocho put his arm around him. "You make me proud, son. You have always been a good boy and I love you. Now let us go back. I am hungry and tired from my long walk."

"Did you bring Lansa home, Father?" Honaw asked.

"No, I did the best I could, but it was not enough. It seems he wants to stay in the woods."

As they walked back to the house, Honaw suddenly stopped and pointed, "Look, Father, who is that coming down the path?"

Tocho looked up, and there was Lansa striding down the path with a deer slung across his shoulders, just as he had done many times before. Tocho smiled and said, "That is Lansa. He has come home after all."

CHAPTER 8

THE RECKONING

Tocho, Honaw, and many other people greeted Lansa as he walked into the plaza. To the women he handed over the deer to be skinned and prepared. All were glad that their best hunter had returned to the village. Tocho was the first to speak to him.

"I was afraid my words had not convinced you to return," he said.

"I heard your words and I understand," Lansa replied. Then he smiled and added, "I think you talk too much."

Tocho laughed and said, "I have found many words to speak."

Then Lansa turned to Honaw, "How are you, little man?"

"I am well and very glad to see you. I have spoken to Father. We have decided to try to find ways to bring balance back to the village. Your being home is a good start," Honaw replied.

"We will work together at this task. But right now I need to go and see my mother." Lansa turned to walk away and suddenly saw Kele across the plaza. She had been grinding corn under the ramada when he arrived. Now their eyes met for the first time. Lansa started to go to her, but Tocho grabbed his arm.

"Do not go to her, Lansa. It will only make things worse for her. Chuchip has been a cruel husband, and if you go to her, his cruelty will only get worse. There will be another time."

Lansa could see the pain in her eyes, but he could also see that the love was still there. Chuchip and Istaga were sitting under the ramada and saw the look in Kele's eyes.

"What are you looking at, woman? Go inside and start my meal!" Chuchip commanded loud enough for Lansa to hear. Kele defiantly looked at Lansa one more time and then disappeared into the house.

Lansa pulled away from Tocho and walked toward his mother's house. He found his mother sitting next to the hearth, stirring rabbit stew. She did look frail. "Something smells very good. I am glad I made it home for the evening meal."

The old woman looked up with a start. "Lansa, you have come home! Oh, thank the gods! My son has come home!"

Lansa went to her and helped her to her feet. He held her close. "Yes, Mother, I have come home, and I am sorry I have worried you. You can thank Tocho. His words brought me home. He reminded me that I made a promise to always be here to take care of you. I let pain and anger cloud my thoughts. I was thinking only of myself and forgot my most important responsibility. I am sorry."

"Do not fret, my son. I was only concerned for your well-being. You brought no harm to me. It pained me to see you suffer. Sometimes a man needs to be alone with his thoughts to understand what the gods are asking of him. I know the pain you feel in your heart. Maybe as the time passes, the pain will lessen. I will pray to the gods to bring you peace."

"I am grateful, Mother," he replied.

Then he looked about. "I see there is work to be done. Your woodpile is small and your water jars are empty." With that, he set to work.

The old woman went back to stirring her stew, but with a smile on her face and a look of peaceful contentment in her eyes. "Everything is right again," she said softly to herself.

The days of winter were upon them now. A cold wind blew out of the northwest and the temperature dropped to well below freezing. Snow covered the frozen ground. The men of the village hunted and worked to keep their woodpiles full. The women spent most of their time grinding corn and caring for their families.

For Kele life had become dreadfully hard. She was sure that all the things she dreamed of would never come to pass. She and Lansa still exchanged glances at each other when they could, but Chuchip watched her closely and reprimanded her harshly when he even thought she was looking Lansa's way.

Chuchip was a poor husband. He was as lazy a man as he had been as a boy. He never hunted or chopped wood. He and his father controlled the communal bins, and as winter passed, the people began to run out of corn. They were forced to trade their labor for corn, but the distributions were meager. Chuchip had them chop his wood, gather seeds, and hunt his meat, but gave very little in return. He had learned this practice well from his father. Some people wanted to protest but were afraid of offending Istaga. They were afraid that if they offended him, Chuchip would cut their rations even more, and their family would go hungry. Corn was power in the village, and Istaga and Chuchip held all the corn.

Chuchip grew tired of forcing Kele to lie with him. She was determined never to submit willingly, but this just made Chuchip even crueler. As the nights grew colder Kele tried to move closer to the hearth for warmth. Chuchip dragged her back to the place next to the wall, saying, "If you are too good to lie with me and give me comfort when it is warm, you do not deserve the warmth when it is cold. You stay against the wall. Maybe the cold will make you think about defying me." She spent many cold nights wrapped in her turkey blanket, but it was still better than giving in to Chuchip.

One day, in midwinter, the skies cleared and the wind ceased to blow. Days like that sometimes came to visit the basin, and the people were glad of it. Most everyone was outside enjoying the warmth while it lasted. Lansa and Tocho were making new arrowheads and sharpening their axes. Chuchip was sitting under his ramada, as he always did, with some men of his clan. It pained Lansa to see Kele serving them food and bringing them drinks.

They are even too lazy to serve their own food, he thought.

Chuchip saw him watching, and with a malicious look in his eye, he stuck out his foot and purposely tripped Kele as she walked by with a pot of hot stew. She fell hard on her knees, spilling the stew. His friends laughed. Looking toward Lansa, Chuchip said, "You are a clumsy woman! Look at this mess. Clean it up!"

Kele stood proudly and said, "If you were not so lazy, you could move your feet out of my path!"

"How dare you speak to me that way!" Chuchip yelled. He picked up the pot of stew and threw what was left into Kele's face. She screamed in pain as the hot stew burned her skin.

Lansa felt the anger explode in his chest and head. Without thinking, he picked up his ax and ran across the plaza at Chuchip. Chuchip did not see him coming until the last moment.

Through his rage, Lansa barely heard Kele yell, "Lansa, no!"

But it was too late. Lansa brought the sharpened ax down on Chuchip. Chuchip staggered back with blood spurting from a deep gash on his head. His eyes rolled back and he fell against the wall.

He was dead. Lansa looked down on him and his rage subsided. He dropped the ax and looked at Kele. "Oh, Kele, what have I done?"

Istaga heard the commotion and emerged from his house. When he saw Chuchip lying there in a pool of blood with a deep wound in his head and the bloody ax at Lansa's feet, it was evident what had happened. "You have killed my son!" he cried.

To anyone's knowledge, except Istaga, there had never been a killing in the village, and no one seemed to know what to do. The people stood frozen at the horror of what had happened. Finally, Istaga took charge."Seize him! Take him to the pit house and pull up the ladder so that he cannot escape!" he commanded.

Chuchip's friends grabbed Lansa and attempted to restrain him, but Lansa began to fight them off. Then Tocho stepped forward. "No more violence," he said. "I will take him."

He calmly laid his hand on Lansa's arm and said, "Come, Lansa. No more blood."

Lansa stared blankly at him, then at Kele. He let Tocho lead him away. The women of the village began to sing the death song. Chuchip was lifted and carried into the house.

As she watched her father lead Lansa away, Kele put her head in her hands and cried. Nova went to her daughter and gently led her across the plaza to their home. She no longer had to stay in the house of Istaga. Nova and Sihu tended to her burns and tried to comfort her.

Through her tears, Kele said, "Mother, all that has happened has been my fault. I refused to submit to Chuchip. I defied him and made him angry. I was not a good wife and look what has happened. Lansa killed him because of me, and now what is to become of him?"

"Even though the marriage was forced upon you by Istaga, it was your duty to consummate the marriage and become with child," Nova said. "I understand that Chuchip did not love you. He did not want you as a wife. He wanted you as a prize to be shown. He was always a lazy, mean-spirited boy, full of himself, like his father. But the village will not see it that way. They will hold both you and Lansa responsible for all that happened."

"I did not submit to him, Mother, but he forced himself on me. I was not strong enough when I fought him. I am so ashamed. Lansa will never want me now! Oh, Mother, what am I to do?"

Nova quietly asked, "He took you against your will?"

"Yes, Mother. I am so ashamed." Kele sobbed.

"My poor child, you have suffered more than most do in a lifetime." She pulled Kele close and reached out to Sihu. They all cried together.

When Nova told Tocho what Chuchip had done to their daughter, he became angrier than she had ever seen him. "I should have killed him myself!" he yelled. "How could the gods let this happen? Why do they hate my family so?"

Then the voice of wisdom came from the youngest of them. Honaw said, "Do not blame the gods for the mistakes of men, Father. We as a people have brought this evil down on ourselves. When Grandfather died, the people forgot how to live the right way, just as they forgot in the time of the Third World. Now it is time to ask the gods for their help in casting out the evil and finding the way back to the warmth and light of Sun Father. Grandfather taught me this."

Tocho smiled at his son and asked, "How can one so young be so wise?"

"He was taught well," Nova answered.

Lansa spent a cold night in the pit house. He prayed to Sun Father and the ancestors, asking their forgiveness. He had returned to the village, hoping he could help in restoring balance and now he had committed the darkest of sins. Sun Father would surely be angry with the people now, and he was afraid many would suffer because of his actions. Nova prepared food for him and Tocho brought it to him, but he could not eat.

He did have one request of Tocho. "You are a fine man, Tocho. You have always lived the right way. Would you pray with me? I fear the gods are not listening to me this night."

They prayed together, and then Lansa said, "All night I have been thinking about what happened today. I keep seeing Chuchip's lifeless body all covered in blood, and I cannot believe I could do such a thing. When I saw him throw the stew in Kele's face and heard her scream, something exploded inside me. I felt the ax in my hand, and the next thing I knew, Chuchip was dead. Tocho, I love your daughter with all my heart and could not stand by and see her treated like that. But to kill is an unforgiveable sin. I will accept the punishment the council decides for me."

"Lansa, your love for Kele is the reason for your actions today. Chuchip was an evil man. He did not live the right way and he did not care for Kele. I must tell you something now that makes my blood boil with anger." He paused and looked down at the floor.

"What is it, Tocho? Tell me," Lansa pleaded.

"Kele would not submit to Chuchip. It was her duty, but she could not bring herself to lay with him. He took her by force! The village knows how you and Kele felt about each other. Istaga will surely use this to condemn you both."

Lansa cried in anguish, "My wonderful Kele, there is no one who has more goodness in her heart! How could this have happened?"

"I know she still held hope that you and she would be together someday, but now she thinks you will not want her because she is no longer pure," Tocho said.

"What happened to her was not her fault," Lansa answered. "She is still pure in her heart. That dog, Chuchip, took her body, but he could never take her heart. I, too, long to be with her someday. I will never love another. Tell her this for me."

"I will. She will be glad to hear your words." He stood and moved toward the ladder. "Lansa, I do not know what the council will decide for you when the sun rises, but I know you are a good man. I know you are not evil. Nova and I would be proud to have you as a son. I will speak for you at council. I will try to make them understand." He climbed the ladder and pulled it up behind him, leaving Lansa in the dark to contemplate his fate.

Istaga wrapped Chuchip's body in his finest robe and dug his grave next to that of his mother in one of the burial chambers of the great house. He made a fine show of grieving, but the death of his only son did not pain him because now he saw his chance to become the sole spiritual leader of the village. He had become so jaded by his lust for power that he saw his son's death only as an opportunity. With no one else to become the Soyala Moiety, he could assume both roles. Istaga prepared to declare himself Tiyamunyi of the village. His long-held plan was about to come to fruition.

At sunrise of the next day, the men of the village again met in council. This was the first time Honaw was allowed to attend. He was still not of age, but Tocho decided it was time because of the wisdom he had shown and because he was fond of Lansa. Honaw sat proudly next to his father. The other men noticed him, but in respect for Tocho and because Honaw was the grandson of the great Kwahu, no one protested. Lansa sat alone on the floor with his eyes cast downward. He did not speak. Istaga led the men in prayer. They asked the gods to join them and to give them wisdom in deciding the fate of their village.

Istaga began. "My heart is breaking today as I grieve the loss of my only son, Chuchip. His time had not yet come to live with the ancestors, but his lifeblood was taken from him by the man we judge this day. He was killed in a most savage way! This day we walk on unknown ground. There has never been a killing in the village, and we must take all steps to assure that this most grave sin never happens again. We must make an example of this killer and show the people that this offense will be dealt with in the harshest manner. But before we decide his fate we must consider another matter of great importance to the village. Because of this man's sin, we again are left without a Soyala Moiety, and this time, no arrangement of marriage will provide one. I see young Honaw here among us today. You are welcome, grandson of the wise Kwahu. If only you were of age to become a Moiety, all this darkness may have never come to pass, but, regretfully, you are not. So this day we must change the custom of our people."

He closed his eyes and raised his hands to the sky. In a solemn and reverent voice he said, "Even now, after I have lost my only beloved son, my heart is filled with pride and joy, for last night as I sat weeping next to my dead son, Sun Father came to me in a vision. He showed me the way forward that will restore balance to our troubled village. He appointed me Tiyamunyi of Chu'a Village!"

A great uproar rose from the pit house. The men of the Bear Clan cheered Istaga and praised his words. The men of the Spider Clan protested, saying, "You have no proof of your vision. It is not the way of the people."

"How dare you question the words of Sun Father?" Istaga replied. "I am a Moiety! I do not lie, but if it will ease your minds, we will let the council decide. Keep in mind that we have no Soyala Moiety. Sun Father, in his great wisdom, has shown us the way to regain the balance we lost after Lansa's offense. I see no other answer!"

The men of the Spider Clan began to shout for Tocho to speak for them. "What say you, Tocho? You, the most respected of our proud clan. What say you?"

Tocho doubted that Sun Father had spoken to Istaga, but he knew the village would suffer greatly without a spiritual leader to perform the rites of Soyala. He gathered his thoughts for several moments and then rose to speak.

"I agree. I also do not see another answer, but I must speak of a matter concerning Chuchip before I can give my consent. The long days of winter are upon us. Many families are running out of food. There are some among us who believe Chuchip was not fair in his distribution of food. He gave to some more than they needed, and to others he did not give enough. A fair way to distribute food must be found before I give my consent."

"Tocho, your words at council have always been wise, but I will not let you question the honor of my dead son," Istaga warned.

"I do not mean to question his honor, but I do speak the truth, and I have a way to solve the problem that should satisfy all. I have heard that in the great houses of White House the Tiyamunyi has someone who helps with the distribution of food. The Tiyamunyi is the spiritual leader and the other controls distribution," Tocho explained.

"You speak of a cacique," Istaga said.

"Yes, a cacique," Tocho responded. "Let the council appoint a cacique and you shall be the first Tiyamunyi of our village."

Istaga did not want to give up any of his power, but he also understood as Tiyamunyi he would receive all of the surplus crop and deer meat. He would also hold all the power to settle disputes. He would be the wealthiest and most powerful man in the village. He could live with the compromise.

"That is acceptable," Istaga said.

The council gave their approval and appointed Tocho to be the cacique. It was a good solution. Both clans would have a say in ruling the village and everyone would be assured of a fair distribution of food. Honaw could not be more proud of his father.

Lansa had been silently sitting on the floor through the debate. He was barely listening. It did not concern him, but now the discussion turned to his fate. Istaga pointed at Lansa, declaring, "My first ruling as Tiyamunyi is to condemn this man to death for the killing of my son. His lust for Kele and hers for him poisoned them both. My son told me Kele would not lay with him and give him a child. She would not perform her duty because of this man and now he has committed the darkest of sins. We need to make an example of Lansa for all to see! What say you?"

Again there was a great uproar. Some yelled that he must be put to death. Others said that only the gods may take the life of a person.

Anger swelled in Tocho when he heard Istaga speak of his beloved daughter, but he held his temper. He knew he must be the voice of reason to save both Lansa and Kele. "Since Kwahu went to the live with the ancestors, the balance of the village has been disrupted," Tocho said. "The gods are angry with us because some have not been living the right way. The winter has already been colder than most, and food is in short supply. I fear the killing of Chuchip has angered Sun Father even more. Killing each other is not the way Sun Father taught us to live. Sun Father punished the people of the Third World for killing each other and if we put Lansa to death, the fury of Sun Father could destroy our village. We must spare his life and begin to restore the balance to our village. My son gained this knowledge from his grandfather and then taught it to me." He smiled at Honaw who beamed with pride.

"For the second time this day, Tocho, your words are wise. But we cannot allow this evil to live among us. I rule we spare his life, but he is to be banished from our village, never to return!" Istaga declared.

Then he added, "I am sorry, Tocho, but Kele must also be punished for her part in this. I rule that she be shunned by the village. She will be allowed to stay in the village, but only her family may speak to her. She will not be allowed to marry again and will live out her life alone. That is my ruling!"

The punishment was harsh, but Tocho knew it would be of no use to argue. It was the best he could have hoped for.

Istaga looked at Lansa. "We will give you until sunset to say good-bye to your mother. I am sure she has suffered great pain by your actions, and this decision will only add to her grief. You should fall to your knees and beg her forgiveness for the hardship you have caused her."

He added one more stipulation. "Other than your mother, you will speak to no one." He wanted to be sure that Lansa did not speak to Kele. He knew that being unable to say good-bye would cause them both great pain. He wanted to inflict as much suffering as he could on the couple, to demonstrate to the villagers his great power over all of them so they would fear him. Guards were placed on Lansa, and the council gave their consent to the ruling. The fate of Lansa and Kele was ordained.

When Tocho and Honaw returned from the council, Honaw was full of excitement. All he could speak of was his father being appointed the cacique of the village and how the lessons he had taught his father helped to save Lansa's life. The pride in his voice was evident, and Tocho hated to dampen his excitement, but more important matters needed to be addressed.

"Honaw," he said, "we will have time to tell all about what happened at your first council, but now we must think of your sister, Kele."

"You are right, Father. I am sorry. We should think of Kele first," Honaw said.

Tocho explained the decision of the council to his family. "Lansa will not be put to death. The council has decided that he will be banished from the village, never to return, and you, my daughter, are to be shunned by the village. Only our family will be allowed to talk to you, and you will never again marry. Lansa has until sunset to put his things together and say good-bye to his mother. At sunset he will be brought to the plaza, where he will admit to his crime in front of everyone in the village. Istaga will then banish him so that all will see his disgrace."

Kele barely heard her father when he spoke of her own punishment. "I do not care what punishment Istaga has ordered for me," she said. "I only care about Lansa, banished in disgrace and all because of me. I must go to him. I must speak with him. He needs to know how sorry I am and how much I love him," she exclaimed.

"You cannot, my child," Tocho said. "Istaga has put him under guard and forbidden anyone but his mother to speak to him. Istaga is now the Tiyamunyi of the village. That gives him great power. His words must be heeded."

Then Kele resolutely said, "It is clear to me that I have no future here in the village. I do not care what these people think of me. I care only for you, my family, and for my Lansa. If I should stay in the village, all of you would suffer my disgrace far more than me. I know what I must do. If Lansa and I are ever to be happy, I must share his banishment. He and I were cheated out of our marriage vows, but I still feel like I am his woman. My place is by his side."

Sihu gasped. "But, Kele, he is banished for life. We will never see you again." She began to cry.

"Do not cry, little sister," Kele said as she hugged her. "There have been enough tears. Remember how, back in the mountains, I asked the gods to show me the way to become the wife of Lansa? I believe they have shown me the way. I must do this, but I will always hold a special place in my heart for my little sister."

Nova then said, "How my daughter has grown. You are not a little girl any longer. The decision you make this day is the decision only a woman could make. Now I know how my parents felt when I moved away with your father. They also feared they would never see me again, but the gods reunited us once more. Forever is a long time. If the gods are willing, we will see each other again."

"I am sure Lansa will be happy about your decision," Tocho said. "He professed his love for you last night. He said he could never love another. He is fine man, but you cannot simply walk out of the village with him at sunset. Istaga would not allow it. We must get word to him."

"I can do it," Honaw proudly volunteered. "I will not go to the plaza. I will hide in the rocks along the path to the mesa and when Lansa passes, I will tell him of your plan. He can wait for you on the path."

Kele smiled, "Little Honaw, when did you become so wise and so brave? How you have grown! You are almost a man. I will miss you. I will miss all of you. The love I carry in my heart this day will always be with me."

After the council, Lansa was escorted to his mother's house as ordered. He had not seen his mother since Chuchip's death, but he could tell she knew what had happened by the pained expression on her face. When he saw her looking so old and fragile, he was overcome with sadness. "Mother, I have brought you much pain. I am sorry I have made you suffer, and now I must break my promise to you. I have been banished from the village. I will not be here to take care of you. I will have nothing. I will not have you, my beloved mother, and I will not have Kele. The gods' punishment is just! I have killed a man!"

"My son, you have brought me only happiness and pride. This punishment is not of the gods. It is man who is punishing you. In time, this village will regret what they have done this day. Chuchip was an evil man, as is his father. I am an old woman, and I can see the evil in Istaga's heart. He has already committed acts of evil and someday they will be brought into the light," she told her son.

"Mother, be careful how you speak. Istaga is now a very powerful man," Lansa said.

"I am not afraid of evil. The gods will see it and protect me," she answered.

"But what is to become of you when I am not here to care for you? You should come with me," Lansa exclaimed.

"Son, I am too old to go into the mountains. I have lived a good life here in this village with you and your father. I intend to end my days here. I will fend for myself for as long as I can. It is time for you to go about living your life. I do not know what the gods hold for you, but I do know that you must go to find out." She smiled and held him close.

There was a knock at the door and a voice called out, "It is time! We must go to the plaza!" Lansa picked up his bow and quiver, slung his pack, and kissed his mother good-bye for the last time.

The plaza was surrounded by the people. All were there except Honaw. No one noticed his absence. Lansa found Kele in the crowd. She looked at him and crossed her arms over her heart, a sign of love. Lansa smiled.

"Confess your sin so that all can hear!" Istaga commanded.

"I stand before you this day filled with sorrow. I have disgraced my family and deserve the punishment that is given me. I have committed the gravest of sins. I have killed a man. I hope that someday Sun Father and all the ancestors will forgive me, and I also hope that you, the good people, will forgive me."

Then Istaga pronounced his punishment. "This day we must rid our village of evil so the gods will not be angry with us. It is my ruling that this man, Lansa, be banished from our village, never to return, for the killing of Chuchip, my son and our Soyala Moiety. It is a fair and just punishment agreed to by the council. Lansa, leave our village and may the gods have mercy on you!"

Everyone stood silent as Lansa left the plaza. He glanced at Kele and she smiled at him. *She does not look troubled by my leaving. She looks almost happy,* he thought, bewildered by her behavior.

His mind was clouded with confusion as he walked up the path when he suddenly heard a small voice come from the rocks, "Lansa, Lansa, I have something to tell you."

"Who is that?" Lansa asked.

Honaw emerged from his hiding place in the rocks and answered, "It is me, Honaw. I have been waiting for you. I have something to tell you."

"Have you come to say good-bye?" Lansa asked.

"Yes, but there is something more. Kele wishes to go with you. She says she has no future in the village. She loves you and her place is by your side. If you want her to go with you, you are to hide here in the rocks and wait for her. She will come to you after it is dark. What say you? Do you want her to go with you?"

"Does your family know of this?" Lansa asked.

"Yes, yes. They are the ones who sent me here with this message," Honaw answered.

"Honaw, you have made me a very happy man. Tell Kele I will wait for her. Tell her to bring something to keep her warm and—"

Honaw interrupted him. "Father and Mother have already given her all that she will need. I must get back now. Oh, I almost forgot."

He scurried back to the rocks and returned with a small bundle wrapped in singed rabbit fur and tied with a thong. "Your mother came to our house and told my parents to give you this bundle. What is it, Lansa?"

Lansa took the bundle from Honaw and held it to chest. "It is a very special gift. Thank you for bringing it to me," he said.

"I must go now," Honaw said. "Good-bye, Lansa. I will miss you. Please take care of my sister."

"You need not worry about that, little man. Good-bye, I will miss you also." With that, Honaw ran down the path back to the village.

Lansa hid himself in the rocks. As he waited he thought, *That is why she did not look troubled when I left. She had already decided to go with me.* He looked at the bundle and again held it tightly to his chest. "Thank you, Mother," he said aloud.

Soon he heard footsteps coming up the path. It was a bright, moonlit night and he could clearly see that it was Kele. He stepped out of the rocks and called out, "Kele, I am here."

Kele ran to him and they embraced. "I have waited so long to be held in your arms. I was afraid it would never happen," Kele said.

"I am here now. I also have waited for this moment. I do not know what the future will bring. I do not have anything to offer. I do not even have a home to take you to, but I promise to love you and care for you until the end of my days."

She held his face in her hands. "I have loved you since that day in the mountains when you first smiled at me. I do not care that we do not have a home. The mountains and forests can be our home. Home will be wherever we are together." They kissed for the first time in their young lives, but it was not awkward. It was as though they had been sharing kisses for many years.

Finally, Lansa took her by the hand and headed up the path. "We must go. I want to be far away from the village by morning. I do not know how Istaga will act when he finds out you have stolen away with me, but I do not want to take a chance. We travel all night. Are you feeling strong?" he asked.

"I am strong and happy. I will go anywhere as long as we are together."

They headed up the path to begin their new life.

CHAPTER 9

◆

SUN FATHER'S WORD

When Istaga discovered that Kele had gone with Lansa, he did not care. He relished his position of power over his little domain. What did he care about two outcasts who meant nothing to him? His plan to become Tiyamunyi had worked better than he imagined. He already held all the power in the village, but with Chuchip still alive, he was not a true Tiyamunyi. Now that Chuchip was gone, he held the power and the title. Lansa had made the last step to Istaga's ultimate goal possible. He was now an all-powerful Tiyamunyi of a great house. He had major plans to put his people to work expanding and beautifying his great house. Soon it would be as grand as the great house he had seen in his dreams.

In some ways, Istaga was a shrewd ruler. One of the first things he did was surround himself with people of his clan who supported him. Members of the Bear Clan became his guards, hunters, gatherers, and servants. He allowed them to live in the great house and assured them they would never work in the fields. By this act, he no longer needed to trade food for the daily upkeep of the great house. Now, when the people needed food, he would put them to work expanding his great house into a palace. He wanted to add a larger ceremonial pit house, one that could hold the entire village. He also wanted to add many more rooms so that visitors would have a place to stay when they came to see his magnificent great house.

Most importantly, he wanted to build walls like the ones in the great houses of White House. The walls he envisioned would symbolically connect his great house to the cardinal directions. One wall would point directly north toward "the heart of the sky" and symbolize a connection to the dark and Earth Mother. The people believed that the dead traveled north to be with Earth Mother and the ancestors of the underworld. Another wall would point directly south and symbolize a connection to light and Sun Father.

Stories of these sacred walls had been handed down for generations. The walls symbolized the essence of the people's religion and beliefs. If the walls could be constructed by his planning and instructions, it would show all who came what a great and powerful Tiyamunyi could do.

Construction was always done in the autumn of the year, after the crops had been harvested and the people had time to do such work. However, Istaga was not a patient man. He ordered Tocho to organize work parties to go to the mountains and get the trees to start construction immediately. Other work parties began to bring sandstone from the mesa to build his rooms and walls. Tocho did convince him that work on the pit house would need to wait until the ground was soft. He was an efficient and fair cacique, making sure all who worked got their fair share of food for their labor.

For a while, all went well. The winter turned mild and there were enough warm days for the construction to progress. The people were satisfied with the food they received. The balance of the village seemed to be restored. All were happy that Sun Father was no longer angry with them. Istaga was quick to take credit for the perceived restored balance. He claimed it was because of his ability to speak to the gods.

Honaw loaded his sling, swung it above his head, and let fly the stone. The shot was accurate, striking the rabbit in the head, killing it immediately. It had been a good morning. He already had two rabbits in his pouch. This made a third. As he scanned the area for another target, he saw in the distance a line of men walking toward the village. He counted ten in the line. He quickly slipped his sling in his pouch and ran for the village.

Tocho was supervising the laying of stone on one of the walls of the great house when he heard his son coming. "Father, Father, there are men coming into the village from the east!" Honaw yelled.

"How many?" Tocho asked.

"I counted ten, Father," Honaw answered, trying to catch his breath.

"Let us go and greet them," Tocho said. He sent one of the workers to tell Istaga that visitors were entering the village.

A small crowd of people gathered around the strangers as they entered the plaza. By the look of them, they had been traveling for many days, Tocho thought.

"Greetings to you, friends, I am Tocho, the cacique of this humble village. Welcome."

"Greetings to you, Tocho. I am called Makya," said a tall man wearing a sheepskin cape tied with a deerskin belt at the waist. The belt was inlaid with bluish-green stones, and he wore a necklace of beads also made of the beautiful stones. "We are travelers from the mining village of Muna, to the east. We have come to trade for corn."

Tocho explained that the beginning of the winter had been difficult for the village. The storage bins of some families were nearly empty. Others had none at all. What was left of the supply was in the communal bins. "You will need to speak with the Tiyamunyi of our village," he said.

"Take me to him, if you will," Makya replied.

Tocho instructed the women to bring Makya's men food and water. Then he led Makya to the ramada outside Istaga's rooms. After a short time, Istaga arrived, accompanied by two of his guards. He was dressed in a fine white robe with a feathered apron. Clearly, he meant to impress the visitor.

"I am Istaga, the Tiyamunyi of this great house and spiritual leader of this village," he announced. "I understand you have come to trade for corn. I am sure you understand that corn holds great value to us. What do you have to trade?" Istaga asked.

"I am Makya, from the mining village of Muna in the mountains to the east. I know the value of corn. It is even more valuable when you have none, and the people of your village are hungry." He removed the necklace from around his neck and handed it to Istaga. "We have ten pouches of these precious stones, dug from our mines, to trade for twenty baskets of corn."

Istaga's eyes lit up when he saw the stones. It was clear how much he coveted them. He did not hesitate to answer. "I am sure a trade can be arranged!"

"Istaga." Tocho cautioned him. "The people have used nearly all of their stores. When that is gone, we will have only what is in your bins of the great house. If we trade that away, I fear the village will run short before the next harvest. If it is a dry season and the harvest is poor, we will surely run out. Are you certain this is wise?"

All Istaga could see were the precious stones. He became irritated with Tocho. "I know how much corn I have! I am not a fool! We have plenty to last us. I have stores in the great house that you do not know of. We will make the trade!"

Makya sent for his men to bring the pouches of stones to be traded, and the baskets to be filled. "My village thanks the great Tiyamunyi. You may keep the necklace as a sign of our appreciation," he said.

"I will see to filling their baskets," Tocho said.

"No, Tocho. You stay and make sure Makya and his men are made comfortable. I will have my servants fill the baskets. You and your men are welcome to stay the night in my great house, Makya. You can then get a fresh start in the morning."

"I am grateful to you, but we must return as soon as possible. Our people are hungry," Makya said.

"As you wish. The baskets will soon be filled," responded Istaga.

The baskets were filled and the visitors started on their way home. That night during the evening meal, Tocho told Nova, "I think Istaga made an unwise trade today. He said there is more corn in storage inside the great house that I do not know about. I do not believe that is the truth. In fact, I think that is why he would not let me fill the visitor's baskets, so I could not see how much corn was left. I believe Istaga's greed may have put the village in peril. If he does not have the corn he says he does, all in the village will surely suffer."

The final days of winter remained mild and the people began to look forward to the coming spring. The winter had been a very difficult time for the village. The balance of all things had been badly disrupted by the death of Kwahu and the killing of Chuchip. Now it seemed the balance was restored. It seemed that Sun Father and the ancestors had answered the prayers of the people.

It was then that the snow began. There had been late winter or early spring snowstorms before, so at first, no one seemed concerned. Then a fierce wind started to blow out of the northwest and the spring snowstorm turned into a blinding blizzard. The storm raged for four sunrises. The light and warmth of Sun Father was taken from the sky and darkness covered the land. Snow piled up against the houses and made it impossible to go outside. The people huddled in their houses and rationed their food, water, and most important, their firewood. The temperature dropped well below freezing. No firewood could be gathered or chopped because the storm made it impossible to see, and the people were afraid of freezing to death if they ventured outside. Suddenly spring seemed very far away. Many began to think that Sun Father was still angry with them, that he had brought this storm to punish them further.

Before Lansa left, he had made sure that his mother was well stocked with dried meat, and Tocho, out of the goodness of his heart, had been bringing her small supplies of corn. Lansa had also left her a good pile of firewood, but as the winter wore on, her pile diminished. By the time the storm hit she was almost out of wood for her hearth. As the storm blew into its third sunrise, she ran out of wood. *I must get more wood or I will freeze*, she thought.

The old woman knew it would be impossible to chop wood, but she thought she might be able to break dry branches off the nearby trees. She draped a rabbit fur blanket over her head, put another over her shoulders, and went out into the storm. The wind and snow blinded her, but she knew where the nearest trees were, and she headed that way. She struggled through snow for what seemed like a long time, and then looked about in confusion. It was as if a cold, white blanket had been placed over her head. She was completely blind. She became frightened and decided to go back to her house, but the snow and wind disoriented her, and she did not know which direction to go. She struggled on a few more steps, but then she realized she could no longer feel her feet or legs. Pushing through the snow had exhausted her, so she dropped to her knees to rest.

Again, she peered through the snow, but this time she saw something. She could not make it out at first, but then she saw a man standing there. She looked closer, and she realized that it was Lansa. Suddenly she was no longer cold. "Lansa, you have come back to care for me just as you promised. I must rest for a while before we go. Come lie with me and keep me warm," she said.

She lay down and pulled the blanket tightly around her, and she was warm. She could still see Lansa standing there smiling at her.

When the storm passed, they found her frozen in the snow.

After the storm broke, the days warmed quickly. No one in the village, even the old ones, could remember such a fierce storm. When the snow began to melt, the wash ran high with cool water and the pond filled beyond what it could hold. The water ran over the top of the small dam, and filled the wash downstream.

Istaga climbed the mesa, watched the shadow of Tuwa Mountain, and determined the day to begin the Planting Ceremony. Unlike the Soyala Ceremony, when there had been much mourning and haste, this time there was dancing and singing as the people enjoyed the joyous spring celebration.

When the Planting Ceremony was over, almost the entire village set about the task of planting the corn, squash, and beans. First, the fields were prepared by digging furrows with digging sticks. Then the precious seeds were brought from the storage bins and carefully planted in the fertile ground. Finally, the irrigation canals were dug, running from the pond at the dam to the newly planted fields. The water the snowstorm left behind made the ground soft and moist, a perfect bed in which to lay the life-giving seeds. The abundance of water brought nourishment to the growing plants. The growing season began well.

The people cared for their fields every day, weeding and repairing the canals. The rain was abundant, with cloudbursts over the mesa almost daily. The plants soon sprouted, strong and healthy. The food from the storage bins ran very low, but Istaga assured everyone that he would provide more when the time came.

Work on the great house was stopped while the people toiled in the fields. The rooms had been completed, but there was still much to be done to complete the walls. Istaga insisted that the work continue, but the people united and refused. He would have to wait until after the harvest for work to begin again.

A steady rain had fallen for two days, and a mighty cloudburst and lightning storm had erupted over the mesa that morning. Honaw carried stones to his father and two others who were working to build up the dam on the wash. As he struggled with a large stone, he noticed Sihu weeding the crop field upstream from the dam. Working in the rain all morning, she stopped to wipe water from her face, using the sleeve of her buckskin dress. He heard her humming a song as she worked. He was glad that the pain of losing Kele was lessening for her. She still missed her sister, but she did not cry so much anymore.

As Honaw walked back to retrieve another stone, he heard a strange, low rumble off in the distance. He had never heard such a noise and had no idea what it could be. He stopped and listened, bewildered by the sound. The rumble grew louder until it became a roar. He could tell it was coming from the wash. He heard Sihu scream and then watched in horror as a huge, muddy wall of water came crashing down the wash. It carried whole trees, broken branches, and other debris. He saw Sihu try to run, but the torrent was on her before she could escape. It swept over her and pulled her down into the black water. Struggling against the current, she was pulled under. She quickly popped back up, but the current was too strong. Again, she disappeared under the black froth. It was the last he saw of her.

He stood frozen as he watched the wall of water sweep down on his father. Tocho scrambled to reach the embankment, but he, too, could not escape. Fighting the power of the flood, he was able to keep his head above water for only a short distance. Looking upstream Honaw saw a large tree tumbling toward his father, its roots sticking above the surface of the water like huge black fingers. Tocho made a tremendous lunge to get out of its way, but the trunk of the mighty tree hit him squarely in the back. He rolled underneath it and did not come back up.

Honaw rushed toward the wash in an attempt to help his father, but the caldron of water roared past, tearing off great hunks of the embankment and sweeping them downstream. The place where Sihu had been working was now part of the wash. He could not see where the dam had been. He saw only ugly, dark water destroying everything it touched. The wash was now three times its normal width, and water spilled out onto the surrounding land. The flood took the crop fields and slammed into the houses that lined the wash, sweeping them away. The people caught inside their houses had no chance to escape and were carried away along with their homes. It took part of the great house. The unfinished walls were washed away, and still the water surged down the wash.

People were running up and down the torrent of water, crying and calling out the names of loved ones. Some people caught in the deluge were pulled to safety. Others desperately tried to reach the embankment, but the water was too strong and swift; it quickly carried them downstream.

Honaw tried again to help the ones caught in the churning water, but it was of no use. He could not get close. The embankment kept breaking away and falling into the cataclysm. He could only stand

and watch in horror as the village disappeared into the muddy, dark current. He realized his mother was standing next to him.

"Honaw, what has happened?" she pleaded.

"The gods have put their anger into the water, Mother, and it has destroyed our village," Honaw said.

Honaw spent three sunrises searching the wash for the bodies of his father and sister, but it was to no avail. It was as if the anger of the black beast had devoured them and would not give them back. Some people did find loved ones, half buried in the mud or hideously wrapped around trees at the bottom of the wash. The dead were laid side by side in a mass grave, far from the wash where the water could no longer torment them.

The power of the flood amazed Honaw. The wash was now far deeper than it had been, and its bottom was filled with sticky, brown mud, broken trees, and huge stones that had been carried from the mesa by the raging floodwaters. The crop fields had been completely washed away. If there was to be any harvest, new fields would need to be prepared and planted immediately. But the survivors of the village were in shock from the disaster they had lived through, and no one seemed to care about the harvest. The survivors could only search the streambed, bury the dead, and sing the death song.

Honaw's home in the great house had been spared by the flood, but that was little comfort to his mother. In just one season, she had lost her father, her beloved husband, Tocho, and both of her daughters. Honaw felt her anguish; he was concerned the pain was more than she could bear. She spent the days secluded in her home, crying and singing the death song. She could not even be sure that Tocho and Sihu would make the journey north to join her father and the other ancestors in the underworld. If their bodies were not found and buried properly, she feared their spirits would be doomed to walk the Fourth World forever, never allowed to go home and live in peace. Honaw tried to assure his mother that Grandfather Kwahu would not leave them to wander forever. He was sure that the old man would find them and take them home.

Honaw had always admired his mother's inner strength, the strength she inherited from Grandfather Kwahu, but now the loss of his father and sister left her weak and confused. He knew caring for her family had been his mother's purpose in life. Now she had no purpose. She sat in the darkness and cursed the gods for the anguish they had inflicted upon her and her family. Honaw was her only comfort. He chopped wood for the fire, filled the water jars, and held his mother while she cried. He mourned the loss of his father and sister, but he held on to his faith.

When Nova began to curse the gods, Honaw spoke softly to her. "Mother, what has happened is not the fault of the gods," he explained. "There is a great evil at work in the village and the people have allowed it to thrive and grow. Since Grandfather died and Istaga became the all-powerful Tiyamunyi, the gods have been angry. We have allowed Istaga to destroy the balance of the village. The people have not been living in the right way. Just as he did in the evil times of the Third World, Sun Father sent Spider Grandmother to warn us of our sins, but we did not heed her messages. We continued to let Istaga lead us down a dark path to destruction. Now is not the time to lose our faith. We must rebuild our world. We must return to living in the right way. That is the only path to restoring the balance in our village and in our lives."

"Honaw, you no longer speak as a child," his mother said. "You speak as a man. Your words are wise, and I hear them. Thank the gods I still have you."

She hugged him tightly and kissed his cheek. After a deep sigh, she firmly straightened up, standing tall. "The time for tears is past. The gods spared us for a reason. Let us honor the memory of our ancestors by rebuilding what evil has taken from us."

Buoyed by Honaw's words, Nova emerged from the gloom of her home and stepped out onto the plaza, followed by her son. When she saw the destruction and suffering in the village, she knew her Honaw's words were true. "Oh, Honaw, we must help our people. They must be shown the path back to living the right way. You are correct; Istaga is the source of the evil that brought this suffering to our village. To follow him further would only bring more destruction and misery. We cannot allow evil to prevail in the village your grandfather and my husband helped build. I know that Moieties have always been grown men, but I cannot think about that now. I can only think about our people!"

Honaw smiled proudly at his Mother's words. She was her father's daughter.

Some of the villagers who had lost their homes had been sleeping out on the open plaza, without shelter. Most had lost almost all their belongings and barely existed. Honaw helped his mother open the rooms of the great house and offer shelter to the homeless. They gathered what food was left in the bins of the great house and began to distribute it to the people. Nova organized the men into hunting parties and sent them out to find meat. Honaw walked among the people and spread his words of wisdom. The people listened to his words, and even though he was still young, they adopted him as their spiritual leader.

Istaga never showed his face after the flood. He hid himself in the great house. He drove away his servants and guards, telling them they were not worthy to live in the comfort of his great house. He told himself that the people had brought this misery on themselves because they did not honor him as a Tiyamunyi. *Did they not refuse to complete the work on the great house as I had commanded?*

He believed the gods were angry because the people did not give him the respect he deserved as their spiritual leader. His lust for power and wealth blinded him from the truth. The secret he carried with him had turned his heart black. He convinced himself that killing Kwahu was what the village needed, that becoming Tiyamunyi was best for the village. He could not see that his actions had destroyed the very thing he wanted most. His mind was so clouded with self-righteousness and blame, he could not see that now was his time to lead his village and fulfill his dream, now was the time his people needed him most. But instead of taking charge and directing his people in their time of need, he abandoned them. He sat in his great house, alone, belittling his people and counting his precious stones.

The small amount of food still left in the bins soon ran out, and the hunters could not bring in enough meat to feed all the hungry mouths. The people gathered on the plaza and demanded Istaga make good on his promise to provide more corn and seed from his stores in the great house. "Show yourself, Istaga! We are hungry! Where is the corn and seed you promised us? If you are truly a great Tiyamunyi, you will keep your word!" they cried. But Istaga would not come out.

They sent a delegation to Nova and Honaw and asked their help in convincing Istaga to give up his stores so that they would not starve. "Your father, the wise Kwahu, and your husband, Tocho, were both fair and honored leaders. We ask that you and Honaw go to Istaga and invoke their names to convince him to keep his word. If we do not replant soon, we will not have corn, squash, and beans for the winter," they pleaded.

"My son has looked into the heart of Istaga, and he has seen only evil. Istaga is not the great Tiyamunyi he makes himself out to be. He is a small, wicked man. Do not look to him to guide you out of the darkness. His vanity has angered Sun Father and brought this calamity down upon our village. We must go back to our traditional ways. We must appoint two Moieties who are just rulers. This is the only way to bring balance back to our village and show Sun Father that we can again live the right way. But first, we must feed our children and replant our fields. Honaw and I will talk with Istaga. We will not let you starve!"

Nova and Honaw went to Istaga's door, and Nova called out, "Istaga, we will speak with you!"

"Go away! You have no words I want to hear!" Istaga yelled in return.

"That does not matter! We will speak and you will listen!" she replied as they walked into the dimly lit room.

Istaga was dressed in his fine Tiyamunyi robe and beautifully decorated apron. He wore necklaces and bracelets made of the precious stones. He sat upon a throne and looked down on Nova and Honaw. He truly believed he was king.

"Why have you come to bother me? I am praying to the gods and ancestors. They tell me they are angry with the people for not honoring me as their Tiyamunyi. That is why all this misery has befallen this ungrateful village. I am asking the gods to show mercy!" he said.

"You have not spoken to the gods in many sunrises," Honaw said calmly. "You make a mockery of praying."

His eyes flashing with anger, Istaga rose to his feet and screamed at Honaw, "You will not talk to me in that manner, boy! I am the Tiyamunyi of this village. I will have you punished!"

"And who will do your bidding?" Honaw replied. "The people will no longer follow a false leader. They know that it is you who have angered Sun Father. They are not at fault. You are the one who disrupted the balance of our village and brought this darkness upon us. It is because of you that the people have not been living in the right way."

"I will—"

"You will do nothing," Honaw interrupted. "I know the secret that burdens your heart and does not let you sleep at night. The balance of our world was destroyed the night you killed my grandfather."

Nova looked at Honaw in amazement. "What are you saying, Honaw? How do you know this?"

Before Honaw could answer, Istaga defiantly said, "Kwahu was old and weak! He lost his footing and fell to his death. Everyone knows this!"

To Honaw it seemed he had rehearsed these words many times. "No!" he said. "Grandfather spoke to me in a dream, as he did with Father. I could not see him, but I heard his words. He told me what you did that night on the mesa. He showed me where to go to find the stone you used to kill him." With that, he reached inside his pouch and pulled out the bloody stone Istaga had buried on the mesa.

Istaga clutched his chest as he stared wide-eyed at the bloodstained rock. By the look on his face, Nova knew the truth. Istaga stumbled back and slumped into his chair.

"He fell, I tell you. I swear by the gods," Istaga stammered.

"Do not worsen your sin by lying," Nova said. "You killed my father, and your lust for power and wealth brought misery and suffering upon this good village. I have no mercy for you. You better pray that the gods have mercy on you when I tell the people what you have done!"

Istaga knew what the people would do if they learned what he had done. He dropped to his knees in front of Nova and Honaw. "No, Nova! Do not tell them! They will kill me! Have mercy!" he begged.

"You had no mercy for my father! Now I have no mercy for you! I will let the people do what they wish with you!" she said as she headed toward the door.

"Wait, Mother, what about the corn and seed?" Honaw asked.

Nova turned toward Istaga, who sat cowering on the floor. "The people are hungry and need seed to replant their fields. Give us what you promised!" she demanded.

Istaga raised his pitiful head and said, "There is no corn. There is no seed. I traded all we had for the precious stones."

"You have doomed our village, and you have doomed yourself! The ancestors will not allow you to join them in the underworld. You will walk this world forevermore. You will never find peace, and that is a fair punishment for the sins you have committed," Honaw said.

"The people will tear you apart when they hear what you have done!" Nova exclaimed.

"No, Mother. There has been enough death. We must not let the people harm him. That will only anger the gods further. We must begin again to live in the right way. Let him live with his guilt. That will be a far worse punishment. Take his precious stones and distribute them to the people. They can use them to trade for food on their journey."

"What journey do you speak of, my son?" Nova asked.

"The people must leave the village, Mother. There is nothing for them here. They must find their own way now. The gods and ancestors will look after them."

Nova considered what Honaw said, and she knew that he was right.

They left Istaga prostrate on the floor before his throne. His tortured mind would find no peace. By his deeds, he had destroyed his dreams of wealth and power. He was left alone in the dark to endure his punishment.

When Nova told the people that Istaga had traded the last of the corn for the precious stones, they flew into a rage. They began screaming and threatening Istaga. "Istaga must be killed for his sins! His selfishness has killed us all! Drag him out to receive his punishment, and then we shall burn the great house!"

They surged toward the great house, but Honaw blocked their way and would not let them enter. "There has been enough killing," he said. "Killing Istaga and burning the great house is not what the gods and ancestors want of us. Istaga killed my grandfather and your great leader, Kwahu." The peoples gasped and began threatening Istaga again.

"How can you not want Istaga punished for his sins?" they asked.

"To die is not the worst punishment," Honaw explained. "Letting him live, to carry the weight of his sins will be a much worse punishment. The death of Grandfather and the killing of Chuchip were sins not of our making. Our sin was to let Istaga become so powerful that he disrupted the balance of our village and pulled us away from living in the right way. That is what angered the gods. They brought the great snow and the terrible flood to punish us for straying away from Sun Father's teachings. If we kill Istaga, it will only show the gods that we have not learned, and the misery will continue. We must show them we have heeded their message and will again live in the right way."

Honaw's words calmed the crowd. Many began to ask, "What do we do now? We have no food and we have no seed to replant our fields. We will surely starve."

"You must take your families and leave this place," Honaw answered. "Our village is done. You must go out into the world and make a new way for yourself. As long as you strive to live the right way, the gods will protect you. Too much evil has been done in this village. We must burn the pit house and destroy the evil that dwells there. The ancestors will never visit there again."

"But we have no food to make such a journey," the people said.

"You must be diligent in your gathering, and your hunters must be skilled in their pursuit. Mother will give you a fair share of Istaga's precious stones. They hold great value. You must trade them for food and seed for your crops when you reach your new homes," Honaw explained.

That night the men gathered shredded juniper bark and greasewood and threw it into the pit house. Then they stacked more greasewood on the roof. They lit the juniper bark and used it to ignite the greasewood. They threw burning greasewood down into the pit house and lit the stacks on the roof. Soon the pit house was aflame. The conflagration burned through the night. By sunrise, the desecrated pit house was destroyed.

Nova and Honaw prepared for their journey. They left most of their belongings behind. They packed what little dried rabbit they had left and the last of Nova's piki bread. "For a time, this was a good place to live, but I am ready to leave," Nova said. "The bad memories would haunt me if I were to stay."

"Keep the good memories in your heart, Mother. We will start a new life. We will regain the balance we have lost and the gods will reward us with happiness once again," Honaw replied.

When they stepped out into the plaza, they were surprised to see the people with their pouches packed waiting there for them. "Why are you standing here?" Honaw asked. "You should start your journeys before the day becomes too hot."

One of the men stepped forward and said, "We go with you, Honaw. You are wise beyond your years and you are our Moiety now. We will go where you go."

So the small boy, still young in age, who once played in the pond and flung stones at the ravens had become a wise Moiety. As he led his people away from the village on Chu'a Wash, he prayed. "Thank you, Grandfather. You prepared me well, but I will need your guidance now more than ever. Help me to bring balance to these good people. Help me to teach them the ways of Sun Father so we all may live the right way."

CHAPTER 10

THE CLIFF HOUSE

On that starry winter night in 1056, Lansa and Kele fled Chu'a Village and walked to the top of the mesa, and then they turned north to Lansa's hunting camp. They walked through the night and reached the camp by dawn. It was a cold morning, but Lansa soon had a fire going, and they sat together wrapped in a turkey feather blanket and ate a breakfast of piki bread and dried venison.

"This is where your father came to find me and bring me back to the village," Lansa said.

"I was afraid you would not return," Kele said.

"When I left, I had not planned on returning. I could not bear the thought of seeing you married to that dog, Chuchip. Your father convinced me I was being selfish and only thinking of my pain. I had forgotten the promise I made to my mother and the pain you were suffering. Your father reminded me of my promise and told me of your marriage to Chuchip. He told me of your suffering and how the balance of the village had been disturbed by all that had happened. His words made me return," Lansa said.

"All of that seems like a bad dream to me now," Kele said. "Being here with you has made me forget all that happened, except for one thing." She paused and looked away.

"I know, Kele. Your father told me that you would not submit to Chuchip, and that he took you against your will," Lansa said quietly.

"Oh, Lansa, how can you take me as your woman now? I am no longer pure! I was the woman of another man!" she cried. "He was a cruel husband, but I made it worse by not being a good wife. The council had approved the marriage, and it was my duty to abide by their wishes. It was best for the village, but I could only think of you. I hated Chuchip and wished he was gone. My thoughts and actions offended the gods, and then you killed Chuchip because of me. I fear my sins will never be forgiven. I do not deserve your love."

Lansa held her close and said, "To wish harm to come to Chuchip and deny him the pleasures of marriage pale in comparison to what I have done. I have taken a life in anger and deserve the punishment that was given me. What happened to you was not your fault. As I told your father, Chuchip took your body, but he did not take your heart. Your heart remains pure. Now we both must live with our punishment. We will never again live among the people, and we will never again be close to the ones we hold dear. But I love you, and we are together. Because of that, I can live with my punishment."

"Back in the mountains, I asked the gods to bring us together. A person never knows how the gods will answer. I feel safe here in your arms, and I am happy," she said.

With that, they kissed. They lay together for the first time that morning, and they both knew their love would sustain them.

They remained in the hunting camp for many sunrises. Kele gathered what food she could find during those winter months, mostly the small nuts that fell from the trees. Lansa was a good hunter and they had plenty of meat for their meals. The days were cold, and the nights were colder. At night, they wrapped themselves in sheepskin blankets and huddled under the lean-to. By day, they stayed warm by the fire. Living in the open was difficult, but they were happy.

One night as they sat by the fire, Lansa noticed that Kele was quiet and did not smile. "Kele, I can see that something troubles you. Do you miss your family?" he asked.

"I do miss my family, but that is not what troubles me," she answered and began to cry.

Lansa put his arms around her and pulled her close. "It pains me to see you cry. What is it, Kele?"

"Lansa," she said through her tears, "I am with child."

"That is not a reason to cry!" he exclaimed. "That is a reason to rejoice. We will have a child!"

"No, Lansa, you do not understand. The time is not right. I carry the child of Chuchip inside me." She buried her head in his chest and shook as the tears streamed down her cheeks. Lansa was stunned and did not know what to say at first, but he did not push her away. He held her even closer. He could feel the pain she was suffering.

"How can you want me now, Lansa?" she sobbed. "I am carrying another man's child. It is the worst punishment the gods could have placed on me. Will their anger continue forever?"

"I promise you on this night before the gods that I will never leave you, no matter what sufferings we may have to face," he said as he wiped away her tears. "I wish we could have been married in the traditional way, but that was not to be. Know, though, that in my eyes and in my heart we are husband and wife, and the child you carry will be our child. I promise to love and protect you both until the end of my days."

"After all that has come to pass, after all the pain and tears, the gods still smile on me. They have answered my prayers and given me a good husband. I also promise to love you until the end of my days," she said.

During their morning meal the next day, Lansa said, "We must leave here, Kele. It is not suitable. You cannot give birth to our child in this forest. We must find a place where I can build you a more permanent home, one with strong walls that will not let in the wind and a hearth to keep you and the little one warm. We must find a place with good water so that we can grow corn and beans."

"But where will we go?" Kele asked.

"I have heard of a great river that lies north and east of here. Hunters and traders tell me there is good land for crops and good hunting in the surrounding mountains. We will go there, and I will build you a fine house before you have our child. In the spring, we will plant corn, squash, and beans. Hopefully the gods will bless us, and it will be a good place to live," he answered.

Lansa went hunting one more time and came back with a deer. They spent the next few days drying the meat. Lansa tanned the hide, and Kele made leggings to keep them warm as they walked. She also made strong walking sandals from yucca plants she found nearby. The gods blessed them with warm days, and soon they were ready to travel. They packed their pouches with what few belongings they had and started their trek northeast. Lansa did not know where the mighty river ran, but he was confident he could find it.

The days remained warm, and being young and strong, the walking was not an effort. They reveled in each other's company and talked about many things as they walked. They shared their dreams and made plans for their future. At night, they wrapped themselves in a sheepskin blanket and slept close to the fire. They ate the dried venison, pine nuts, and a few seeds they were able to gather. They did not eat the corn, squash, or beans that Nova had given Kele. These precious seeds were sealed tightly in a jar to be used to start their crop fields in the spring. Kele's belly continued to grow, and she glowed with happiness. Lansa would sometimes lay his hand on her belly and feel the little kicks. He was sure it was a boy because of the strength of the kicks.

Lansa and Kele had traveled many sunrises since they left Chu'a Wash. The moon had grown full four times. When their journey began, they walked from sunup to sundown and only stayed in camps for a matter of a day or two, just long enough to hunt and gather what they needed to sustain themselves. But as Kele's belly grew, she tired more quickly. They were no longer able to walk all day and sometimes they stayed in a camp five or six sunrises. The gods had been kind to them. They blessed them with fairly warm days, but on this morning, the sky was gray and a cold wind blew out of the northwest.

"I pray we come to the river soon," Lansa said as he ate the rabbit stew Kele had fixed for their morning meal. "You cannot have our child out here in the forest. I need time to build you a good house."

"Do not worry, my husband, it will be many sunrises before our child is born. You will have time to build our home and plant our corn before she comes," Kele replied.

"You mean before he comes." Lansa teased her.

Kele smiled. "We will see my husband. We will see …"

"The sky is dark and the wind is cold today. Maybe we should stay in camp another sunrise," Lansa said.

"No, let us walk today. I feel strong. I know we will reach the river soon," Kele replied.

"As you wish," Lansa said as he began to pack their pouches for the trail.

As they walked, the sky grew darker and a light snow began to fall. They did not worry at first because they had traveled on snowy days before. But as the day wore on, the wind began to howl and the snow intensified and began to accumulate. Soon the icy, wind-driven snow bit at the exposed skin on their hands and faces.

"We must find shelter!" Lansa yelled above the din. He looked around, but they were crossing a mesa and there were no trees against which they could build a lean-to. He wrapped a cape around Kele and tied a thong around her waist. He then tied the other end around his waist.

"Keep the cape wrapped tightly around you and your face out of the wind. Let me lead you!" Lansa instructed. Kele looked at him with fear in her eyes and nodded her head.

The wind blew the heavy snow horizontally, and it became difficult to see even a few feet ahead of them. Lansa pushed with determination against the blizzard. He hoped he would find some place where they could get shelter enough to protect them from the storm. Then he was jerked to a stop by the thong around his waist. He turned to see Kele on her knees in the snow. He knelt by her side and looked into her eyes.

She said in a weak voice, "I can no longer feel my legs. I cannot walk. I must rest."

"We cannot rest here. We will freeze to death if we stop now!" Lansa shouted against the wind.

"Just let me lie here awhile. I am too tired to continue today," Kele mumbled as she lay down in the snow.

Lansa picked Kele up and struggled on. He prayed. "Please Earth Mother, help me find a place that will protect us from this storm."

Fatigue began to overtake him, and his legs grew weak, but he knew he could not stop. He summoned all of his strength and fought hard against the gale. Suddenly, the wind let up enough for him to see a few hundred feet. He had walked into a box canyon. He scanned the canyon looking for any kind of protection and caught a glimpse of a trail leading up a crevice in the canyon wall. He followed the trail with his eyes, and he was amazed to see that it led to a stone house built into the canyon wall.

"Thank you, Earth Mother, for not abandoning us," he said to himself.

"Kele, Earth Mother has saved us," Lansa said as he pulled the cape from her face. In anguish, he saw that she was unconscious and could not hear him. He wrapped the cape tightly around her and tied it with the thong. He gently placed her over his shoulder and started up the crevice. His legs ached, and he faltered as he climbed, but he reached the house in the cliff and entered through a T-shaped door. The wind carried the cold in through the door and windows, but the house offered some protection. He was grateful.

He gently laid Kele on the floor and looked about. It took a moment for his eyes to adjust to the darkness. He peered about and saw that the house had been abandoned for many seasons. As he looked around, he noticed a hearth and a pile of wood in the back corner of the room. "Again you smile on us, Earth Mother!" Lansa marveled.

As he carried some wood to the hearth to light a fire, he noticed there were three planks covering a depression in the floor. As he removed the planks to add to his stack of firewood, he saw a partially decayed bed mat, and below that, a body of what he thought was a man. The house had become a burial chamber when its inhabitants had left.

"I am sorry to disturb your sleep, friend. But I need your burial box to save my wife and unborn baby," he said softly. "I promise to return you to your restful sleep when the storm has passed."

Quickly Lansa started a fire and stripped Kele out of her wet clothes. She momentarily stirred from her lethargy and looked at him through glassy eyes. She began to shiver violently; her breathing was slow and shallow. He stripped off his own clothes and wrapped a dry rabbit skin blanket around them both. He held her close as they lay next to the fire. Her skin was extremely cold and she continued to shiver. He rubbed her arms and legs, trying to bring the warmth back to her body. Eventually she stopped shivering, and her breathing became stronger. Lansa was exhausted, but he tried to stay awake as long as he could, until, finally, the weariness overtook him, and he drifted off to sleep.

"Lansa, wake up, wake up!" Kele cried as she shook her husband. Lansa stirred from his sleep and looked up to see Kele staring at him with a worried look. "Oh, thank the gods!" Kele said. "I thought you had left me." She gently kissed him and hugged his neck.

"I will never leave you. I will always be here when you awake," Lansa smiled.

Kele returned his smile and looked around. "What is this place? How did we get here?"

"Earth Mother saved us from the storm. I will tell you all about it soon, but now we must shut out the storm or we will need her to save us again."

The storm continued to howl outside as they started the fire again and covered the windows and door with turkey feather and rabbit-skin blankets. Soon their little shelter was warm and dry. They sat next to the fire and Lansa told her all that had happened.

"You were very cold and could not stay awake. I feared you and the little one would freeze to death. I prayed to Earth Mother to show me a shelter from the storm. She showed me this abandoned house built into the side of a cliff. Only it is not just a house." He took her over and showed her the body lying in the burial bed. "It was once a home, but now it is a burial chamber. I needed the wood that covered him for the fire. When we leave, we must find wood to replace it and restore his place of rest," he said.

"You saved my life once again, my husband. But this time you saved more than just my life." She reached out for his hand and laid it on her belly. They both felt the little one kick.

That night as they lay in their bed listening to the storm blow, Lansa said, "When I laid with you next to the fire today, my mother came to me in my dreams. I saw her sitting in the snow and the storm swirled all around us. I asked her why she was sitting out in the wind and cold."

"Lansa, you have come back to care for me just as you promised. I must rest for a while before we go. Come lay with me and keep me warm," she answered.

"I moved toward her to keep her warm, but the wind blew her away and she disappeared in the snow. What do you think this dream means, Kele?"

"I do not know, my husband. Maybe it was just a dream," she answered.

It took three sunrises for the storm to blow itself out. When they awoke on the fourth day, they could no longer hear the wind. They pulled down the blankets and felt the warmth of Sun Father's light. The new fallen snow glistened under his brilliance.

They prayed. "Thank you, Sun Father, for returning your light and warmth to us." They stepped out onto a small overhang and stood under a bright blue sky. From their vantage point high on the cliff face, they could see a long distance. They looked upon a beautiful valley off to the northeast. Running through the valley was the river they had been searching for.

Lansa held Kele close and said, "We are home. Thank you, Earth Mother, for showing us the way."

Before leaving the cliff house, Lansa kept his promise. He cut and shaped three stout planks and fitted them tightly over the body in the small depression. He also replaced the firewood he and Kele used during the storm. In completing these tasks, he felt the balance of the burial chamber had been restored and the spirit that dwelled there could again rest in peace. They packed their pouches, made their way down the cliff, and started toward the river.

CHAPTER 11

THE RIVER

Lansa and Kele planted their crop fields along a bend in the river where the water slowed and it was easy to build a small dam. They dug irrigation canals from the river that nourished the seeds that Kele had brought from Chu'a Wash. Before very many sunrises, they had healthy sprouts of corn, squash, and beans growing in their fields.

They found good straight trees in the nearby forest that would make fine corner posts and ceiling beams for a house, but they could find none of the tabular stones that could be cut for the walls. The stones they found were not shaped well and were too hard to cut. To remedy this problem, Lansa decided to build a different type of house, like the ones he had seen as a boy hunting with his father. His father told him the old ones had built these types of houses in the days before the village on Chu'a Wash.

First, he dug a pit twenty feet long, fifteen feet wide and two feet deep. Next, he cut a number of the small white trees and fitted them vertically around the interior of the pit. These would act as a framework for the walls. Then he cut bigger logs that acted as corner

108

posts to support a log and brush roof. He and Kele mixed grass and mud from the river and covered the walls and roof, both inside and out, to seal the structure.

Inside, he built a wall toward the back of the house that divided the interior into two chambers. The front chamber was used for living space and the cooking area, and the back room was used for sleeping. He built two hearths, one in each room. The house was entered through a ground level opening that had a stone placed in front of the interior door to deflect the wind and cold. There was a hole in the roof to let the smoke escape.

Last, he dug the sipapu, a small hole next to the hearth, in the floor of the front room and placed a turkey feather and a small piece of the beautiful bluish-green stone at its bottom. This was an entryway to the underworld so that the ancestor gods could visit them. The turkey feather and small stone were offerings to let the ancestors know they were welcome. When the house was completed, Lansa was sure that it would be cool in the summer and warm and dry in the winter. Lansa was satisfied that he had built a secure home for his family.

He and Kele continued to work in the crop fields and started construction on a storage bin to hold their stores of food during the winter. Kele's belly grew, and it became harder for her to work in the fields, but she did not complain and helped as much as she could.

One day in late summer as they worked, Kele said, "The little one is very restless today. I think it may be time soon."

"Time for him to come out?" Lansa asked excitedly.

Kele giggled at his question. "Yes," she answered, "time for him to come out."

That evening when they had finished their day's work, Kele walked up and down the rows of corn stopping periodically to pull an ear of corn from a stalk. She shucked each ear of corn until she found one that had big, full kernels and perfectly straight rows. This perfect ear of corn would be needed when it came time to name their baby.

That night the pains in her belly came more often, and there was less time between each spasm. By early morning, before dawn, she knew it was time. "It is time, my love," she said. "Give me your sharpest knife."

"How can I help you, Kele? What should I do? This is your first child and you have no mother or grandmother to help you," Lansa asked worriedly.

"Do not worry, Lansa. Women have been having babies since the beginning of time. I know what to do. I will be fine. Once I go into the back room, you must not enter, no matter what you hear. You must promise me this."

"I promise," Lansa reluctantly agreed.

With that, Kele took the perfect ear of corn and the knife and went into the back room. Soon Lansa could see the light of a fire coming through the door. Then he started to hear Kele moan and cry softly. This went on for what seemed like hours. He wanted to rush in and hold her, help her through the ordeal, but he had promised he would not. He remembered Kele's words, "You must not enter, no matter what you hear."

He heard Kele cry out. He jumped to his feet and rushed to the door. It took all his strength to keep himself from entering the room. *She is dying!* he thought.

It was then that he heard a different cry. It was small and weak at first, but then it grew loud and strong. By the sound of the strong cry, he knew that Kele had given them a son. The thought of him not being the baby's father did not enter his mind. He had promised Kele that he would claim the child as his own, and in his heart, he already had.

All that day and into the night, Kele stayed in the back room, caring for and nursing the baby. Lansa prepared for the naming ceremony that would take place at dawn the next morning. From the perfect ear of corn Kele had picked, he ground a fine meal and used it to draw four lines on the floor pointing toward the sacred cardinal directions. Where the lines intersected he placed a turkey feather and a small piece of the bluish-green stone. This was an offering to the gods so that they would bless their child and consecrate his name. He then prepared a bowl of yucca-root suds and placed it on the offering. The room was then ready for the naming ceremony. He joined Kele and the baby in the back room and waited for dawn.

"Everything is ready," he said. "Now we wait for Sun Father."

"There is one thing I do wish we had for the ceremony," Kele said.

"What is that, young mother?" Lansa asked.

"It is the tradition of the people that a new mother wears her wedding dress for the naming ceremony. I wish I had a wedding dress."

Lansa smiled and left the room. When he returned, he handed Kele a small bundle. It was wrapped in charred rabbit fur and tied with a thong. "What is this, my husband?" she asked curiously.

"Open it and you will see. I hope it will do," he replied.

Kele carefully opened the small package to reveal a beautiful white buckskin dress with bright yellow disks hanging from tassels that encircled the collar, sleeves and hemline. She held the dress up and was overwhelmed by its beauty. "It is the most beautiful dress I have ever seen!" she exclaimed. "Where did it come from? How did you get it?" The excited questions came so quickly that Lansa did not have a chance to answer.

"Calm yourself a moment and I will tell you. It is a long story," Lansa said gently.

Kele sat with the baby sleeping in her arms. Lansa sat next to her and held her as he went on with the story. "Do you remember when we went to the mountains to cut logs for the new rooms?"

"Yes, I remember," Kele, answered.

"It was then I knew that I loved you and wanted you for my wife," Lansa continued.

"I remember you went hunting and came back with a buck draped around your neck. Sihu and I marveled at your strength. You carried the buck so easily. I also remember you would not allow the women to work the skin. You insisted on doing it yourself," Kele said.

"Yes, you remember well. I took the skin to my mother and asked her to make this dress. It was to be my gift to your mother when I asked for permission to marry you. Only I never got the chance to give it to her. The night before I was going to present it to her, your grandfather fell from the cliff and died. To present it to her then would not have been proper. It was then my long nightmare began. At the council that night, Istaga arranged the marriage between you and Chuchip. Your father and I fought for you, but we could not sway the council. When I realized I had lost you, I was filled with anger and despair. I did a very selfish thing. I ran to my house and grabbed my bow and quiver. All I could think of was just getting away to the mountains. But before I left, I saw the small bundle I brought you tonight. My mother had wrapped it so carefully. She was proud of the work she had done. I was so full of rage that I threw the bundle into the cooking fire and ran out the door. I thought I had destroyed the beautiful dress."

"How did you come to have it tonight?" Kele asked.

"Your brother brought it to me when I was banished from the village. He was waiting for me along the trail. He told me of your plan to leave with me and gave me the bundle. He said my mother had given it to your parents and asked that they find a way to get it to me."

He held up the rabbit skin and showed Kele where the fur was charred. "My mother must have saved it from the fire and kept it for me. I was waiting for the right time to give it to you. I can think of no better time than now. It was meant for your mother, but I hope it will do for your wedding dress. You can wear it when we name our son at dawn," he said.

"It is the most beautiful dress I have ever seen. I will be proud to wear it," Kele said happily.

The baby squirmed in her arms and fretted a little. She lay on her mat and nursed the little boy. Lansa lay next to them and held them close. The yellow disks of the dress reflected the light from the fire and made the room shimmer. They waited for Sun Father. Kele had never been happier.

When Lansa awoke, the room was still dark, and there were only warm ashes in the fire pit. He went outside and could see that the eastern sky was just beginning to lighten. He went back inside and spoke softly to Kele. "It is time, Kele. Sun Father will soon show his face over the horizon."

Kele opened her eyes and smiled at Lansa, "I have been waiting for this day for a long time. Take the little one out next to the fire. I will join you when I am ready."

Lansa gently lifted the sleeping baby and went out to the other room. He lit a torch and placed the baby on a small bed mat next to the warm coals in the fire pit. When Kele emerged, she was wearing the white buckskin dress. The fit was snug, but Lansa had never seen her look more beautiful. Her hair hung loosely around her shoulders and the yellow disks shimmered in the light of the torch. He had never loved her more than he did in that moment.

Kele knelt next to the bowl of yucca-root suds in the middle of the offering. She removed the blanket that covered the baby and held his little naked body in her arms. He began to cry because of the cold. She dipped her hair into the yucca suds and gently washed the baby with her hair. She then rubbed ashes from the fire pit on him and sprinkled his face with the corn meal Lansa had prepared.

Then Lansa took an ear of corn, dipped it in the yucca suds and lightly touched the child's head. "I name you Moki, for the deer whose life's blood feeds us and gives us strength. We promise to care for you and teach you so that you may grow strong and wise," he said.

They placed little Moki in a cradleboard, his face carefully covered with a tiny blanket, and walked to the top of a nearby hill. When Sun Father appeared above the horizon, Kele removed the blanket from the cradleboard and allowed the light to shine fully on his little face. She presented the infant boy to Sun Father and recited the ancient prayer:

> On this day
> Our child
> Into the light of Sun Father
> You are standing.
> This is the beginning of your days,
> Our days have passed.
>
> On this day
> The ancestors have come
> To stand in their sacred place.
> Sun Father has come to look upon you.
> This is your day.
>
> On this day
> We offer this prayer
> And this prayer meal to Sun Father.
> May your life be fulfilled, and

In your thoughts may we live.
For this, on this day
We name you Moki.

The days of summer turned to fall. The river ran high, and there had been ample water to nourish their crop fields during the growing season. Lansa and Kele worked side by side with little Moki strapped in a cradleboard on Kele's back. Their harvest was good. They had plenty of corn, squash, and beans to feed them during the winter. Now they just needed to lay in a supply of meat, and they could be assured of a comfortable winter.

"I must go hunt deer before the cold comes and the snow flies," Lansa said. "I have seen their tracks and droppings in the mountains to the west. It should not take me long. I should be back within three or four sunrises. But I do not like leaving you and Moki here alone for that long."

"Do not worry about us, my husband," she said. "We have plenty to eat and there is a good stack of firewood right outside. We will care for each other, and Moki will protect me," Kele said with a laugh.

That night Lansa made new arrowheads and sharpened his ax and his knife. Kele packed dried venison and piki bread into his pouch. At dawn the next morning, Lansa kissed both Kele and Moki good-bye and walked off toward the mountains.

Kele kept busy grinding corn and making piki bread. By evening, she was tired and the house was hot from the hearth burning all day. She wrapped Moki in a blanket and went outside to sit in the breeze. She sat with her back against the house and held Moki in her arms. He was soon asleep. The breeze was cool against her face. Kele closed her eyes and drifted off to sleep herself.

She woke with a start when she heard something move in the crop field. The evening had turned to night while she slept, and she strained to see in the darkness. Then she heard a low growl, and suddenly she could see glowing eyes piercing the darkness. She heard more growls and counted three, four … no, five sets of eyes moving slowly through the grass. Her heart pounded in her chest when she realized what she was looking at: wolves.

Backing slowly into the house, Kele laid the sleeping Moki on his bed mat. The fire had gone out, so she quickly rekindled it. She could hear the wolves prowling right outside the door opening. She picked up a burning log and started another fire on the floor just inside the door. As she was building the fire, she looked up and saw a large wolf staring at her through the door. She threw a burning log out the door and quickly jumped back. That startled Moki, and he began to cry. She cradled him in her arms, and tried to quiet him. "Be still, little Moki. We are in trouble," she whispered.

Through the night, she heard the wolves snarling and moving about just outside the walls of the pit house and on the roof. She kept a larger-than-normal fire going in the hearth and fed logs into the fire she had built by the door. Moki could sense her fear and was restless. He slept fretfully, and she did not sleep at all.

At daylight, she checked her store of water and wood. She was glad that Lansa had filled the water jars before he left. He had also brought in a good pile of firewood, but burning wood all night had depleted the pile quickly. She knew that the fires had kept the wolves away during the night. She also knew she had enough wood to keep the fires going through the day, but she would have to bring in more for another night. She hoped that the wolves would move on in search of easier prey.

She prayed. "Please, Earth Mother, help me and my child. Let the wolves be gone."

She listened carefully and was filled with hope when she could no longer hear the wolves prowling around. Moki finally fell asleep for longer than just a few minutes, so Kele sat quietly and listened intently for any sounds of the wolves. She heard none. Looking at her small pile of wood and with Moki sound asleep, she decided that now would be a good time to bring in more wood from outside. She picked up the ax used to chop kindling. It felt heavy in her hand, but she was sure she could swing it forcefully if she had to. She snuffed out the fire in front of the door and, tense with fear, slowly crawled outside.

Kele shaded her eyes from the bright sun and looked about. She saw wolf tracks all around the house, but she heard no sound and saw no sign of them.

"Thank you, Earth Mother," she whispered to herself.

Holding the ax up ready to strike, she worked her way over to the woodpile. She picked up as much wood as she could, but it was awkward, because she still held the ax. She was able to carry only a few pieces.

She carried what she had into the house and went back for a second load. *It will take too many trips carrying just a few sticks at a time*, she thought.

She lay the ax down just outside the door. She went to the woodpile and began to load up her arms, when suddenly she saw a very large black wolf staring at her from the crop field. It snarled at her and showed its teeth. Fear gripped her, and she froze. Then she heard Moki cry. She turned and saw another wolf standing at the door of the house.

Dropping all but one log, she ran toward the door, yelling at the wolf, "Get away from my child!"

The wolf snarled and turned to face her. She threw the log at the beast, distracting him long enough for her to pick up the ax lying by the door. The wolf lunged at her. She brought the ax around in a sweeping arc and caught the wolf on the side of the head. It was a fierce blow. Blood spurted from the wound. The wolf yelped and ran off.

She was halfway through the door when she felt a hard tug on her foot, and a searing pain shot up her leg. She screamed as the wolf began to pull her back out the door. Kicking her leg hard, she broke free and turned to see the black wolf staring at her, blood running from its mouth. She scrambled to the fire, and picking up a burning log, she thrust it in the face of the animal. It yelped and backed out the door.

Moki was still crying, so she dragged herself over to him and cradled him in her arms. She was relieved to see that he was not hurt. Her burned hand hurt badly, but the pain in her foot and leg was intense. She looked down and saw that her foot was badly mangled. Blood was beginning to pool on the floor.

"I will die if I do not stop the blood. What do I do? How do I stop it? Oh, help me, Earth Mother. Show me what to do."

Seeing the fire still burning, she remembered a time when the people were cutting wood and a man had cut his arm. It was bleeding badly, and Grandfather Kwahu heated the blade of a knife in the fire until it was hot and pressed it to the wound. The man yelled out in pain, but the blood stopped flowing. She gently placed Moki on his bed mat. Then she calmly placed the blade of the ax in the fire until it was white hot.

She prayed. "Give me strength, Grandfather."

Kele pressed the searing blade to her foot. The pain was almost more than she could bear. She screamed, and Moki began to cry again. Bracing herself, she held the hot blade to her wound until the sweet smell of burning flesh filled her nostrils. She dropped the ax and fell back next to Moki. She became light-headed and thought she would black out.

"No! I must stay alert. I will have to protect Moki until Lansa returns. Oh, Lansa, please return soon."

She mixed a bowl of yucca suds and gently washed her foot and burned hand. She cut a piece of rabbit fur and washed it thoroughly in the suds and wrapped her lacerated foot. She did not wrap her hand because she would need both her hands to care for Moki. When these tasks were finished, she again took stock of her supplies. She still had a full jar of water, but the few logs she had brought in would not be enough to keep two fires going all night. She knew the fire in front of the door was the only way to keep the wolves from entering the house. Rekindling that fire, she wrapped Moki in a blanket and nursed him until he slept.

The horrible pain in her foot radiated up her leg and into her body, but she would not cry out. She knew Moki's crying would attract the wolves and embolden them to enter the house. She kept feeding the fire, watching fearfully, as her pile of wood grew smaller and smaller.

Oh, Lansa, return soon. Your family needs you. I cannot fight these wolves alone.

For a second night, she heard the wolves prowling outside the walls and on the roof. When dawn broke, she was down to her last few sticks of wood. Soon the fire would burn itself out, and there would be no way to keep the wolves from entering. She had no choice but to face them, and fight the best she could. Protecting her child was her only thought. With tears in her eyes, she gently kissed her Moki. "Good-bye, my son. You have been the greatest joy of my life. Grow into a fine man like your father and make us proud," Kele whispered.

With that, she put him in the cradleboard and placed him in the corn bin, leaving the lid cracked open to allow him to breathe. She prayed that this would protect him until Lansa returned. Left in the dark, Moki started to cry.

"I am sorry, little Moki. Be strong!"

The fire had gone out, and she heard the wolves right outside the door. She picked up the ax and prayed one last time. "Sun Father, give me strength. I do not fear death, for I know Earth Mother and the ancestors will welcome me home. My life has been good. I have the love of the strongest, bravest man I have ever known. We have been given your greatest gift, a child. Thank you. I will gladly give my life for him. Protect him, Father, and comfort Lansa."

With that, she crawled out the door and stood as erect as she could. The wolves glared at her, their teeth bared and hackles standing straight up. "Come and do battle!" she yelled at them. "I know you only do what is natural to you. I do not hold it against you, but you will not take my life easily!"

The large black wolf stood a few steps in front of her. The fur and skin on his face was singed and one of his eyes was milky white. He emitted a low growl and watched her menacingly. She braced herself against the house and raised the ax. The wolf exploded toward her and lunged to get at her throat.

Then the first arrow struck. It hit the black wolf in the neck and went straight through. The wolf rolled once in the dirt and was dead. The second arrow struck a wolf in the side; it yelped and bit at the arrow as it ran away. Astonished, Kele looked in the direction from where the arrows had come and saw Lansa running toward her, pulling another arrow from his quiver. He let fly. The arrow stuck a third wolf in the chest and stopped him in his tracks. Lansa then dropped his bow and pulled his ax from his belt. The last wolf attacked him. It struck him and knocked him down, but he quickly rolled and swung his ax at the animal again and again. When he stopped flailing, the wolf lay dead at his feet.

Kele collapsed to the ground. All the fear and pain of the last days exploded, and she cried uncontrollably. Lansa rushed to her and held her in his arms.

"Lansa, I did not think you would be here in time. I did my best to fight them and protect our son," she sobbed.

"I am here, Kele. I am sorry I left you. I will never leave you alone again." Her foot was bleeding through the bandage she had made. "Kele, you are hurt!"

"It will be all right," she said. "Everything will be all right now that you are home."

Lansa carefully lifted her and carried her into the house. He laid her on a bed mat and looked around for the baby. "Kele, where is Moki?" he asked.

"He is in the corn," she answered weakly, and blacked out.

It took Lansa a moment to figure out what she meant. He knew she would not have left Moki in the crop field, and the only other corn was in the storage bin. He removed the lid and there was Moki, lying safely in his cradleboard. Moki smiled when he saw his father's face.

CHAPTER 12

THE BEACON

During the autumn and winter of 1060, little snow fell in the mountains that surrounded the basin, and even less rain fell on the parched land that spring and summer. The years had been difficult since Honaw led his people southwest away from Chu'a Wash. They settled near a small wash that at first provided enough water for them to cultivate a small crop field. They built a village along the wash, but it was nothing like the village they had left behind on Chu'a Wash. It did not have a great house. They saw no need for one. It was simple, consisting of twenty small houses that surrounded a ceremonial pit house.

Honaw had grown into a strong young man of sixteen growing seasons. He was much like his father, lean and muscular. His dark hair was long, and he tied it back with a single thong made from the sinew of a deer. Most of the time he wore a simple white robe of a Moiety; when he hunted or worked in the field, he wore a deerskin loincloth. His mother, Nova, often told him he was as handsome as his father.

Over the years, Honaw had led his people well. He did his best to guide them and instruct them in the right way Sun Father wanted them to live. He diligently marked the sacred ceremonies and was careful to prepare the prayer sticks and recite the prayers just as Old Kwahu had taught him. But for the past two growing season, there was very little water in the wash. The storage bins were nearly empty, and he worried that there would not be enough food to last the winter.

One morning as he scooped cornmeal from the communal bin to give to the people, his jar struck the bottom of the bin. He knew there was only enough corn to last a few more sunrises. "Father, have I not been a good Moiety? Have I not done my best to instruct the people to live the right way and keep the balance? Why have you forsaken us? Without rain, the crop field has not flourished. There is no food for these good people during the cold months ahead. I fear many will die. I do not know what to do. I need guidance. Please answer my prayers. How do I save my people?"

Nova had aged well since they left Chu'a Wash. Silver streaks now ran through her dark hair, but she was still strong and possessed a keen mind. She devoted herself to taking care of her people. She made sure that all had their fair share of food; she nursed them when they were sick or injured and, above all, she showed them how to be kind to one another.

Honaw had always loved his mother dearly, but after the loss of Tocho and Sihu, he had come to depend on her for many things, not the least of which was her strength in times of despair. She always provided sage advice and encouragement in difficult situations or when Honaw doubted himself. She was much like Old Kwahu. Honaw felt as if he was still connected to his grandfather through her.

"Mother, the corn bins are almost empty," he said as he watched her grind the last of their corn. "I go to spend the night on the mesa."

"You go to pray again, son?" Nova asked.

"Yes, Mother, maybe the gods will answer my prayers this time and give me a sign as to what to do. Our hunters will not be able to bring in enough meat to last the winter, and with no corn, I fear many will starve. The people also know this. They look to me for answers, but I have none for them. I hope the gods have not abandoned us."

He stuffed his turkey feather blanket into his pouch and picked up his prayer sticks. "I will return at sunrise, Mother." He kissed her and started toward the mesa.

That night atop the mesa, he prayed to Sun Father to give him guidance and to Earth Mother to provide them what they would need to survive the long winter ahead. But this night, he also prayed directly to Old Kwahu.

"Grandfather Kwahu, you who taught me so well, do you remember when I led our people out of the old village? I told you then that I would need your guidance more than ever if I was to bring them to a safe place where they could be happy. I thank you for showing me the way to our little village. For a time we have been happy and safe here. The people have lived in the right way, and all has been in balance. But now Sun Father is angry with us. He holds back the rain, and the wash runs dry. You know better than I do what this means. What am I to do, Grandfather? Show me the way."

He sat looking out over the landscape hoping for a sign but saw none, only the shadows moving across the land and the stars in the sky. His eyes grew heavy, but he fought sleep. He wanted to stay awake and pray. There might yet be a sign.

Suddenly, there was Grandfather Kwahu floating in the air just beyond the edge of the mesa. He could see him clearly. Honaw was not afraid. He rejoiced.

"Grandfather, you have come! Thank you! You heard my prayers. What am I to do? How do I save our people?" he pleaded.

The old man did not speak, yet Honaw heard his voice. Pointing north, Kwahu said, "Follow the light in the darkness."

Honaw looked in the direction the old man was pointing, but saw no light. "What light do you speak of, Grandfather?"

"Follow the light in the darkness, Honaw," Grandfather said gently, and then he smiled and faded away.

Honaw woke and found himself curled up on his turkey blanket. It was still dark. He did not know whether Grandfather had really been there or if it had been a dream. It did not matter. He knew it was the sign he had so badly needed.

"What did Grandfather mean? Follow the light in the darkness?" he asked himself.

He looked north but saw no light. He climbed higher up the mesa where he could get a better view north, and there it was, one single beacon far off on the northern horizon! He was filled with joy. Grandfather Kwahu had answered his prayer. Honaw did not know how the light got there, or what it marked. He only knew that he and his people had to follow it. He stood there until sunrise. He became concerned because, as it became lighter, the beacon faded until it could no longer be seen.

As he walked back down the mesa, he was filled with questions. "Are we to travel only by night? What if the light does not return? I must have faith!" he told himself. "Grandfather told me to follow the light in the darkness and showed me the way. We will follow the light."

For two more nights, Honaw climbed the mesa and looked to the north. The beacon appeared both nights. He aligned the light with a bright star in the northern sky. He stayed on the mesa until dawn, when the beacon faded with the morning light. He then selected landmarks that aligned with the beam. In doing this, he assured himself that he would not get lost and lead his people astray.

On the morning of the third day, he told his mother of his plan. "Mother, there is little corn left in the bins. Our people will not survive if we stay here. It is time to move again."

"I agree," she replied. "You must lead the people to a better place, but where will we go? What will we do?" she asked anxiously.

"Grandfather Kwahu spoke to me in a vision. He has instructed me to lead the people north toward a light in the darkness."

"What light in the darkness, my son?"

"On the night Grandfather came to me, he told me to follow the light in the darkness and pointed to the north. I looked and at first, I did not see the light. I climbed higher on the mesa and that is when I saw it, a bright light glowing in the darkness far to the north. I have spent the last two nights on the mesa to make certain the light was there. It is there, Mother, and I must lead the people to it. I do not know what we will find when we reach the light. I only know that Grandfather instructed me to lead the people to the light in the darkness."

Honaw called all the people to the plaza and told them of his vision. He asked them to trust him as they had trusted Old Kwahu. He also told them that if some wanted to stay here in the small village, he would understand and wish them well. No one wanted to stay. They all pledged to follow him because they had trusted him once before and they would trust him again. They did not burn the pit house this time since there had been no evil in this village. They simply packed their pouches with what they could carry and walked away, abandoning the little village.

CHAPTER 13

❖

JOURNEY TO WHITE HOUSE

Honaw very carefully marked the trail heading north. Each night he climbed a mesa that gave him a clear line of sight to the north, and each night, the beacon continued to shine. He was thorough and exacting as he marked the bright star in the northern sky and then aligned landmarks that he could follow the next day. The going was slow because they had many children and old ones who tired easily. Along the way, the women were able to gather pine nuts, roots, and berries, and the men successfully hunted rabbits, but it was barely enough to stave off starvation.

Ten sunrises into their journey, they reached a mountainous area. The landscape changed from low-growing piñon and juniper trees to tall pine, fir, and spruce trees. It was good ground for hunting deer. Honaw decided to camp for a few days in order to rest and send out hunting parties to bring in deer. The people were happy for the rest, and they had all grown tired of rabbit stew. They stayed in camp for five sunrises. During that time, the men were successful in their hunting, with Earth Mother giving them four deer. The camp celebrated with plentiful meals, and everyone filled their pouches with dried meat. The people were refreshed and ready to resume the journey north.

On the morning they were preparing to leave, Honaw noticed his mother frequently rubbing the back of her neck. He could see that she was very uncomfortable. "Mother, what is wrong? Why do you rub your neck?" he asked.

"It is nothing," she answered. "One of Earth Mother's insects has bitten me, and it is has become bothersome."

"Let me look at it. Maybe I can make a poultice to give you some comfort." Honaw parted her long hair and observed a large red spot with a small darker red spot at its center. It felt warm to the touch. "I can see why you are bothered. I think one of Earth Mother's little creatures has decided to make a home for itself under your skin. I will see if I can remove it. This may hurt a little. I am sorry."

"Do not worry about hurting me," she said. "It will be a relief to be done with this discomfort."

With that, Honaw pinched the skin around the small dark spot and the body of a tiny insect appeared. He grasped the body between his thumb and forefinger and pulled it loose from the skin. Nova jumped when he did this, but she did not cry out. He then made a poultice from a plant that Old Kwahu had shown him and placed it on the reddened area.

When he finished, Nova said gratefully, "Thank you, my son. It feels better already. Do not give it another thought." They finished their preparations to leave. Honaw got a fix on the landmarks he had memorized the night before, and the people resumed their trek north.

Two sunrises out of the mountains, Nova started to complain of severe pain in her head, and she would not eat. Then the fever came. She became too weak to walk, so Honaw carried her. Sweat poured from her body as she slept against his chest. He could not keep up with the others. They left them far behind. When the people stopped for the night and noticed that Nova and Honaw were not with them, they sent two young men back who offered to help carry Nova, but Honaw would not let them. He feared for her life. He could feel her strength slipping away.

Honaw carried her into camp and laid her on her bed mat. He bathed her head and neck in cool water to comfort her. She moaned in pain every time he touched or moved her arms or legs. When he was pouring cool water on her burning feet, he saw that they were covered with small red spots. He had never seen this before, and Grandfather had never taught him anything about red spots on the skin. He did not know what to do.

Again, that evening he tried to get her to eat, but she refused. The fever continued through the night and her breathing became shallow. He sat by her side until sunrise. When she awoke, she seemed to have recovered a little. She still had severe pain in her head, but she was more alert and talking. Honaw hoped the fever had broken, and she would recover. When he looked at her legs, his heart and his hope sank. The red spots now covered both her legs and had become darker.

When he looked at her, she smiled and said weakly, "Why do you have such a look of worry on your face, my son? I feel better this morning. My legs do not hurt. I do not even feel them, but I am tired. Just give me a little more time to sleep, and I will be ready to follow you to the light in the darkness."

"Yes, Mother. You just rest. Soon we will all go together," Honaw replied. He sat by her side and held her hand when she drew her last breath. Tears rolled down his face as he sang her death song. The people gathered around when they heard him sing, but he never felt more alone. His mother had been his strength since Grandfather, Tocho, and Sihu had passed to the ancestors. Without her, he was lost.

Honaw wrapped Nova in a blanket and carried her to the top of the mesa. Many of the people wept and sang the death song. They all loved Nova. They wanted to accompany Honaw to the top of the mesa and help with the burial, but Honaw would not permit them. His grief manifested itself through anger, anger at everything and everyone.

"I will bury my mother alone!" he snapped. "Where were you when she was dying? Only I cared for her, and only I will bury her!" Since Honaw could not strike out at the gods, he vented his anger at his people.

It pained Honaw that he could not lay his mother to rest in a sacred burial mound, and that he had so very few of her things to bury with her. He lay her facing north, so that her spirit would be able to find its way home. Even though he was angry with the gods, he still recited the death songs and preformed the rituals. She had won her place with the ancestors long ago. They surely would not deny her.

When he finished with the burial, he tried to pray, not just to recite the words, but to talk to Grandfather and all the gods. Try as he might, he could not restrain his anger. He exploded and shook his fist at the northern sky.

"How could this have happened, Grandfather? How could you and the ancestors take her from me? I do not deserve this punishment! The people do not deserve this punishment! Mother gave me purpose. She gave the people comfort and wise counsel. Now all is lost. Your light in the darkness is not a beacon of hope. It has only led us to death and suffering! I have always heeded your words and led the people the right way, but I no longer believe in what you say. I will no longer heed your words! I will no longer follow your beacon!"

He kneeled alone by her grave all through the night. The women brought him food, but he would not touch it, or even acknowledge their presence. He simply stared out into the darkness, not speaking or moving.

Well past daybreak, when they should have already been on the trail heading north, a small group of men came to talk with Honaw. "Honaw," they asked respectfully, "when do we resume the journey north? There is no water here, and the little ones grow thirsty."

Without looking at them, Honaw answered. "You do not need my permission to leave. Take the people and go."

"Go without you? We do not know the direction. We do not know the landmarks that will lead us to the light in the darkness. We will be lost," they pleaded.

"I do not care about the light in the darkness. I will no longer lead you to it. Stop depending on me! It is long past the time for you to take care of yourselves!"

"Honaw, how can you say these words? You have always showed us the way, and we have always faithfully followed. We have trusted you. We will perish without you to lead us."

"In leading you, I neglected my mother, and now she is dead. I will lead you no more. Now go!"

"Honaw, please—"

"Go! Leave me alone!"

From the top of the mesa, he watched the small band of people head north. He watched them until they disappeared over the horizon. He felt no pity for them. He felt no responsibility for them. He completely lost faith in all his grandfather had taught him. He was no longer a Moiety. He was just a man alone, filled with sorrow and self-pity.

The sun rose high in the sky, and heat pushed down on him. He had not had water in almost two sunrises and had not eaten in almost three, but still he would not leave his mother's grave. He grew weak and light-headed. He raised his hands to the sky and shouted, "I will never leave you, Mother! I will remain here next to your grave and join you again in death!"

The world went dark, and he collapsed over his mother's grave.

❖◈❖

Honaw felt cool water on his face and lips. He opened his eyes and was blinded by a bright light. When his eyes adjusted to the light, he saw the face of a beautiful young girl.

She smiled at him and said, "Welcome back to the Daylight World. I feared you had already started your journey to the underworld."

He tried to speak, but his lips and mouth were so parched, he could not form the words.

She noticed his discomfort, and lifting his head, she said, "Here drink this." The water felt cool as it filled his mouth and ran down his throat. He grabbed the jar and tried to gulp the water to quench his excessive thirst, but she pulled the jar away.

"Slowly, slowly," she said. "You will tie your belly into knots if you drink too quickly." She lifted his head and gave him a few more swallows.

His head finally cleared, and his thirst abated somewhat. He looked at her again and was startled by her beauty. "Who … who are you? Where am I?" he stammered.

"I am called Lenmana, and you are with the people of the Snake Clan," she answered.

"How did I get here?"

"We found you slumped over a grave on top of a mesa off to the west. At first, we thought you had already passed to the underworld, but when we felt your heart, it still beat weakly. We carried you here, and I have cared for you."

"How long have I been here?"

"You dwelled between the world of the living and the dead for three sunrises. I am glad you have returned." She lifted his head and gave him a few more sips of water.

"Now it is my turn to ask the questions. What are you called?" she asked.

"I am Honaw of the Spider Clan."

"We have heard of a boy Moiety called Honaw, who led his people into the wilderness. It is said he saved them from an evil Tiyamunyi. They say he is a great Moiety who can speak to the gods. Are you the Honaw we have heard of in these stories?"

"I was chosen by my people to be Moiety, and I did lead them away from a village along Chu'a Wash, but I am no longer that man. I am just Honaw now."

"Why are you not a Moiety? What happened to your people?" she asked.

"I have no people!" he snapped. "I am tired. Let me rest." He rolled over and pretended to sleep. He did not want to answer any more of her questions.

At sunset, he smelled the deer meat cooking. Lenmana had made a fire and was busy cooking a stew. His empty belly growled with hunger.

"You must be hungry," Lenmana said. "Our hunters brought in deer, and I have a fine deer meat stew cooking. Get up from that bed mat and let us have a meal."

Honaw tried to stand, and was surprised by the weakness in his legs. He stumbled back and almost fell, but Lenmana steadied him, and helped him to the fire. She handed him a bowl, and the aroma of the stew made his belly growl even louder.

"Eat slowly," she admonished him. "It has been many sunrises since you last ate."

Honaw forced himself to eat slowly. He savored each bite. "This is very good," he said. "You are a fine cook."

He looked around and saw many other cooking fires. There were children playing and women busy with their own evening meals, but there were no houses. It was a night camp.

"What is this place?" he asked.

"We have been camped here for three sunrises. We are travelers on the Great North Road. We were called to the Soyala Ceremony at White House," she answered.

Astonished by her words, Honaw stopped eating. "You travel to White House?"

"Yes," Lenmana told him excitedly. "We saw the beacons and followed them to the Great North Road. None of us has seen White House, but we know it is a beautiful place with large plazas and flower gardens. It even has a large pond with fish."

"I know of White House. They say it is the center of all things. You say you followed the beacons. What beacons do you speak of?"

"At the Time of Soyala, great fires are lit at White House. The light from the fires can be seen from a far distance. When they are seen, those who keep other great beacons light those fires to signal people from an even farther distance away. All are summoned to come to the Soyala Ceremony."

Honaw now understood the light in the darkness. Old Kwahu had been directing him to lead his people to White House. There, Honaw would find the answers that would save his people, the people whom he had left stranded in the wilderness. He stood and peered north, and there was the beacon shining brightly in the dark sky. *The light in the darkness comes from White House,* he marveled to himself.

"The Soyala Ceremony will begin soon," Lenmana said excitedly. "We follow the North Road. It leads to White House. The ceremony lasts for sixteen sunrises. I have heard stories of Soyala at White House. They say it is beautiful, filled with feasts, dancing and song. There are many wonders to behold. I can hardly wait to get there!"

Honaw dropped the bowl and walked off into the darkness. He was ashamed, and his heart was heavy. He spread his arms to the northern sky and prayed. "Grandfather, Mother, I have failed you and I have failed our people. I have been so full of anger and self-pity, that I forgot all that you taught me. I have abandoned our people in the wilderness and left them without a Moiety to help them into the coming year. I forsook the sign you gave, Grandfather. I did not understand the meaning of the light in the darkness, and now I fear our people will never find the safe home you meant for them. When Mother left to live with you, I was angry and lost my faith. I know how much you cared for our people, Mother. I know you would have never left them alone to die. I was given the great honor of being a Moiety, and I failed. Forgive me, Grandfather! Forgive me, Mother!" He fell to his knees and wept.

Lenmana heard him crying. She came and knelt by his side. "Why do you weep, Honaw? What is it that burdens your heart?"

He looked at her and saw the concern in her eyes. "I am not the brave Moiety you have heard about. Maybe I was brave when I was boy, but I am a coward as a man. I have committed a terrible sin," he said. "You asked what happened to my people. I will tell you! I left them to die in the wilderness! I, too, saw the beacon. My grandfather, who was truly a great Moiety, appeared to me in a dream and instructed me to lead my people to the light in the darkness. I did not know it was coming from White House, or that it was calling all who saw it to the Soyala Ceremony. I led my people toward the beacon for many sunrises, but I lost my faith in Grandfather and all the gods when my mother crossed over to the underworld, as you call it."

He dropped his head into his hands and cried. "I was given a great responsibility to lead my people home, and I failed them! I abandoned them!"

"You must find them, Honaw," Lenmana said calmly.

Honaw was surprised by her words. Then he realized she was right. It was the only way to correct what he had done.

"Yes," he said. "It might not be too late. They might yet be saved."

"Where did you leave them?" she asked.

"They were walking north from the mesa where you found me, but that was many sunrises ago. I am not sure I can find them. I am not sure they will follow me if I do find them."

"You must try, Honaw. The great Moiety of whom I have been told would not abandon his people. I will go with you. We will leave in the morning."

"You will go with me? What of your parents? What of your family?"

"I have no parents. I have no family. There is only me. No one will care if I am gone," she said. "Come. We must sleep so we will be strong in the morning."

Honaw woke at dawn to a cold and windy day. Lenmana was already awake and packing a large yucca-fiber basket with packages wrapped in deerskin and tied with sinew. There were large water jars standing nearby.

"I was about to wake you," she said. "It is time we start our journey. We must find your people soon if they are to be saved."

After a hearty breakfast of deer stew and piki bread, Lenmana pointed to the yucca basket and instructed Honaw to help her lift it onto her back. Honaw lifted the basket and was surprised by its weight. He noticed it was mounted on a backboard and had three deerskin straps attached to the board. "This basket is heavy. What have you packed?" he asked.

"Things we will need for our journey," Lenmana answered. "It is not so heavy. I am used to carrying this pack." She leaned forward, and Honaw placed the pack on her back. She looped the bottom strap around her waist and asked Honaw to tie it tightly behind the backboard. Another strap went around her chest under her arms and was tied in the same way. The top strap she looped around her forehead, and Honaw tied it to the backboard. She shifted the pack on her back until she was comfortable with the weight.

"I cannot allow you to carry such a burden while I carry nothing," Honaw exclaimed.

Lenmana pointed to the water jars and said, "Do not worry; you will carry your share."

The water jars were placed in two yucca baskets with loops at the top. She instructed Honaw to insert each end of a stout tree limb through the loops. She then lifted the limb with the jars dangling from each end onto Honaw's shoulders. She placed rabbit fur under the limb where it crossed his shoulders to cushion the load. With their loads situated, they started their trek to find his people.

It took them until midday to reach the top of the mesa where Nova was buried. Honaw put down his load and stood quietly by her grave for a moment. He then lifted his arms to the northern sky and prayed.

"I have come back to right a terrible wrong, Mother," he said. "I pray that you and Grandfather can forgive me for abandoning our people. Thank you for sending me this good woman who saved my wretched life and revealed to me the path I must take to bring our people home. I stand humbly before you now, Grandfather, and all the gods, and I ask that you help me in this task."

He then collapsed to his knees. Lenmana rushed to his side and helped him to stand. "You are still weak from your ordeal," she said. "We will camp here tonight and rest."

"No, Lenmana!" Honaw exclaimed, "We must push on! We must find them."

"You will be no use to them if you are weak and feeble. We will rest here tonight and get a fresh start in the morning," she said. The wind grew bitter cold that evening. They built a fire and sat close wrapped in blankets and sheepskin capes.

"Where did you last see your people?" Lenmana asked.

Honaw pointed to the northwest and said, "They walked north across that open plain. I do not know how long ago. I pray that we find them."

"We will find them, Honaw," she said. "I want to thank you for the kind words you spoke about me to your mother. I did no more than anyone would do. To help other people is the way of our people. It is the right way to live."

"I also was taught about living the right way, but I failed when I left my people to wander the wilderness."

"Your mother must have been very kind and wise. I know that you loved her very much. What happened to her? Why did she go to live with the ancestors?" she asked.

"That was very strange. One morning, as we were packing to leave, she rubbed her neck again and again. I thought she was injured, but she showed me where a small insect had buried itself in her skin and was causing her discomfort. I pulled the creature out, and she seemed to be all right. Within two sunrises, she became weak and could not walk. A fever ravaged her and red spots appeared on her legs. Her heart beat weaker and weaker. I was holding her hand when she went to live with Grandfather." He wiped away a tear.

"My people have seen this disease," Lenmana said. "It is caused by the insect you pulled from your mother's neck. The insect is very small, but its poison is strong. It burrows under the skin and pushes its poison into the body. The poison shows itself in red spots, an aching head, and a high fever." They sat in silence for a time.

Honaw finally broke the silence. "You know much about me, but I know very little about you. You said you have no family. What happened to them?"

"My parents passed when I was very young. I was raised by a man and woman who had no children of their own. They treated me well, but they were old, and they also passed when I was just thirteen growing seasons old."

"You are young and strong. Why have you no husband?" Right away Honaw chastised himself. He knew that was not a proper question to ask. "I am sorry, Lenmana. It is not my place to ask such a question."

"I do not mind," she said. "I did have a husband. I had two husbands. They both live with the ancestors now. One died from the bite of the snake that rattles its tail. The other was killed crossing a river. Now all the men believe that I have angered the gods, and that I am cursed. I was happy to go with you. There was no future left for me with my people."

"I do not think you are cursed, Lenmana," he said.

She smiled at him and pulled the blanket more tightly around her. The next morning they followed the trail left by the people. It led north into the wilderness. The days were cold and the nights were colder. The only vegetation was saltbush and cacti. They found mostly dry washes, and in the ones that did have small pools, the water was foul.

"The people left the forest with their pouches full of dried deer meat and piki bread, but that would only last them a few sunrises," Honaw said. "They will not survive long in this land."

"All the more reason to keep traveling and find them," Lenmana replied.

On the sixth sunrise since they left the mesa, they began to find burial mounds along the trail left by the people.

"They are dying!" Honaw exclaimed. "Grandfather, what have I done? Our people die because of me."

"Honaw, do not give up hope," Lenmana pleaded. "We will find them. They travel slowly. They cannot be far ahead. Let us climb the mesa. We could see them in the distance."

They climbed a nearby mesa and gazed northward, looking for any sign of the people. Suddenly, their hearts filled with joy when they saw Honaw's people on the plain below the mesa. They were camped along a wash that twisted its way through the dry land.

"We have found them, Honaw! There are your people!"

"There are so few. I fear many have died," Honaw said sorrowfully.

"Thank the gods we have found them. Let us go to them and help the ones we can," Lenmana replied.

As they walked into the camp, they were shocked by the condition of the people they saw there. There were only twenty-five or thirty people in the encampment. Almost half the people had been lost. Many lay on bed mats too ill to care for themselves. They stared at Honaw with dark, hollow eyes. Lenmana immediately took one of the water jars and began to give water to the thirsty people, coaching them not to drink too fast.

"People, I have returned. I ask your forgiveness for what I have done!" Honaw said.

An old woman Honaw remembered as Yamka looked at him with anger burning in her eyes and said, "Why should we forgive you? You left us here in the wilderness. Many have died."

"I remember you, Yamka," Honaw replied. "You are the mother of Honani. I remember you are a strong woman and Honani is a fine man. Where is your son?"

"Honani was chosen to be the leader of our people when you abandoned us, but he passed to the ancestors on the trail. I speak for these people now."

"We saw many burial mounds on our way to find you, and I know they all died because of me," Honaw replied. "There is no way I can bring back the dead. I can only ask your forgiveness. We can save all who still live, if you will follow me again."

"We followed you once because we had faith in your words. The light in the darkness was to be our salvation, you said. After you left, we could no longer see the light. We were lost and forsaken by the gods. Now, you have returned to ask our forgiveness and want us to follow you again? You ask much from us, Honaw!"

"I know I have committed a great wrong. When my mother died, darkness filled my soul. I thought only of my own pain and was angry with the gods. I turned my back on you and lost my faith. I forgot all that I was taught about living the right way."

Pointing to Lenmana, Honaw continued. "This woman is Lenmana of the Snake Clan. Her goodness and wisdom brought me back to the correct path and restored my faith. If you will permit me to lead you again, we can take you to the place Kwahu spoke of. The light in the darkness is calling us to White House, to celebrate the Time of Soyala. It is not too late. We can follow the North Road to White House. I believe our future waits for us there. I need to correct the great wrong I have done you. The gods did not forsake you. The fault is all my own. I have asked the gods to forgive me, and now I am asking you. What say you?"

"If we stay here in the desert, we will all die," Yamka answered. "So we will follow you, but we will see if there is forgiveness in our hearts."

Handing Honaw the jar of water, Lenmana said, "Honaw, give your people water. Do not let them drink too quickly. They are hungry and we must feed them."

She began to take the packages from the yucca basket. They were filled with dried deer meat and piki bread. There was enough for everyone to eat, and more left over for future meals.

"Where did you get so much food?" Honaw asked.

"The Snake Clan is generous. When I told them of your people, they all gave what they could. To live the right way means to share your food with the hungry," she answered.

"Now I see why you carried such a large, heavy basket," Honaw said. "Your people truly are generous, and you are a fine woman. I am grateful to the gods for sending you to me. First you saved my life, and now the lives of my people." Wrapping his arms around her, he said, "You saved my life and you saved my soul. I thank you, Lenmana."

She smiled at him and began to hand out food to the people.

PART THREE

CENTER OF THE WORLD, SPRING AD 1060

CHAPTER 14

❖

WHITE HOUSE

After three days of food and fresh water, most of the people had regained enough strength to travel. Those who still could not walk were carried. Honaw climbed the mesa and again found the beacon. He and Lenmana led the people northeast to White House. Each night the beacon became brighter until it seemed Honaw could reach out and touch it. He knew White House was close.

After five sunrises, they were still making their way northeast across small hills covered with saltbush and cut by washes. As they topped a small hill, Honaw saw something moving on the plain to the east. It was a clear day, and he could make out what looked like people walking north toward a gap between two high mesas.

"Lenmana, come quickly, what is this I see?" he asked.

Lenmana moved up next to him and peered into the open plain. Her eyes widened when she recognized what she was seeing. "We have found it, Honaw, the North Road to White House!"

Honaw turned to his people. "Rejoice good people, our journey is almost at an end. There is the North Road to White House! We will be home soon!" When the people saw the North Road, they raised their hands to the northern sky and thanked the gods for delivering them.

As they moved closer, the road became clearer. They could see it headed directly north, straight as an arrow shaft. There were many men, women, and small children traveling the road. They were all walking north, only north. They carried all manner of bundles and baskets. They looked as if they had been traveling for many days.

One man on the road suddenly stopped and looked in their direction. It was evident that he saw them. He waited on the road as they approached. When Honaw saw him clearly, he could see he was an older man dressed in a sheepskin cape with a deerskin belt inlaid with the precious stones tied around his waist. He was surprised to see that he wore his hair in the same bobbed style as the people of Chu'a Village.

"Greetings, fellow travelers," he said. "Why do you walk over that rough country when you have this fine road to follow?"

"Greetings to you. We only just discovered the road when we reached the crest of that small hill off to the west. We come from the southwest and have traveled many days, following the light in the darkness to Soyala at White House," Honaw explained.

"The light in the darkness?" the man asked. "You must mean the beacon that burns at House of the Southern Sky atop the South Mesa. I have never heard it called the light in the darkness."

"Yes, the beacon," Honaw replied. "A wise old Moiety once called it the light in the darkness. It guided us here to White House. If the gods are willing, we will make White House our new home. It will be our salvation. We have nothing to return to."

"All who enter White House are welcome," the man said. "If your people are willing to live the right way and share in the work that glorifies the gods, they will be provided for. They will live safe and secure within White House.

"I am Pakwa, the Soyala Moiety of the Eagle Clan." Pointing to the people walking on the road, he said, "These are my people. This is the second time we have made the pilgrimage to White House for the Soyala Celebration. It is a wondrous and beautiful celebration. Come walk with us. Let us be the first to welcome you to White House, the center of all things."

"I am Honaw, Moiety of the Spider Clan." Gesturing to Lenmana, he said, "This good woman is Lenmana of the Snake Clan. These are our people. Thank you. We will walk with you. Our journey has been difficult. We are anxious to reach White House and join in the Soyala Celebration."

"You say you and your people are of the Spider Clan?" Pakwa asked.

"Yes, we are the Spider Clan from Chu'a Village far to the south. Our village was destroyed by a flood. We now seek a new home," Honaw answered.

"This is Honaw, known as the boy Moiety, who speaks with the gods," Lenmana said with pride. "He vanquished an evil Tiyamunyi and led his people away from their destroyed village. There are many who know his name."

"Then you will be more than welcome at White House," Pakwa replied. "The all-powerful and most holy Qaletaga, Tiyamunyi of White House, is of the Spider Clan. He dwells in House of the Sun. I am sure he will be most anxious to meet you. I will take you to him. Let us go!"

Farther along the North Road they entered a canyon. A small stream wound along the canyon floor. Piñon trees, juniper trees, and greasewood grew along its banks. Mesa walls, hundreds of feet high, towered over them on both sides.

In the distance they saw what looked like a huge rock standing at the base of a mesa to the north. The rock was a brilliant white that stood in stark contrast to the brown sandstone mesa wall. As they moved closer, they could see that it was not a rock at all. It had straight vertical walls and there were doors and windows in the walls. Finally, they could see people walking about in front of the walls and, to their amazement, on top of the walls.

Honaw stopped and stared in wonder. "What in the name of the gods …?"

"It truly is a wondrous sight. Is it not?" Pakwa said. "It is House of the Antelope, home of the Antelope and Hawk Clan Moieties and their families. Every time I see it, I am filled with awe and amazed at what the people of White House have done. Know, too, that this is only the edge of the city. There are many more wonderful things to see."

As they moved deeper into the canyon, it began to widen, and then they emerged into another, even grander canyon that ran east and west. A larger, wider stream ran down the middle of the canyon. Across the stream, two other great houses rose from the canyon floor. The one to the west was just as large and beautiful as House of the Antelope, but the one to the east was larger and even more spectacular. Two elevated platform structures rose twenty feet high in front of the magnificent great house.

"What are those platforms?" Honaw wondered.

"They are monuments to Sun Father. They guard the entrance to House of the Sun where Qaletaga dwells," Pakwa explained.

They crossed the shallow stream, and Pakwa led them down a gravel pathway. The pathway lay between the stream on the south side and the wall of the immense platform on the north side. The path was crowded with people dressed in colorful robes of deerskin and sheepskin. Many wore jewelry made from the bluish-green stones. Honaw and his people walked in silent wonder as they gazed at all the beautifully adorned people.

On the south side of the stream, they saw many small houses with ramadas. They saw women grinding corn, preparing meals, making baskets, and molding pots and then firing them in their kilns. Men were weaving blankets and chopping wood. Old men lounged in the sun and children shrieked with laughter as they played.

The pathway led to a corridor between the two platforms. Pakwa led them down the corridor. There before them rose the immense front wall of House of the Sun. They walked between two walls and up a covered stairway. At the top of the stairs, they emerged onto a giant plaza surrounded by more walls and raised terraces. Smoke curled up from pit houses built into the plaza floor, and a wall down the center divided the plaza into two parts, forming a second plaza with many more pit houses. There were many rooms opening onto both plazas. The most astounding feature of the great house was the gigantic back wall. There were two tiers. One rose ten feet above the plaza floor, ending in a terrace, and the other rose another fifteen feet above that, forming a second, higher terrace. Honaw and his people gazed in astonishment at what they saw.

"I never would have thought people could build such a place as this," he muttered. "It truly is a monument to Sun Father and all the gods. I am humbled to be in a place such as this."

Lenmana stood gazing at a single pine tree standing in the far southwest corner of the plaza. "Pakwa, why does that tree stand alone?" she asked.

"That is Earth Mother's sacred tree. It will stand in her honor for as long as the Fourth World endures," he said.

The plaza was alive with activity. There were women making piki bread and drying rabbit and deer meat. Men were tanning hides, weaving turkey feather blankets, and making sheepskin capes. They watched as two women made fine jewelry from bluish-green stones and tiny shells. Trading kiosks stood along every wall. People traded with each other for many goods: finely painted pottery jars, woven blankets, baskets, turkey feather blankets, bows and arrows, beautifully adorned robes, deerskin belts, and bracelets inlaid with the bluish-green stones. Honaw had never seen such a collection of finely made items all in one place.

One man traded small, exquisitely made bells from a material that was unknown to Honaw or Lenmana. Honaw picked one up and it tinkled sweetly. Lenmana giggled when she heard the perfect sound. He rubbed his thumb against the surface of the bell and could see it was not made of wood or stone. Bewildered, he asked, "What is this material?"

"It is called copper," the trader answered. "It comes from great cities far beyond the southern horizon."

Honaw felt a tug on his arm and turned to see Lenmana pointing to a row of cages filled with large, beautiful birds. They had feathers of gold, blue, red, and white. They held to their perches with talons and they had elegantly hooked beaks of many colors. Astounded, Lenmana said, "I have never seen such birds. Earth Mother's world is truly wondrous!"

"I have seen their feathers, but this is the first time I have seen the birds," Honaw replied. They stood, fascinated, trying to comprehend all that surrounded them, when Pakwa approached. He was with a man dressed in a fine white robe.

"Honaw!" Pakwa called. "This is Pavati. He is the cacique of House of the Sun."

"Greetings," Pavati said. "Welcome to White House. My friend Pakwa tells me you and your people are of the Spider Clan. We did not know there were other Spider Clans within our realm. Qaletaga is most anxious to meet you. But first, I know you have traveled far and are tired and hungry. I have ordered the keepers to prepare rooms and food for you and your people. We will let you rest and recover, and then Qaletaga will call for you."

"Your hospitality is greatly appreciated," Honaw replied. "My people have traveled far and endured many hardships. They are in need of rest."

"Then rest they shall have. Follow me," Pavati directed.

Honaw and Lenmana stood wrapped in a turkey feather blanket on the terrace outside the room they were given by Pavati. Their people had been housed and fed and were resting in the rooms provided by the keepers. The sun had set, but there was still a tinge of light on the western horizon. From their viewpoint, they could see most of the canyon of White House. Cooking fires dotted the city like stars in the sky, from the Mount of the Dagger of Light in the east, to the West Mesa. Soyala Ceremonies were going on in the pit houses of House of the Sun. They could hear the foot drums and the chanting.

"I would not have believed our people could build such a place as this," Lenmana said.

"It shows what can be done when people live in the right way and devote themselves to Sun Father and all the gods. They built White House to maintain balance in the world and honor the gods. In return, the gods have provided them with a good life, free from pain and suffering."

"Grandfather Kwahu was not speaking only of the beacon at House of the Southern Sky when he told me of the light in the darkness. He meant all of White House is the 'light.' It is the 'light' that showed us the way out of our pain and suffering. It truly is our salvation. We must strive with all our strength to live the right way, and add to the glory of White House. In this way we can show our gratitude to Old Kwahu, Sun Father, and all our ancestors," Honaw said.

"I have only one regret," he added softly. "I wish my mother were here to see this."

"She is here with us, Honaw. Our ancestors are always with us," Lenmana replied.

He turned and looked into her eyes. "The gods were smiling on me the day you came into my life," he said, and kissed her.

A light snow had fallen in the night, but the morning broke cold and clear. White House sparkled in the brilliant sunlight. Pavati called on Honaw just after the morning meal. Qaletaga was ready to see him.

As they walked across the plaza, Honaw asked, "What do I call him? I have never addressed a real Tiyamunyi before." He tried not to show his nervousness.

"Call him by his name, Qaletaga," Pavati answered. "He will welcome you. He was very glad to hear that there are other people of the Spider Clan."

Pavati led him into a room lit by the sun coming through open windows. Qaletaga sat by a hearth that burned brightly in the middle of the room. He was making a prayer stick. He stopped what he was doing when Honaw and Pavati entered the room.

"Sorry to interrupt, Qaletaga," Pavati said. "This is Honaw, the one we spoke of earlier."

Qaletaga smiled and rose to meet them. He wore a radiant dark red robe with intricate gold stitching on its hem and sleeves. He wore a headpiece made of yellow and blue feathers. Honaw was sure that they had come from the birds he and Lenmana had seen in the cages. Around his neck he wore an exquisite necklace made of tiny, colorful shells.

"Greetings, Honaw," he said. "Come sit with me and warm yourself by the fire."

"If you do not need anything further from me, I must meet with the stonemasons and plan today's construction," Pavati said.

"That is all, Pavati," Qaletaga answered. "You may leave us."

Pavati bowed and left the room, leaving Honaw standing alone, unsure of what to do.

"Please sit, Honaw. There is much I would like to discuss. I have heard a great deal about you. I am told you and your people are of the Spider Clan, as am I. Where do your people hail from?" Qaletaga asked.

"We are from a small village along Chu'a Wash, a far distance south of here. We left there a long time ago because it was destroyed by a flood."

"I am speaking of before that time," Qaletaga said. "What about your ancestors?"

"The stories passed down in our clan say that we first came to Chu'a Wash from some place up north. I do not know exactly where. Four generations of our people lived in Chu'a Village before it was destroyed," Honaw answered.

"There is a story my clan tells of a time when White House was just a small village, and a group of our people left to find land of their own. It is said they traveled south. I believe that your ancestors were those people. I believe that we have the same blood flowing in our veins. It is good that you are a great Moiety to your people," Qaletaga said.

"It would be an honor beyond compare to be of the same blood as the all-powerful Qaletaga, but I am just a humble Moiety. Grandfather handed down my position to me. I was not anointed by Sun Father, in the way that you were."

"You are too humble, Honaw. I know of your deeds. I know that as a boy you saved your people from an evil man who falsely claimed to be a Tiyamunyi. I know you led them into the wilderness and eventually led them here, back to the home of your ancestors. I also know you speak to the gods. We are of the same blood, and that is good."

"I thank you for your kind words. That I am Moiety at all is because of what I learned from my grandfather Kwahu. He truly was a great Moiety. I still have much to learn. I do not claim to be my grandfather and do not have the right to walk in the footsteps of the great Qaletaga."

"You are correct, Honaw. You are young and have much to learn, but I believe the gods smile on you. They have plans for you that have not yet been revealed."

Honaw was stunned by his words. "I am honored by your words, Qaletaga, but I—"

Qaletaga interrupted him. "Let us see what the future brings. For now, you have only seen a very small part of White House. Let me show you what our people have accomplished in the name of Sun Father."

They walked out to the gravel pathway and Qaletaga led Honaw east along the wash. People lowered their eyes and bowed reverently as Qaletaga passed. He greeted his people fondly and frequently stopped to engage them in conversation. It was evident to Honaw that the people loved their Tiyamunyi.

They passed House of the Bow where the Moieties of the Bow and Lizard Clans dwelled. Farther east, they passed House of the Rabbit where the Moieties of the Rabbit and Horn Clans lived. All the great houses were covered with a luminous white plaster that made them shine beautifully in the morning sun, but none were as large or as beautiful as House of the Sun.

Finally, at the far eastern end of the canyon, Qaletaga led Honaw down a trail heading south. Honaw saw a massive butte rising up into the crystal-blue sky. He was awestruck by its size and majesty.

"That is the Mount of the Dagger of Light, home of the gods," Qaletaga explained. "It is the most sacred place in our world. It is the place where the gods mark the center of time. The Dagger of Light tells us when we should begin the Time of Soyala and the Time of Niman. It tells us when to plant and when to harvest. It keeps the world in balance so that the people may live well and prosper."

"My grandfather told me of the Dagger of Light and how it marks time on the Sacred Circle," Honaw replied.

"Let me show you, Honaw," Qaletaga said. "You must see to understand." They climbed the great butte, and Qaletaga took him to the place where three vertical stone slabs cast a shadow on two replicas of the sun chiseled onto the rock face behind the slabs. He showed Honaw how the position of a dagger of sunlight shining between the slabs marked the time of Soyala and where it would be at the time of Niman.

"Earth Mother placed these stones here so that we would not stray from the path of Sun Father, and so we would always mark the time when our ancestors come to renew our world," Qaletaga explained.

"This is the most sacred place of our people, Honaw. Not all can come here. Only those who are one with the gods may come here. I believe you are such a person. Think about what I have told you. I will show you more of White House in the morning." They descended the mount in silence. Honaw was overwhelmed by what he had seen and heard.

The next morning Pavati again called on Honaw, and again he took him to Qaletaga. This time, Qaletaga was not alone. A woman dressed in a beautiful buckskin dress and a boy who looked to be nine or ten growing seasons were with him.

"Welcome, Honaw," Qaletaga greeted him. "It is good to see you this morning. I would like you to meet my wife, Mansi, and my son, Honovi."

"It is an honor to meet you," Honaw said shyly.

The woman smiled and nodded her head in recognition, but the boy stared at Honaw with cold, angry eyes. "He does not look like a great Moiety who speaks with the gods. He is just a simple man!" the boy said loudly.

"Honovi," Qaletaga snapped. "Your rudeness is embarrassing to your mother and me. You will apologize to our guest!"

"I will not apologize to him!" Honovi said defiantly. "I should be walking with you when you go among the people, not this homeless one!"

"Mansi, take this boy from my sight. I will concern myself with him later," Qaletaga said. The boy's mother moved to guide him away, but Honovi was already striding from the room. She followed after him.

"Forgive my son, Honaw. He is headstrong and already considers himself a Tiyamunyi. He has much to learn."

"I have not been harmed," Honaw replied. "I remember when I was much the same."

"Come walk with me again today. I enjoyed our time together yesterday, and there is more I want to show you," Qaletaga said. This time they walked west from House of the Sun, still following the wash. They passed many small houses where one or two families lived. They passed House of the Antelope on the south side of the wash, and then House of the Sand, where the Moieties of the Sand and Hawk Clans lived with their families.

A variety of trees grew on the banks of the stream. Honaw could identify piñon, juniper, willow, and cottonwood. He imagined how beautiful it would be in the summer when the grass was high and the trees and flowers were in full bloom.

Just beyond House of the Badger, the wash widened, and Honaw was taken aback by what came into view. A lake cradled between the canyon walls shimmered in the sunlight. Men threw fishing nets into its water, women washed clothes, and children played on the lake's shoreline. "White House truly is a place of wonder and beauty!" Honaw exclaimed.

Qaletaga agreed. "The gods have blessed us with many favors. These great houses are built by the people to thank and honor the gods. With every log that is cut or stone that is placed, the people give thanks and praise."

They crossed the lake on a footbridge and continued west. The sun was warm and the walk was easy as they moved along the southern shoreline of the lake. At the west end of the canyon, Qaletaga turned and led them southwest along a path that brought them to a stairway cut into the mesa wall. They climbed the steep stairway and emerged on top of the West Mesa. From here, Honaw could see another white great house looming before them.

"That is House of the Western Sky," Qaletaga explained. "No Moieties live there, only the keepers of the Western Beacon." When they reached the house, a few men came to greet them. They bowed to Qaletaga and kissed his hand. "Welcome, Qaletaga," they said. "We are honored by your visit."

"Greetings, friends. I bring a visitor. He is anxious to see the fine work you have done here. But first, bring us water and food so that we may refresh ourselves."

After a small meal, Qaletaga gave Honaw a short tour of the great house. Much of it was not yet completed. Groups of workers were busy erecting walls and placing ceiling beams. He showed him the huge torch that was lit twice a year for sixteen days during the Time of Soyala and again during the Time of Niman. The torch's fire called all the people of the western realm to the celebrations at White House.

Finally, Qaletaga led Honaw to a ladder that took them up into a tower where they could see a great distance in all directions. Honaw looked down and saw the shimmering lake stretching east and the great houses at the center of White House. He could see House of the Southern Sky atop the South Mesa. He could see travelers along the North Road. To the north, he saw another great house on the mesa above House of the Sun. Qaletaga explained that it was House of the Northern Sky, the place of the northern beacon. To the west, he saw another perfectly straight road that led to distant mountains.

"That is the West Road," Qaletaga explained. "It leads to those mountains you can barely see in the west. Those mountains are where the gods of the western sky dwell. Our people who live there make a pilgrimage to White House each year during the Time of Soyala." Honaw stood awestruck by the grandeur that lay before him.

"Behold the realm of White House, Honaw!" Qaletaga exclaimed. "White House is the center of all things. It is built to worship Sun Father, Earth Mother, and all the ancestor gods. North, south, east, and west come together here. The sky, the Fourth World, and the Third World all meet here in White House. Everything is in balance here. Our world and our people would perish if White House were to fall."

"It has been the task of my family through the generations to make sure that White House never passes from the Fourth World; now it is my task." He continued, "It is a heavy burden. I need help to carry it. This has been weighing on my mind for a long while. I had a dream that a Moiety from a long-forgotten branch of the Spider Clan would come to White House to help me carry my burden. You are that Moiety, Honaw! Sun Father has sent you to me!"

Honaw was shocked by what he heard. "I am but a simple Moiety," he said. "How can I help with your burden?"

"For all these many years I have been both the spiritual leader of all the clans of White House, and also the Soyala Moiety of the Spider and Corn Tassel Clans. When the people of White House were small in number, I was able to balance the responsibilities, but now we are many. The people of the Spider and Corn Tassel Clans are good people. They deserve a Soyala Moiety who can guide them in their spiritual lives, one who can devote all of his energies toward their happiness and success. I have found it more and more difficult to maintain a balance, and I fear that my people will suffer. I need you to watch over them," he said.

"Your people can join with mine, and the Spider Clan will be reunited once more," Qaletaga continued. "Together we will build new homes for all your people. Your women will join mine in grinding the corn and making the piki bread for House of the Sun. Your men will work alongside mine in the many building projects of White House. You and your wife, Lenmana, will live in House of the Sun with me and my family."

"Lenmana is not my wife," Honaw said.

"It is obvious that you care very much for her. I just assumed that she was your wife," Qaletaga replied.

"Now that we have come home, I will ask her. She has no mother for me to offer a gift to."

"That will not be an obstacle. If you want her as your wife, and she consents, we will make it so. What say you, Honaw? Will you help me with this burden?" Qaletaga asked again.

"What you offer is beyond anything I could have ever imagined. It would be an honor to hold such a position. I have just one question. What of your son?" Honaw asked.

"I have given that much thought. He is still too young to be a Moiety. He is next in line to become Tiyamunyi. His time will come. I need you now. So what say you?"

"When my grandfather appeared to me that night on the mesa, he smiled and told me to follow the light in the darkness. As we began our journey, I thought the light he spoke of was just the distant beacon. Now I understand that Kwahu meant much more. I will help you with your burden for as long as there is strength in my body," Honaw said.

CHAPTER 15

HONOVI

Honaw and Lenmana stood on the terrace watching their son, Alo, play with the other children in the plaza below. Now in the summer of 1064, Alo was four growing seasons old. Honaw could already see that he was a bright child blessed with his mother's good nature.

The years at White House had been good to Honaw and his family. The people of the Spider and Corn Tassel Clans had accepted him as their Soyala Moiety. His blood ties to the Spider Clan gave him stature. Qaletaga, the great Tiyamunyi, praised him for saving his people and for his unique ability to speak with the gods. His people were happy to have their own Soyala Moiety to say the prayers and perform the rituals that would ensure good crops and prosperity in the coming year.

Honaw was much like his grandfather. He enjoyed being with the people. He worked alongside the men as they laid the stones and timbers of new additions to the great house. His judgments in arbitration were considered just. Both he and Lenmana became known for their kindness and willingness to help. He was grateful that he did not need to collect the tithe or redistribute food to the people. These tasks were the responsibility of Pavati. Honaw only concerned himself with his role as arbitrator and with the spiritual lives of the Spider and Corn Tassel Clans.

The people of the Spider Clan who had followed him from the village on Chu'a Wash prospered at White House. As Qaletaga promised, the men were given work on the many construction projects in White House, and the women who chose to worked in House of the Sun. Lenmana held a very prestigious position as a healer. She had learned to make potions and poultices when she was with her people of the Snake Clan, and now she used that skill to heal the people of White House.

There was one, however, who had no love for Honaw. It was evident that Honovi, Qaletaga's son, despised him. As time passed, Qaletaga grew very close to Honaw. They spent many hours together walking among the people and speaking of many important issues. When Honaw suggested that he should be talking to his son about such matters, Qaletaga argued that even though he continued to groom Honovi for the day he would become Tiyamunyi, he felt Honovi was still too young and could not yet speak as an adult on the vital issues of White House. He said he needed Honaw's sage advice on such things. Honaw was not surprised that Honovi disliked him.

Honaw felt Honovi's animosity and tried to befriend him, but Honovi would have none of it. When Honaw spoke to Qaletaga about Honovi's feelings toward him, Qaletaga blindly told him not to be concerned. Qaletaga said that Honovi was just a boy and acted as a boy.

On one occasion when Honaw and Qaletaga returned from one of their walks, Honovi confronted Honaw as he was leaving the great house. "Honaw," he said, "I know what you are attempting to do and you will fail. No matter how you try to manipulate my father, I promise you, I will be the next Tiyamunyi of White House, not you!"

Honaw tried to convince Honovi that he had no interest in being Tiyamunyi and that the position was rightfully his, but Honovi would not listen. He was convinced that Honaw was conniving to usurp his position. Honaw watched with deepening distress as father and son drifted further and further apart. He felt Honovi's pain and disappointment. Qaletaga did not realize that his son was no longer a boy. Honaw felt Qaletaga was wrong, but he had promised to help him with his burdens. He could not go back on his word.

In the spring, the people of White House came to House of the Sun for the Planting Celebration. Lenmana happily dressed little Alo in a fine robe for the Planting Celebration. All the people dressed in their finest clothes and stood on the terraces surrounding the plaza to watch the ritual dances and hear all the traditional songs

Little Alo was filled with excitement as his family took their place on the terrace to watch the celebration. Soon they heard foot drums pounding out a beat as flutes played a mystical melody. Men and women began dancing in two rows circling the plaza. Some wore the mask of the god Kokopelli, the little hunchbacked god who traveled from village to village in the spring playing his flute. The melody of his flute on the spring breezes brought warmth to the land, melting the snow and bringing the rain to assure a successful crop. Other dancers wore beautiful headdresses made from the feathers of birds that traders from southern lands brought to White House. The dancing and singing would go on all night, a joyous celebration that praised the gods and renewed the land.

Qaletaga sat on a platform in the plaza with his wife and son by his side. He would rise periodically during the celebration to recite the prayers that would bring the rain. He always rejoiced in the celebration of the planting season, but this night he felt disturbed and uneasy. A dull ache in his arm and sharper pains in his chest were keeping him from enjoying the celebration. Mansi had noticed he was not well. Sweat beaded on his forehead, and there was a look of pain in his eyes. "What is wrong, my husband? I can see you are in pain. Why do you hold your arm?" she asked.

"It is nothing," he answered. "A small pain in my shoulder, that is all."

When it became time for him to speak again, he rose but was unable to stand erect. He faltered and fell back in his chair. "My husband, you are not well!" Mansi exclaimed. "Rest in your chair, let someone else say the prayer."

"I know the prayer, Father. I can do it!" Honovi said excitedly.

"No, I will do it," Qaletaga replied, still not realizing how his refusal to include his son was causing Honovi so much disappointment. "My people need their Tiyamunyi to speak the prayer."

Honovi could only remain silent again; his father did not notice the anguish on his face. Qaletaga struggled to his feet and stepped forward. He always spoke in a powerful voice so that all could hear the sacred prayers, but this time only the few standing close by could hear his words.

"Send forth massed clouds to stay with us
Stretch out your water hands
Let us embrace—"

He stopped abruptly and clutched his chest. He turned to his wife, and in a weak and feeble voice he called to her, "Mansi." The blood drained from his face and he collapsed to the ground.

The crowd gasped and then fell silent. Mansi and Honovi rushed to his side. Honovi pressed his ear to his father's chest. Then looking at his mother, he said, "His heart does not beat, Mother. He has passed to the ancestors."

Mansi knelt by her dead husband and cried as she sang the death song. Honovi rose and turned to the silent crowd. "Good people of White House!" he exclaimed in a loud voice. "The gods have taken my father, your Tiyamunyi, to live with our ancestors. Sing the death song! Light the signal beacons! Tell our people that the great Qaletaga is dead!"

Honaw rushed down from the terrace when he saw Qaletaga fall. He knelt down by his side and held Mansi to comfort her in her grief. When Honovi saw him there, he angrily cried, "Get away from my father, Moiety! You have no right to be here. I will send Father to the ancestors and comfort my mother. We do not need your help!"

"I, too, loved your father, Honovi," Honaw answered. "I only want to—"

"Leave us!" Honovi commanded. Stunned, Honaw rose and walked away.

The women of White House sang the death song all that night. Honovi and Mansi prepared the body for burial. They washed his hair in yucca-root suds and adorned it with the bird feathers. They dressed him in a beautiful red robe and wrapped him in white deerskin.

As dawn broke, the Moieties from each house gathered in the plaza of House of the Sun. Many people watched from the terraces. Honaw joined the other Moieties in the plaza, but he was not given a place of honor, even though his being the Moiety of Qaletaga's Spider Clan should have allowed him to share in the death ritual. The body of Qaletaga lay on a platform in the middle of the plaza. Honovi stood by his father and sang his song of death.

> Do not weep for me, for I am still with you.
> I am the gentle breeze that blows across the mesa.
> I am the spring rain that sustains the young corn.

I am the warmth of Sun Father upon your face.
You can still hear my voice in the laughter of your children.
Do not weep for me, for I am still with you.

Six chosen Moieties gently lifted Qaletaga's body and carried it to a burial chamber deep inside House of the Sun. They buried him with offerings of food, water, cornmeal, and prayer sticks. Exquisite copper bells, elegant jewelry made of the precious stones, and three of the magnificent, sacred birds were also placed in the chamber. A stick was pushed into the soil covering the body, so that his spirit could depart and begin his journey to join the ancestors.

That evening Honovi called his first council of the Moieties of White House. Honaw took his place in the pit house, just as he always had. Honovi wasted no time establishing his rule and striking out at Honaw. He still perceived Honaw as a threat to his rule and took this opportunity to exact revenge.

"The Spider Clan of House of the Sun is the oldest and most revered of all the clans of White House," he told the council. "Its first patriarch led his people to this valley. He was anointed by Sun Father to be the first Tiyamunyi, and that honor has been passed down to the eldest son of his family for all these many years. With the passing of my father, I now humbly hold that place of honor and pledge before Sun Father to guide my people as my father did.

"But there is one among us who brings dishonor to the Spider Clan and all of White House. He beguiled my father with false oaths of love and devotion, all the while seeking to drive a wedge between our great Tiyamunyi and his only son. He coveted the position of Tiyamunyi and worked to rob me of my rightful position. I accuse Honaw of sins against Sun Father and all of White House. He is no longer worthy to hold the position of Soyala Moiety of the Spider Clan! I rule that he should be stripped of this sacred position of honor and banished from White House!"

The council erupted in angry shouts, some in agreement with Honovi, and some in support of Honaw. Choovio, the well-respected Niman Moiety of House of the Sun, rose and lifted his hands to silence the council.

"Hear my words, Moieties of White House!" he said as the men quieted. "I have worked closely with Honaw since he came to White House. He possesses great knowledge of the prayers and rituals that honor the gods and maintain the balance in our world. His rulings are always well thought out and fair. His people think much of him. The sins Honovi has accused him of are grave indeed. Honaw deserves to speak for himself and defend his honor. What say you, Honaw?"

Honaw began. "It is true. I did love Qaletaga. He showed me the correct path when I was lost. His words and actions saved me and my people, but I have never wanted to be Tiyamunyi. Honovi is also correct when he says that I had no right to such a holy position. When I came here, I was but a humble Moiety, and I am still just a humble Moiety. To be a Tiyamunyi takes someone far greater than me. If it is the wish of Honovi, our Tiyamunyi, that I can no longer be Moiety, and that I must be banished from White House, so be it. He is anointed by Sun Father. He knows best."

Again there was a great clamor in the pit house. Some still spoke against Honaw, but this time, many more spoke in favor of him.

Once more Choovio silenced the Moieties. "Honovi, it is true you are anointed by Sun Father, but so was your father. Honaw did not seek out the position of Soyala Moiety for House of the Sun. Your father sought him out and appointed him to the position. I do not believe you have the power to undo what your father has done. In his honor, you should uphold your father's wish."

Honovi was annoyed that his first command should be questioned, but he knew that the ultimate decision must come from the council, and he could see that it was not going to go his way. After much discussion the council ruled in favor of Honaw. Honaw would remain in White House and continue as Soyala Moiety of the Spider Clan.

"So be it, Honaw," Honovi angrily snapped. "You can keep your minor position, but I will not have you and your family living in my father's house. Go live among your people where you belong!"

The council chose to defer to Honovi on this issue, in the interest of keeping peace and balance among the clans of White House. Honaw and his family were cast out of House of the Sun and went to live among the people of the Spider Clan.

Thus began the reign of Honovi.

CHAPTER 16

DAY OF THE WARM SNOW

The time since Qaletaga's death had been difficult for the people of White House. For two growing seasons, there had been very little spring and summer rain in the basin, and the surrounding mountains were not capped with snow in the winters. The rivers and streams held very little water. By summer of 1066, the beautiful lake of White House had shrunk to little more than a small pond. With no water, crops failed and game became scarce. The caciques of the great houses distributed the food they had in storage, but without plentiful crops to replenish the bins, the people were facing a winter of hardship and starvation.

Honovi proved to be a harsh Tiyamunyi. Unlike his father, he was not a guardian of the people. He ruled from a throne in House of the Sun, surrounded by servants and guards who groveled at his feet. He seldom walked among his people and refused the wisdom of his Moieties at council. He demanded that new construction projects on White House continue throughout the year, with no consideration for the needs of the workers.

He banished Pavati from House of the Sun, saying he did not need a cacique. He proclaimed that only he would control the collection and distribution of food from the great house to the people. Honovi's bins had adequate food to last at least part of a winter, but he distributed meager amounts to the people, while making sure that he and his household would not go hungry.

He was obsessed with expanding House of the Sun and other building projects. He personally planned and supervised all construction projects. He worked his people every day for long hours and distributed very little food in payment. The people began to question his motives. They felt he was not building for the glory of Sun Father, but only for his own power and authority.

Honovi's decisions caused many arguments between him and his mother. Mansi tried to advise him. "My son, I fear you have forgotten the lessons your father taught you," she warned. "He believed the most important duty of a Tiyamunyi was to be the guardian of the people. Their well-being should always come first. Sun Father has become angry with us and holds back the rain. The people fear the coming winter will bring hunger and death to White House. You must forget about your construction projects. Pray to Sun Father and Earth Mother. Ask their forgiveness. Plead with them to return the rain to our fields, so that their people might live. Send your caciques to distant villages to trade for food. You have a bounty of the precious stones and copper to trade. Send them, my son. This is what your father would have done."

Honovi's eyes flashed with anger. "I am not my father, old woman! I know what is best for White House. Sun Father is angry because the people do not work hard enough to beautify my city …" He paused and attempted to correct himself when he heard his own words. "To beautify his city. That is why he has stopped the rain and the crops have failed. The people only think of their own stomachs and not the glory of Sun Father! If they obey my commands, Sun Father will provide all that is needed. If they do not, then they deserve to starve!"

Mansi continued to try to advise him away from this course of action, but he paid her no heed. Finally, he would hear no more. He confined her to the far side of House of the Sun. There she lived with a few of her loyal servants, mourning the loss of her husband, and the son she once knew.

As Honovi's prominence waned, Honaw's grew. Honovi meant to punish him when he exiled him from House of the Sun, but Honaw, Lenmana, and Alo enjoyed living among the people of the Spider Clan. As before, Honaw adhered to the lessons taught to him by his grandfather. The other Moieties of White House did not understand his practice of working alongside his people. When the people traveled to the mountains to gather the timber needed for construction of corner posts and ceiling beams for the new buildings ordered by Honovi, Honaw accompanied them. He worked at mixing mud and laying stones on new walls. Honaw knew only one way to be a Moiety: the way his grandfather had taught him. He became well-known throughout White House for his kindness. His arbitrations were fair, and at council he acted as a strong advocate for the people.

Lenmana was also well known throughout White House. She was a great healer. Often she could be seen walking the footpaths with little Alo tagging along, on her way to someone's house to bind a wound or soothe a fever. Her kindness and gentle healing endeared her to everyone. She and Honaw were beloved by the people of White House

While other Moieties feared Honovi and did not dare speak against his decisions, Honaw stood unafraid and always spoke his own mind. He argued strongly for Honovi to release more of the food held in the storage bins within House of the Sun. He pleaded with him to send parties to the outlying villages to trade for food. A number of times at council, Honovi flew into a rage at Honaw, trying to silence him, but Honaw would not be silenced. Honovi's hatred of him grew with each passing day.

Eventually, many people became angry with Honovi. They feared starvation and death would soon come to haunt White House. Councils were held secretly in clan pit houses to discuss what should be done. Delegations were chosen to go to Honovi and demand something be done about the food shortage, but Honovi refused to even meet with them. Within all of the clans there were some people who began to rebel, refusing to work on the great houses.

Honovi sent an order to all the Moieties of White House, which they were then to communicate to their people. Honovi decreed that only those who worked on the great houses would receive their allotment of food. He claimed he had a vision in which Sun Father had said that he was angry with the people because they were refusing to work. In his vision, Sun Father told him that if the people returned to work on the great houses, the rain would fall and snow would return to the mountains, but the people had lost faith in their Tiyamunyi. They no longer believed Sun Father spoke to him.

Almost no one returned to work. The caciques of the great houses, except for House of the Sun, pooled all the food in the family bins and began to ration it out to their people. It would not be enough to last the winter, but it would allow them some time to work out a compromise with Honovi.

Honovi was in no mood to compromise. He was incensed. "How dare these ungrateful insects defy my orders!" he bellowed. "I am the Tiyamunyi of White House. They will obey or they will pay for their impudence."

The people of the basin had known very little violence. There had been instances where raiders had come down from the north to ransack outlying villages in search of food, copper, and the precious stones. At those times, some people in the northern villages had lost their lives, but this happened only on rare occasions. Most of the time, White House was a place of peace.

Honovi changed that. He began to send out his guards to round up laborers to work on the great houses. When the people refused, they were beaten and their families were threatened. The guards bound their hands and dragged them to the great houses, where they were forced to work. Guards stood over them as they worked, and lashed out at anyone who did not do his share. A few Moieties protested, but many more feared Honovi and aided in his actions or did nothing. The people did not know how to react to such violence. Fear and despair settled over the people of White House.

In time, some began to search for a new leader to find a solution, and some looked to Honaw. Secret councils were held where people spoke in support of him. "Was he not also a member of the Spider Clan?" some said. "Did he not also have visions?" All agreed he had been taught well by his legendary grandfather, Kwahu, and that Qaletaga himself had taken him under his wing and groomed him to be a Moiety. It was clear to everyone that Honaw cared for his people. Soon the voice of a few became the voice of many. The people looked to Honaw for their salvation.

Honaw doubted himself and resisted their pleas. He told them that he had not been called by Sun Father to be Tiyamunyi. He told them Honovi was the rightful Tiyamunyi. But the people were persistent and pleaded with him. They said White House was doomed if Honaw did not step forward.

Honaw was torn. He looked to Lenmana for help and advice. He valued her words more than any other's. He knew she would give sound counsel. One night, as they ate their evening meal, he spoke to her.

"My heart is heavy, Lenmana, and my mind is filled with many troubling thoughts. It is plain to see that the people of White House are suffering, and I fear more suffering in the coming winter. Many will die. I do not understand how Honovi can let this happen to his people. He has become a cruel tyrant much like the tyrant I knew as a boy. He is obsessed with building larger and grander great houses, not for the glory of the gods, but for his own glory. He has forgotten all that his father taught him, or maybe he never learned. Qaletaga taught that the first duty of a Tiyamunyi is to care for and protect his people. How can he starve them and do them harm?"

"Honovi is not his father, my husband," she replied. "He learned little from him. Qaletaga held great power, but power was not important to him. He cared only for the welfare of his people. He built grand great houses for the glory of Sun Father and Earth Mother, knowing that they would bestow their blessing on the people if he did so. He guided the people so that they would come to know the kindness and love of Sun Father, and the people prospered under his rule. Honovi cares only for power. Your words are true, my husband; he does not build for the glory of Sun Father. He builds for the glory of Honovi. He does not deserve to be Tiyamunyi!"

"I hear your words, Lenmana, but I also do not deserve to be Tiyamunyi. I was not chosen by Sun Father. I do not have the heart of a Tiyamunyi. Honovi feared from the beginning that I was trying to take away his rightful place. I cannot just step in and take away what is rightfully his. Sun Father is already angry with the people. The balance of White House has already been terribly disrupted. If I do what the people ask of me, I fear it will anger Sun Father more, and the people will suffer even more."

Lenmana went to Honaw and held his face in her hands. She looked into his eyes and Honaw could see the love she felt for him, and he could feel it in her words. "You do have the heart of a Tiyamunyi, Honaw. You have shown that many times over. We do not know what is in the heart of Sun Father. Perhaps he became angry because Honovi became Tiyamunyi. Is it not true that he sees all and knows all? He sees the black heart of Honovi. He sees the way he is treating his good people. He stopped the rain from falling soon after Honovi became Tiyamunyi. It could be that he guided you to White House to learn from Qaletaga so that you would become Tiyamunyi and show his people how to live the right way. Maybe if you are Tiyamunyi, the balance of White House will be restored."

"You give me much to think about," Honaw replied. "Before I sleep tonight I will ask Grandfather for guidance. He has helped me before when I was troubled. Maybe he will look kindly on me once again and show me the path I should take."

Honaw did not have to wait for a sign or a vision to show him the path. His future was determined that very night when he and his family were awakened by the loud voices of men and a hard rapping on their threshold.

"Honaw, show yourself! Honovi, our great Tiyamunyi, has summoned you! You will come with us!"

Lenmana was startled out of her sleep, and Alo began to cry. "Honaw, why do these men come in the night? What does Honovi want with you?" she asked.

"Calm yourself, my wife. I will go and see what they want. You tend to Alo. He is frightened," Honaw answered.

Again the men called to him and banged loudly on the door. "Come out, Honaw, or we will come in to get you!" they shouted.

Honaw stepped out of his house to face a number of Honovi's guards. Some carried torches. Some carried clubs. "What do you want? Why do you come to my door in the middle of the night? You have frightened my wife and child," he said.

"I am Machakw, commander of our Tiyamunyi's guards. Honovi has summoned you. You will come with us."

"Whatever this is about, I am sure it will wait until morning. You can tell Honovi I will come to House of the Sun after my morning meal. Now leave us. You have already caused enough disturbances for one night," Honaw said.

He turned to go back into the house. Machakw grabbed his arm roughly and held it tightly. "You will come with us now," he said in a threatening voice.

"Release me! You have no right to force me!" Honaw shouted.

Lenmana heard the struggle and stepped out of the house. "Unhand my husband!" she pleaded. "The people of White House are not treated in this way!"

One of the guards stepped forward and pushed her toward the door. "Go back in your house, woman. This is not your affair!" he said.

Honaw's face and body tensed with anger and he shouted at the guards. "How dare you put your hands on my wife?" He broke away from Machakw and moved to protect Lenmana, but Machakw raised his club and struck Honaw, who fell unconscious. Blood seeped from a wound on the back of his head.

"Take him!" Machakw ordered. The guards seized Honaw and dragged him away. Lenmana was left frozen in the dark. She heard Alo crying in the house.

When Honaw awoke, he was cold and his head ached terribly. He looked around and found himself lying on a dirt floor in a small room. The only light came from a small window. The room smelled of wet earth and smoke. He touched the back of his head and felt a large, painful lump. His hair was matted with blood.

Suddenly a door opened and daylight filled the room, blinding him. "Finally, you have awakened. Honovi has been waiting." Honaw shaded his eyes and looked toward the sound of the voice. He saw Machakw and two guards standing above him. "Take him!" Machakw ordered. The guards pulled him to his feet and pushed him toward the door.

Honaw pulled away. "Take your hands off me," he said defiantly. "I do not need your assistance."

They stepped out the door onto the plaza of House of the Sun. There was a large crowd of people held back by the guards. They gasped when they saw him. His clothes were soiled, and the back of his robe was covered with blood. He felt weak and his head throbbed with pain, but he stood strong and proud before the people. Machakw led the way across the plaza and the two guards walked on either side of him with their war clubs at the ready.

A few in the crowd called out to him, "Honaw, what is happening? Why have you been taken?" Honaw scanned the crowd and saw Lenmana holding Alo, tears streaming down her face. He smiled and raised his hand to show he was all right. The crowd surged forward as the guards strained to hold them back. "Where are you taking him? What has he done?" they shouted.

"This one has committed treacherous crimes against our Tiyamunyi. Honovi will decide what is to be done with him!" Machakw replied.

"No," the crowd yelled. "He is a good man! He is a good Moiety! Release him. Release him!"

He was led into the same room where he had first met Qaletaga. This time, however, guards armed with axes and war clubs stood against the walls. Honovi, dressed in an opulent red robe, sat in a raised chair.

Machakw forced him to his knees. Honaw looked up at Honovi in defiance. "I do not remember your father having any guards, and you have guards everywhere I look. What do you fear, Honovi?"

"You will not speak of my father!" Honovi snapped. "You will not speak at all! Since you came to White House you have coveted my position of power. You have schemed and connived to become Tiyamunyi from the very beginning. You tried to turn my father against me, and now you try to turn my people against me. I know of your plan to overthrow me. I am no fool!"

Honaw spoke softly, but his voice did not tremble. "I never wanted to be Tiyamunyi, and I did not try to turn your father against you. The trouble you had with your father was of your own making. He tried to teach you how to live the right way and keep balance in all things. He showed you every day how to care for the people, but you would not see; you would not learn. You cared only for the power, beautiful robes, and precious stones. I did not need to turn the people against you. You were able to do that on your own. You are a fool, Honovi."

"Silence him!" Honovi shouted.

Machakw kicked Honaw in the back, and with his hands bound, he could not break his fall. His face slammed hard on the stone floor. The blow pushed the wind from his lungs, and his nose spurted blood. He struggled to breathe, but he forced himself up from the floor and glared at Honovi. He was not afraid of Honovi, or his guards. He was determined to show no weakness. He would not give them the satisfaction.

Honovi stood and looked down on Honaw. "I have been praying to Sun Father for guidance in this time of suffering, and he has spoken to me. He has told me I must rid White House of a terrible evil. I must sacrifice the source of this evil to him. When the sacrifice is done, he will bring the rain, the crops will grow, and the deer will return to our mesas. You are the evil, Honaw! It is because of your treachery that the people suffer!"

"You sound much like a false Tiyamunyi I knew as a child," Honaw calmly replied. "Like you, he knew nothing about living the right way, and like you, he also claimed to speak to Sun Father. His words were false and so are yours. Sun Father has no time for men like you. Do with me what you wish, but hear me when I say, it will not end your troubles. I will be happy to go to live with the ancestors, and I know in my heart you will never be welcome with them. You are the evil, Honovi."

Honovi shook with rage and he screamed at Honaw, "I will not listen to any more of your evil words! Sun Father has spoken to me! You will be sacrificed to him when he shows his face in the eastern sky. I will cleanse White House of your evil and be done with your treachery! Take him away!"

There was a dim light in the eastern sky when Honaw stepped out onto the plaza. Machakw looped a rope around his neck. Using the rope, he led him to a table that had been placed in the middle of the plaza. In the shadowy light, Honaw could see people standing all around the plaza. People on the terraces held torches. There was not enough light to see their faces. The crowd was strangely quiet. All he could hear was the sound of a few women crying.

He was not afraid. His only regret was that he was not able to see Lenmana and Alo. It would have been comforting to say good-bye and hold them one more time. He would have liked to tell them how much he loved them and not to mourn him long. Honaw knew he was going to live with his mother, father, Old Kwahu, and all the ancestors. He would have told his living family to rejoice, that he would see them again in the next world, but Honovi was cruel and would not allow it.

As the sky began to brighten, Honaw saw Honovi standing on a raised platform. He wore a beautiful robe and an elaborate headdress made of feathers. He had several necklaces made of the precious stones strung around his neck, and he was surrounded by his guards. The guards picked Honaw up and placed him on the table. They bound his hands and feet to the four corners of the table, and ripped away his shirt so that his chest was bared.

Honovi stood and raised his hands to the eastern sky. "Sun Father!" he said. "I have heard your words, and what I do today, I do in your name. This man is evil. He has brought suffering to our people. Through his treachery, he has tried to turn these good people away from their Tiyamunyi. He covets my power and works against your teachings!"

With this, a great uproar came from the crowd. Honaw could hear many voices all denying what Honovi was saying. "No, no," they cried. "This not true! Honaw is a holy man! Your words are false!" The crowd surged forward. Some tried to break through the guards, but they were beaten back.

"Hear my words, people!" Honovi said in a loud voice. "Sun Father came to me in a vision and told me that this man is evil! This man is the reason Sun Father is angry with his people! He wants Honaw's blood! Only by his blood will the rains return to our thirsty land. Only by his blood will crops grow again and the deer return to our land. Sun Father has instructed me to sacrifice this man to him! That is the only way the balance of White House can be restored."

Again the crowd surged forward shouting their protests, but the guards held them back. Suddenly Honaw's voice could be heard above the cacophony. "Be calm, my people. Let them do with me what they will. Do not sacrifice yourselves for me. You know how to live the right way. Remember, and Sun Father will show you the way out of these dark days. I will still be among you!"

"Silence him!" Honovi shouted.

Machakw moved to stuff a piece of deerskin in his mouth, but

Honaw smiled at him. "There is no need," he said. "I am through. I will speak no more."

The rising sun was a red dot through the smoke-filled air on the eastern horizon. "Sun Father has shown his face in the eastern sky. It is time!" Honovi shouted. "Do what Sun Father has commanded. Drive the blade into his heart!"

Machakw picked up the blade and raised it above his head, but then he looked at the face of Honaw and hesitated. He lowered the blade and turned to Honovi. "It was your vision, not mine," he said.

"How dare you defy me?" Honovi shouted as he ran to the table.

He pushed Machakw away and grabbed the dagger. He raised it above his head ready to plunge it into Honaw's chest. Suddenly, Earth Mother trembled beneath his feet, and a great rumble rose up from deep inside her. Honovi stood frozen with the dagger still raised above his head. Earth Mother trembled again, this time more violently. Then there was a muffled explosion and the horizon to the southwest was suddenly aglow like Earth Mother herself was on fire.

Honovi dropped the knife and ran for the great house as Earth Mother continued to tremble. Honaw heard screams and saw the people running in all directions. In the chaos, he realized Lenmana was standing above him. She cut his hands and legs free. Honaw rose from the table and held her close. She was shaking with fear. Little Alo was hanging on to her dress. He had a look of astonishment on his face, but he did not cry.

"What is happening, Honaw?" she cried.

"I do not know!" he answered.

They stood there clutching each other until Earth Mother stopped trembling. The fire in the sky grew until there was a great red dome covering the southwestern sky.

As Sun Father rose in the east, the red dome seemed to fade, but what took its place was even more terrifying. A huge black-and-gray cloud rose from the sky and grew until it covered the entire western horizon. Lightning flashed across its ominous face as it bubbled up higher and higher into the sky.

By midday, a strong, hot wind began to blow from the direction of the cloud, and it was evident that the black cloud was moving closer. Some people ran about wailing and shrieking in fear, while others raised their hands to Sun Father and begged his forgiveness. All believed it was the end of the Daylight World. They believed that Sun Father and Earth Mother had come to destroy their world, to punish them for their sins.

When the cloud engulfed the entire sky, blocking out Sun Father's life-giving rays, the world grew dark and a gray snow began to fall. The snow was not cold. It was warm, and it covered the ground in a layer of gray ash. The air was hard to breathe. The people huddled in their pit houses and prayed for salvation.

Honaw, Lenmana, and Alo took shelter in their house. They covered the door and windows with turkey feather blankets. They sat pressed together under the dim light of a single torch. "Oh, Honaw, is this to be the end of our days? Has Sun Father come to destroy the Daylight World?" Lenmana asked.

"I do not know," Honaw answered.

He could see the fear in her eyes.

Alo looked up at his father. "I am scared," he said. "You said Sun Father was all good. Why does he do this to us?"

Honaw sat Alo in his lap and pulled Lenmana closer to his side. "I know that Sun Father is merciful and loves his people," he said. "I do not think he would destroy us in this way. I believe that this is a warning. A harsh warning indeed, but I do not think he means to destroy us. We have allowed Honovi to lead us down a trail of darkness. We have strayed from the path of Sun Father, and he is very angry with us. He is telling us that we must return to living the right way and restore the balance to all things. If we accomplish these tasks, I believe he will lift this terrible curse."

"Honaw, I love you with all my heart," Lenmana said. "I thought I had lost you forever, but Sun Father and Earth Mother saved you from the dagger. They must have saved you for a reason. I think they must have plans for you."

"You also had a hand in saving me. Without you, I would still be tied to that table with gray snow covering my face. Thank you, and I love you, too, with all my heart," he replied.

"I love Mother and Father, too. I am not afraid anymore," Alo said. They sat together in the dim light and prayed to Sun Father to take away the curse.

The warm snow continued for four sunrises. On the fourth day it stopped falling, but the sky remained dark. The people who ventured from their houses had to carry torches to see. The ash lay like a dirty, gray blanket covering White House and all the land. The water in the pond was black and gritty. There was no fresh water to drink.

No one had seen Honovi since the morning of the fire in the sky. A crowd of men began to gather outside his chamber. They spoke among themselves and many blamed Honovi for the plight that had befallen White House. They believed that Sun Father became angry with them when Honovi became Tiyamunyi.

Cheveyo of the Bow Clan spoke angry words to the crowd. "Honovi does not care for his people like a true Tiyamunyi. Did not Sun Father hold back the rain when he became Tiyamunyi? He has brought this curse down upon us. Earth Mother started to tremble and moan and the sky caught fire when he lifted the dagger to kill Honaw. Sun Father stopped the evil deed! It is Honovi's fault that Sun Father has taken his light from us! It is his fault that Sun Father is angry with us!"

As the crowd grew, it became more and more furious, as fear overwhelmed their thinking. "We must purge this evil from White

House! It is the only way Sun Father will show his face again! It is the end of our days as long as Honovi lives. We must kill Honovi or all is lost!"

Many in the angry crowd brandished clubs as they surged toward Honovi's chamber. "Pull him from his hiding place!" they screamed. "Kill him before it is too late!"

"Kill him! Kill him! Kill him!" they chanted.

Suddenly, Honaw appeared on the terrace above Honovi's chamber. He raised his voice above the incensed crowd. "Hear me, good people! I beg you to stop what you are about to do!"

The angry throng stopped and grew silent when they saw Honaw standing above them. Honaw continued. "I know you are angry and afraid, but killing Honovi will not lift this curse from us. It is true that his heart is black. He is not his father. His father cared for his people and taught you how to live the right way. Honovi is not a true Tiyamunyi. He cares only for power, beautiful robes, and the precious stones, but killing him is not the answer. Sun Father has brought this darkness down upon us to teach us a lesson. We have not been living according to his teachings. We have strayed from the path. We must now show him that we have learned the lesson well. Sun Father does not teach us to kill. Show him that you have learned his lesson by sparing Honovi. Killing him will only make Sun Father angrier, and then, in his wrath, he may truly destroy White House and all his people."

Machni, Niman Moiety of the Antelope Clan, stepped forward and pleaded, "Then what do we do, Honaw? How do we get Sun Father to lift this curse? We have very little food to eat and almost no water. Help us, Honaw."

"I will go to Honovi. I will tell him what we have decided. He is not a fool. He knows in his heart that his evil has brought this curse down upon us. He also knows that because of the evil in his heart he will never be allowed to live with the ancestors. In death he is doomed to walk between the worlds for eternity. He does not want to die. We must banish him from White House. He will carry his evil and the guilt for what he has done with him for the rest of his days. That will be punishment enough."

Honaw came down from the terrace, and the crowd parted to let him pass to Honovi's chamber. He stepped into the outer chamber and called to Honovi, "Honovi, it is Honaw. I will speak with you. May I enter?"

"You may enter," a voice replied, but it was not the voice of Honovi. It was a soft, frail voice of a woman.

As Honaw entered the chamber, he saw Mansi sitting on the floor. She was crying. She cradled Honovi's head in her lap. A red bloodstain covered the front of Honovi's robe. Honaw could see that he was dead.

Mansi looked up at Honaw. "My son tried to live up to the image he held of his father, but he saw only the surface," she said through her tears. "He did not understand what it meant to be a Tiyamunyi like his father. He saw only the power and none of the kindness. I lost both my husband and my son when Qaletaga fell. I heard the chants and anger in the voices of the people. I knew what they would do to him. I could not bear to see him suffer in such a way. I took his life. May Sun Father and the ancestors have mercy on us both."

Honaw knelt next to Mansi and put his arm around her. "You have suffered greatly. You are a good woman. You were a good wife and mother. I am sure the ancestors see your virtues and feel your pain. They will be merciful."

Machakw was standing nearby. "Bring him so that the people may see," Honaw said to him. Machakw gently lifted Honovi from his mother's arms and followed Honaw out of the chamber.

The crowd stood frozen when they saw Machakw holding Honovi's lifeless body. "Good people of White House, Honovi, your Tiyamunyi, is dead! We will bury him in a place of honor next to his father!" Honaw called to the crowd.

Some in the crowd cried out in anger, "No! Leave him for the dogs and the black ravens. He does not deserve a place of honor."

"There has been enough pain and suffering in White House," Honaw replied. "We must return to living the right way. Sun Father is merciful and he teaches his people to be merciful. We do not have the right to judge Honovi, only Sun Father and the ancestors have that right. We will be merciful and bury him according to the teachings of Sun Father, like all the Tiyamunyis before him."

Lenmana helped Mansi prepare the body for burial. They buried Honovi next to his father in the inner burial chamber of House of the Sun. The women of White House stood on the plaza and sang the death song. The crowd filled the plaza. The people were merciful and Sun Father was pleased.

When Honaw, Lenmana, and the burial party emerged from the chamber, a rainstorm began. The rain was not black and tepid. It was cool and fresh. It washed White House clean of the gray ash. The stream ran clear and fresh water filled the pond. The people rejoiced. Sun Father was no longer angry with them. The curse was lifted.

In the days that followed, the sky cleared and the light and warmth of Sun Father returned. The pond was again clear and there was fresh water for the fields, but the growing season was more than half over, and the crops were stunted. The harvest would be meager, not nearly enough to feed the people of White House in the coming winter.

Councils were held to discuss a solution to the vexing problem, but the Moieties of the different houses argued among themselves and accomplished little. Some wanted to send out large hunting parties to the far mountains in hopes of bringing in enough meat to last the winter. Others proposed sending a party laden with copper and the precious stones westward to trade for food.

Through the years, they had always looked to their Tiyamunyi in times of crisis. Only he could ask Sun Father for guidance. Without a Tiyamunyi, some feared White House would be doomed to suffer hunger and death in the coming winter.

Honovi left no son to inherit the post, and a solution through marriage could not be found. A council was called. The Moieties from all the great houses came to the pit house in House of the Sun to appoint a Tiyamunyi. Smoke curled up from the fire in the hearth, and the foot drums pounded a solemn rhythm as they assembled. Honaw took his place among them.

Ahote, the old and wise Soyala Moiety of the Badger Clan, was first to speak. "Hear me, Moieties of White House," he said. "The decision we make today will determine the future of White House. Let us pray to Sun Father that he may guide us in our choice of Tiyamunyi. There is one among us who led us through the dark days when Earth Mother shook beneath our feet and Sun Father set the sky ablaze. He alone set us back on the path to living the right way, His words made clear to us why Sun Father was angry. Through his guidance, the curse was lifted and Sun Father again blesses us with his light. But the balance of White House is not yet restored. We do not have enough food to last the long winter to come. So again we need his wisdom to show us the way. We need him to be the guardian of the people. We need him to be our Tiyamunyi."

Honaw realized Ahote was speaking of him. A knot rose up in throat. *No, not me,* he thought. *I am not worthy. Many others are far wiser. I was not chosen by Sun Father.*

Ahote continued. "The one I speak of is of the Spider Clan, and Qaletaga, our most beloved Tiyamunyi, had faith in him. Qaletaga took him into his heart and taught him what it meant to be a true guardian of the people. He learned his lessons well. He has already proven his worth as a leader. The people trust him and his love for them cannot be denied. I submit that Honaw of the Spider Clan be appointed Tiyamunyi!"

The pit house erupted in cheers of approval. All looked at Honaw, who did not know how to respond to the honor of their support.

"What say you, Honaw?" Ahote asked. "The council has chosen. Do you accept?"

Honaw stood and walked to the center of the pit house. He was awestruck as he looked upon the smiling faces of the Moieties. "This is a great honor and a grave responsibility you have bestowed on me," he said. "I am not sure I am worthy of the task. I am just a humble Moiety."

"Qaletaga knew you were worthy," Ahote said. "From the time you came to White House, all could see your greatness. Sun Father became angry when Honovi became Tiyamunyi. Honovi led us into darkness. You led us out. We need you again, Honaw. Become Tiyamunyi and show us the way. We have faith in you."

Now in the days after the warm snow, the boy Moiety of Chu'a Village became the Tiyamunyi of White House. Sun Father was again pleased.

Honaw was reluctant to move into House of the Sun. He argued with Lenmana as she was packing their belongings to move. "I would rather live here among the people," he said. "I would not feel comfortable in House of the Sun. The people need a Tiyamunyi to walk beside them, not lord over them."

"No, Honaw," Lenmana replied. "The people need to believe that there is something greater than themselves. They need to know that Sun Father is watching and looking out for them. They need to believe that through you, Sun Father will show them the way to live the right way and keep their world in balance. They will expect you to live in his house, where his visions will be clear to you."

"But Sun Father has never spoken to me. I have had no visions of him."

"But you have had visions. Did not the old man, Kwahu, speak to you in a vision? Did he not reveal to you the evil in your village when you were a boy? And was it not Kwahu who told you to follow the light in the darkness?" she said.

"That is all true, but Grandfather is not Sun Father," Honaw answered.

"Oh, my husband," Lenmana gently said. "Do you think that Sun Father did not know when Old Kwahu appeared to you? Just as he sent old Spider Woman to the people in their hour of need, he sent Kwahu to you so that you could bring the people back to the correct path of living the right way."

"You speak words of wisdom, my wife. As I have said before, Sun Father was smiling on me the day you found me in the wilderness. I thank him every day. But no matter how you try to convince me or how many visions I have of Sun Father, I will not wear the bejeweled robes and I will not sit on a throne!"

Lenmana smiled. "As you wish, my husband," she said.

Honaw made it a point to walk among the people every morning. He would take little Alo and walk the path along the pond. The people were always pleased to see him. Sometimes he would sit and converse with them until it was time for the afternoon meal. The people said he had learned well from Qaletaga.

One of the first persons to ask for an audience with Honaw was Pavati. Honovi had dismissed him as cacique of House of the Sun, and now he returned to offer his services to Honaw. With the food crises looming, Honaw was happy to have him back to help deal with the problem.

Honaw's first charge to him was to organize trading parties to be sent out in every direction in search of corn. The parties took with them precious bluish-green stones, copper bells, and knives, axes, and arrowheads made from the hard black-and-red stones. Pavati himself led the party heading northeast. Honaw asked the people to pray that they would be able to bring back enough corn for the winter.

Another one to ask for an audience was Mansi. She came one morning as Honaw, Lenmana, and Alo were finishing their morning meal. She looked frail and troubled.

"Please, forgive the intrusion of an old woman, great Honaw," she said.

"It is just Honaw, dear Mansi, and it is no intrusion. How may I help you?"

"I have come to ask for food for a journey I must take."

"What journey do you speak of, Mansi?" Honaw asked.

"I must leave White House, Honaw. There is nothing for me here."

"There is no need for you to leave. You will always be welcome here. This is as much your house as it is ours. You can stay here with us," Honaw replied.

"Thank you for your kindness, but I cannot stay here. The spirits of my fallen husband and son will forever haunt me in this house. I must leave."

"Where will you go?" Lenmana asked.

"I do not know, but I am sure Sun Father will travel with me."

"Of course we will give you food. How much do you need?" Honaw asked.

"Enough to last two people a few days," Mansi replied.

"Two people?" Lenmana asked.

"Machakw will accompany me," Mansi answered.

"I am glad you do not travel alone. Machakw is a good man. It shall be done," Honaw said.

Lenmana packed two pouches of corn meal, piki bread, and

dried rabbit and deer meat, enough to last for many sunrises. Mansi was grateful.

A few days later, Honaw asked, "What is the news of Mansi and Machakw?"

"They were seen climbing the north mesa," Lenmana answered. That was the last anyone would see of them.

CHAPTER 17

❖

TEZCATLIPOCA'S WAR

In 1056, when the boy Honaw and his mother led their people away from Chu'a Village, they left the false Tiyamunyi, Istaga, alone in his destroyed great house. He remained there for many days, immersed in self-pity. In his sick mind, he was convinced that he had done no wrong and that his actions were only for the good of the people of Chu'a Village. He took no responsibility for his own actions and blamed Honaw for his plight. As the days passed, his self-pity turned to hate and revenge. Hate and revenge are strong motivators, and eventually he emerged from his ruined great house, swearing he would seek vengeance on Honaw and the people who abandoned him.

Istaga stood in what was left of the plaza, spread his arms to the northern sky, and proclaimed, "By Sun Father and all the ancestors, I will vanquish my enemies and regain my power. I will again be a great leader and take my place next to the ancestor gods of old!"

He gathered what little food he had, and with a small pouch of the precious stones he had hidden away, he began to wander the wilderness. He knew that Honaw had taken the people north, and he did not want to confront them yet. He needed to find a way to regain a position of strength and power before he met his hated enemy. So he drifted south, trading his precious stones for food in small villages and with fellow travelers.

Istaga told all the people he encountered that he was once a Tiyamunyi of a magnificent great house who had been betrayed by his people. He told of how he had cared for his people and provided for them and asked only that they help build and beautify his great house for the glory of Sun Father. But, he said, his people were lazy and greedy. He said they would not work and stole from him. They fought among themselves and refused to live the right way.

He had no choice but to punish them for their trespasses. He told of how he prayed to Sun Father to send a calamity that would chastise his people, and Sun Father sent a great flood that destroyed his village and struck down all the evil people. He furthered his lies by saying that after the flood, Sun Father appeared to him and told him of another village somewhere to the south where the people would love him and appreciate his goodness, but it was his penance to wander the wilderness until he found this village. He said that Sun Father would again appear to him when he found what he was searching for.

Istaga told this story so many times, he almost began to believe it himself. He was such a convincing liar that soon the word spread about a great holy man traveling the land in search of a village where he would build a magnificent, powerful city to rival White House.

As he left each village, he told the people that Sun Father had not yet appeared to him and, regrettably, their village was not his place. In reality he assessed each village to see if it was suitable for him to exploit. But the villages he passed through were small and poor. It became obvious to him that he was not going to regain his status in these small, impoverished places. He began to rethink his plan.

By the summer of 1066, Istaga had wandered south for many growing seasons until he came to the land of the god Tonatiuh. Tonatiuh was the sun god worshipped by the people who lived in this land. He kept the sun moving across their sky and ruled over the Tonatiuh world. But Tonatiuh was very much different from Sun Father of White House. He was a fierce warrior god who demanded human sacrifice to keep the sun moving across the sky. His priests acted as warlords and led brutal warrior-cults that collected tribute from the people and killed all who did not pay.

When Istaga reached the land of the Tonatiuh, the people were starving and a civil war between the warrior-cults over control of what little food there was had been raging since the crops failed two growing seasons ago. As the war progressed, the people continued to worship Tonatiuh, but the warrior-cults attempted to establish their own identity by pledging allegiance to one of many different warrior gods. Each of these warrior gods was more fierce and brutal than the next.

The warrior-cult in the land that Istaga entered followed the horned serpent god, Tezcatlipoca. They were fierce warriors, but their priest was a poor leader. He had led them in a number of battles in which they were defeated at the hands of what they considered much lesser warriors. After the defeats, they were driven north by the victors. The warriors became angry with their priest and sacrificed him to Tezcatlipoca in the hope that doing so would help them regain their power and defeat their enemies. Istaga found them in the desert, leaderless and starving. He had always been a shrewd man, and in those warriors, he saw his chance to become a wealthy and powerful leader again. He laid his plan to become the priest of the warriors of Tezcatlipoca.

He talked to the people and learned as much as he could about Tonatiuh and the warriors of Tezcatlipoca. He mastered their prayers and rituals. When he determined he had gained enough knowledge, he put his carefully laid plan into effect.

One morning before dawn, Istaga climbed a small rise that overlooked the camp of one hundred or more Tezcatlipoca warriors. He had dressed to impress the warriors. He wore his finest robe and an apron inlaid with the precious stones. He also wore a necklace and bracelets made of the bluish-green stones.

As dawn broke, the light of the sun shown radiantly at his back, and he cast a long shadow across the camp. In his loudest voice, he called out, "I am Istaga, a holy man from the north. I have been sent by mighty Tezcatlipoca to lead you out of this desert and to reveal to you a future of wealth and power the likes of which you have never known!"

The warriors in camp shaded their eyes and looked to the top of the hill to see who was speaking. The sun glistened beautifully off the precious stones Istaga was wearing, and in his regal robe, he truly did look like a messenger from the gods.

"Tezcatlipoca has told me of your plight," Istaga shouted down to them. "I know you have been defeated in battle through no fault of your own. Tezcatlipoca knows you are great warriors. He has sent me to you so that you may once again be the powerful warriors your enemies fear!"

The warriors stared in amazement at Istaga, and no one uttered a word until one man stepped forward and called back to Istaga, "Come down so that we may see the holy man sent to us by Tezcatlipoca."

The man watched skeptically as Istaga descended the hill and walked boldly to the center of camp. The warriors gathered around him. Some were awestruck by him, while others were suspicious. Istaga knew this was the moment of truth. If his plan was to succeed, he could not show any fear or weakness. He stood straight and looked each man in the eye.

The man who called him down approached Istaga, stopping only inches from his face. He was a big man, tall and muscular. He had scars on his chest and arms. He looked down on Istaga and said, "You may be a holy man, but I do not believe you were sent by our great Tezcatlipoca. You look to me like an old fool with no more power than a woman grinding her corn." Some of the warriors laughed. Others stood silent, waiting to see a reaction from Istaga.

With cutting sarcasm, the warrior said, "If you were sent by Tezcatlipoca, you must surely have immense power. Show us your power, holy man."

Istaga gripped the handle of a blade he had hidden in his robe. "I will show my power, and I will show you who is the fool!"

With a quick motion, Istaga raised the blade and plunged it into the man's throat. It penetrated through until the point protruded from the back of his neck. With a look of shock on his face, the man staggered and fell, clutching his throat. Blood poured from the wound and ran down his chest. He lay in the dust with blood pooling around his head and breathed his last. Istaga walked up to him and placed his foot on his chest, pulling the blade free. Reaching down, he thrust the blade into the man's chest. Cutting out his heart, he held it above his head for all to see.

"This is how Tezcatlipoca has instructed me to treat all enemies that stand before us. This is how you will regain your power. We will crush all our enemies under our heels and cut out their hearts!" Istaga roared.

Istaga's demonstration was effective. The warriors of Tezcatlipoca understood blood. They all stood silent, stunned by what they had witnessed.

Finally, another warrior stepped from the crowd. "I am Zaca," he said. "I was second in command to our last priest. We sacrificed him to Tezcatlipoca because he betrayed us in battle. We cut out his heart and burned it. We then cut off his head and stuck it on a staff so that all might see what we do to worthless jackals." He pointed to a pole standing at the entrance of their camp. At its top was a decaying skull turned black by the sun.

He continued. "I tell you this so that you will know what awaits you if your words are false. You said you could lead us to more wealth and power than we have ever known. We are listening, priest. Speak your words." The warriors moved closer so that they could hear. They formed a tight circle around Istaga.

"I have traveled long and far," Istaga began. "I come from a land to the north beyond the great mountains. I was once a high priest of a village, but I, too, was betrayed. I was betrayed by the very people I cared for and loved. Greed and laziness turned them against me. They would not work the fields and stole from me and each other. That refused to follow my teachings on how to live together in peace. I prayed to Sun Father, who ruled that land and sky, but he did not listen. He gave me no answers. It was then that the great horned serpent, Tezcatlipoca, first appeared to me in a vision. He told me that Sun Father was weak and no longer held power over the land. 'Follow me,' he said. 'I will punish those who betrayed you and lead you out of the darkness.'"

"Tezcatlipoca kept his word. He sent a great flood that destroyed that evil village and all who dwelled there. He then told me to travel south and I would find the mighty warriors who fight in his name. He said that I should lead his warriors on a quest to destroy all the followers of false gods and evil teachings. He said that if we did his bidding, he would reward us all with vast wealth and power, that we would vanquish all our enemies, and through him, we would rule all the world. So what say you, warriors of mighty Tezcatlipoca? Will you do his bidding and follow me in this great quest?"

"Climb back up your hill, priest," Zaca said. "We will consider what you have said."

Istaga climbed back up the hill and sat in the hot sun while Zaca talked to his men. He knew they were deciding his fate. Either he became a priest of Tezcatlipoca, or his head would rest on the end of a staff.

After what seemed like an eternity, Zaca finally called him to come down. "We have decided, priest. We are poor and hungry in this cursed desert. We have nothing. You lead and we will follow. What is your plan?"

"You will not regret your decision," Istaga said.

"You better hope we do not regret our decision. If you fail in your promise, your head might end up on the end of a staff," Zaca replied.

"We will not fail. Ready your men. We go north in the morning," Istaga instructed.

"North? Our enemies are to the south, in Tonatiuh," Zaca argued.

"We must regain our strength before we meet our enemies to the south. We need food. There is food for the taking in the lands I passed through. We will raid the villages to the north and demand tribute. We will sacrifice their spiritual leaders to Tezcatlipoca. We will take food, copper, and women. We will make them fear us. They are weak and their Sun Father is weak. When we have fed the men, and they are again strong, we will attack the mines at Muna. You see these bluish-green stones I wear?"

"We know of the stones. They are greatly coveted by the priests of Tonatiuh," Zaca replied.

"They are mined at Muna. We will take all that we can carry. Like you say, they are precious to the people of Tonatiuh. They will make us wealthy and powerful. Only then will we return and destroy our enemies to the south."

Istaga and his warriors moved north, raiding villages as they went. At each village, they struck fear into the people by brutally sacrificing the Moieties to Tezcatlipoca. They told the people of each village that Sun Father had lost his power, and that Tezcatlipoca now ruled the land, demanding blood to keep the sun moving across the sky. They proclaimed that Tezcatlipoca was the only true god, and that all followers of Sun Father had to convert to Tezcatlipoca or die. They forced the people to watch as they cut the hearts out of their Moieties and burned them, and then they cut off their victims' heads and displayed them on staffs. They commanded the people to denounce Sun Father and pledge their allegiance to Tezcatlipoca.

The warriors took food, women, and anything of value from the villages. They vowed they would be back in the spring to collect a tithe of food from the villages, and if not paid, everyone would be killed and the village burned. The placid people of the basin had no experience with war or violence; they were helpless under the onslaught.

Thirty sunrises into their bloody incursion, they came to a beacon tower great house called Takala. The people of Takala were led by two devout Moieties who acted as the keepers of the beacon. The Moieties refused to denounce Sun Father, and even as they were tortured, they emboldened the people to defy Istaga and his vicious warriors. A daughter of one of the Moieties was especially outspoken and stood unafraid before the killers. They tied her to a pole and pierced her body with arrows. Even after this there were many who still would not bow to Tezcatlipoca. In the end, Istaga's warriors slaughtered sixteen men, women, and children. They threw the bodies into the beacon tower and burned the tower.

Word of Istaga's rampage spread across the land. The people began to leave their villages and take refuge on top of the mesas or in the mountains. After his complete subjugation of Takala, Istaga made plans to attack the village of Muna and take control of the mines that produced the precious stones. He had promised his warriors that they would possess more riches than they had ever known, and now he would keep his word.

To this point, his raiders had met with no resistance. The people of White House had no concept of war or a standing army. The mines at Muna had a few guards armed with clubs and axes, but they were no match for the merciless warriors of Tezcatlipoca. The warriors descended upon the village and massacred all who stood in their way. The guards fought bravely, but in the end, they stood no chance. Many were killed in battle, and those who survived the attack were sacrificed along with the Moieties. The rampaging warriors seized many baskets of the precious stones and coerced men and women of the village into carrying them. Istaga kept a good amount of the stones for himself and distributed the rest to his men. Again, they vowed to return in the spring to collect more.

Caught up in their bloodlust and strengthened by their triumphs and profits, the warriors swore their allegiance to Istaga, who believed in his heart that he was chosen to destroy White House and rule all the world in the name of Tezcatlipoca. He finally had the power he had always coveted, the power he thought he justly deserved.

In the fall of 1066 Pavati stood on a ridge overlooking a peaceful valley with a river winding its way down its center. There was a stone house standing in a bend of the river and well-irrigated crop fields nearby. With luck, this would be the last place he would visit to trade. Thirteen of his men already carried full baskets of corn, squash, and beans. They had only two more baskets to fill, and they would be starting back to White House. They had been traveling for many sunrises, and his men were anxious to go home. Noticing a small trail, he started down the ridge to the farm.

Moki looked up from his work in the crop field. "Look, Father," he said. "There are many men coming down the trail from the ridge!"

Lansa stopped his work and shaded his eyes to better see the men approaching. "I see them, my son. They are carrying heavy," he said to Kele.

"Stay here with your mother, Moki. I will go to meet them." He picked up his bow and quiver and started toward the men just as they emerged from the tree line. Moki and his mother watched as Lansa reached the men.

The men stopped and talked with Lansa for a few moments, and then they all headed to the field. "Traders or hunters, maybe," Kele said to Moki.

"Kele, we have visitors," Lansa said. Kele and Moki stepped to the edge of the field and waited.

"Greetings," Pavati said. "My name is Pavati. I have been sent by Honaw, the great Tiyamunyi of White House, to trade for food. Sun Father has held the rain for two growing seasons, and the storage bins of White House are empty."

Kele and Lansa were stunned when they heard the name Honaw. "Could it be, Lansa?" Kele asked.

"Did you say Honaw is your Tiyamunyi?" Lansa asked.

"Yes, Honaw of the Spider Clan. Do you know him?" Pavati asked.

"He may be my brother. Tell us about him," Kele said excitedly. "Does he hail from White House? Does he have a sister? Are his—"

"Wait," Pavati said. "I will be happy to tell you about him, but one question at a time. He does not hail from White House. He, and what was left of his clan, came to us from the south on the Great North Road at the Time of Soyala six growing seasons ago. He is the boy Moiety who saved his people from a false and evil Tiyamunyi. He speaks with the gods and saved us from the darkness. He is loved by all."

"Do you know the village he came from? Please tell us," Kele asked.

"He came from a village along a wash called Chu'a. Yes, Chu'a Village," Pavati answered.

"Oh, Lansa," Kele gasped. "It is our Honaw! It is my brother!" She started to cry.

Lansa held her and Moki asked, "Why do you cry, Mother?"

"You know of your uncle Honaw?" Lansa asked him.

"Yes, Father."

"Well, now we have learned a truly marvelous thing has happened. He has become the most holy Tiyamunyi of White House. Your mother cries tears of joy."

"Sun Father surely works in mysterious ways," Pavati said. "When did you see him last?"

"It has been ten growing seasons. He was just a boy then, but wise beyond his years." Lansa answered.

"You and your men must be tired and hungry. Please stay with us tonight, and tell all about Honaw," Kele said.

"Thank you, but no," Pavati said. "The people of White House are hungry and wait for our return. We have a few of the valuable bluish-green stones and some blades made from the hard black stone. We would like to trade for corn, squash, or beans. Most of our baskets are full, but we still have two that are empty. We hope we can fill them here and start back for home."

"Sun Father has been good to us; the river has run full for many growing seasons. We have corn, and you can keep your stones and blades. We will fill your baskets and are happy to do so," Lansa said.

Lansa took the two men with empty baskets to the storage bins, and Pavati sent the rest to the river to fill the water jugs.

"Are you sure you will not change your mind and stay with us tonight?" Kele asked. "I do wish to hear more about Honaw. I cannot believe that my little brother is Tiyamunyi of White House."

"I thank you for your courtesy," Pavati answered. "But like I said, my people are hungry and my men are longing to be home. The day is still young and good for traveling. We must go.

"But I must say I am always amazed by Sun Father's kindness," he added. "I believe he led us here so that you could know of your brother. Honaw is a great man, Kele. You should travel to White House. Go to see him. Have you made the pilgrimage to White House?" he asked.

"No, we have never been there," she answered.

"It is a wondrous place, and I am sure Honaw would be pleased to see you." Then with their last baskets and water jars filled, Pavati and his men headed southwest toward home.

The years along the river had been good to Kele and Lansa. Moki had grown into a strong, intelligent boy, full of curiosity and eager to learn. He did not know that Lansa was not his real father. Kele and Lansa agreed that the time would come when they would need to tell him, because it is important to know your ancestors, but that time had not yet come. They told him of his grandmother Nova, his grandfather Tocho, and his aunt and uncle. And they spent many nights sitting around the hearth, telling stories of his great-grandfather Kwahu, but said nothing about his father's family.

Lansa traveled far to the surrounding mesas to gather enough sandstone to build Kele a stone house to replace the pit house. Earth Mother continued to smile on them. Even in times when rain was scarce, the river always carried enough water for their crops to flourish.

Kele never fully recovered from the wolf attack. Her mangled foot healed but was deformed, and she used a walking stick to move about. The pain grew worse as the years passed, but she did not complain and always did her share of the work. Though Kele and Lansa tried, Sun Father did not bless them with another child. Kele felt guilty that she could not give Lansa a son of his own blood, but Lansa always reassured her that he already had a son in Moki. He never wavered from the very beginning in his insistence that Moki was his son.

Two sunrises since Pavati and his men visited their farm, Lansa and Kele sat in the shade of the ramada watching Moki fishing the river. Lansa could see that Kele had something on her mind. "What is bothering you, my wife? You have had a distant look in your eye since Pavati's visit."

"I am sorry, Lansa. I know I have not been myself. There is something that I need to talk to you about."

"I think I know," said Lansa. "You want to make the trip to White House to see your brother. I, too, want to see him. It has been many years. I long to hear what has happened to your mother, father, and sister. I wonder if my mother still lives. She would be quite old now."

"Yes, my husband, I need to see Honaw. I still cannot believe that he is the most holy man in all the land, Tiyamunyi of White House! It takes my breath away. And I must know what has happened to my family. Maybe they live there with him."

"It is a great distance," Lansa said. "It will take many days walking on land that is hard to cross. It will be very difficult for you because of your leg. Do you think you will be strong enough for such a journey?"

"It will be painful, but with you and Moki to help, I am sure I can make it. I must see my brother," she said.

"All right, we will go. It will take a few sunrises to prepare. I must hunt and you must make piki bread and dry meat."

"Thank you, Lansa. I knew you would take me."

Lansa stood and waved to Moki. "Come, Moki, we have much to do. We travel to see your uncle!"

After two days of preparation, they were ready to leave. They left at sunrise so they could get a good start before the heat of the day. Lansa carried his bow and quiver, and both he and Moki carried packs of food and water. He made Kele a new crutch from the branch of a strong oak tree. He padded the top with rabbit fur and covered it with deerskin. It fit snuggly under her arm and gave her good support. He knew the trip would be hard on her, but he also knew she would never complain. He would have to watch her closely and stop when she tired.

Five days into their journey, as they walked along the base of a mesa, Moki stopped and covered his mouth and nose. "What is that smell?" he asked.

"I smell it too," Kele said. "It is awful."

"I have smelled it before when I was hunting, but never this strong," Lansa answered. "Something nearby has died and lies rotting in the sun."

They continued to move around the base of the mesa and suddenly came upon a hideous sight. Laying there in a small clearing were the bodies of several men. Some had arrows protruding from their bodies and others had gaping wounds in their heads. Dried blood mixed with the sand around them. They were all dead. Kele screamed, and Moki fell to his knees and vomited.

"Oh, Lansa, who could have done this?" Kele cried.

"I do not know," he stammered. Pointing back up the trail, he said, "Take Moki away from here. Go back to those trees and wait for me." Kele helped Moki to his feet, and they moved back up the trail to a small stand of piñon and juniper trees.

Lansa went in among the bodies, and it was then that he recognized the dead. They were Pavati's men. He looked around for Pavati, and he found him leaning against a rock. He had three arrows in his chest. There were no sign of their pouches or the baskets of food. It was evident that they had been robbed and killed for what they carried.

Who would do this? he thought.

Then he heard Moki call out, "Father, come!" And then he heard Kele scream.

Pulling his ax from his belt, he bolted toward the trees. He saw Kele with a frightened look on her face. A man stood behind her with a knife at her throat. Another man held Moki from behind with an arm around his throat. Filled with rage, Lansa lifted the ax to strike, and then he felt a sharp blow to the back of his head, and everything went black.

When he woke, his head was pounding and his mouth was dry. He tried to lift his hand, but found that he was bound to a tree. His hands were tied behind the tree and his feet were tied at the ankles. He struggled to free himself, and then he heard a voice. "Struggle if you wish, farmer, but you will not break your bonds."

Looking up he saw a man standing over him. He was like no man he had ever seen. He wore a feathered helmet and breastplate with an image of a horned serpent. In one hand he held a colorful shield and in the other a spear. The man turned to two warriors standing beside him. "Take him," he ordered.

They cut the thongs holding Lansa's hands and legs and roughly pulled him to his feet. Lansa's head throbbed, and he became dizzy. He lost his balance, stumbling as he was pushed along. Putting their arms under Lansa's, the warriors pulled and dragged him some distance and then threw him hard to the ground. Lansa came up spitting dirt and blood. He shook his head to clear his vision and looked around. Kele and Moki were standing nearby. Kele tried to come to him, but a guard standing behind her, grabbed her by the hair pulled her back. She stifled a small cry.

"Stay where you are!" the guard said.

A man sitting in a throne-like chair, wearing a beautiful red robe adorned with the bluish-green stones, looked down on Lansa and said, "Tezcatlipoca truly is a generous god. He has delivered my enemies to my feet. First, he brought word to me that Honaw, the impudent boy, who thought himself a god, sits as Tiyamunyi of White House, and now he has delivered these worthless creatures to me. I did not think I would ever see you again, Lansa."

Lansa looked at the man, struggling to focus his eyes. Suddenly he recognized who he was looking at. "Istaga?" he asked. "How can it be?"

Speaking to his warriors, Istaga raised his arms and said, "Behold, the murderer of my only son, his adulteress wife, and their bastard son." The warriors laughed and shouted insults at the captives.

Facing Lansa, Istaga sneered. "Yes, Lansa, I have returned as a high priest of mighty Tezcatlipoca. I have come to take my rightful place as ruler of this land. The people of Sun Father are weak. They scatter like turkeys when we approach. I am not surprised, since all they have is that cowardly Honaw to guide them. The warriors of Tezcatlipoca have swept through these lands like the wind blowing through the grass. We have crushed all who follow Sun Father, and now we go to White House where we will trample Honaw and his people under our feet! Your beloved Sun Father has lost his power. No one can stand before us! Honaw will grovel at my feet before I put the blade to his chest," he said.

"Istaga, you were a worm that crawled on its belly in Chu'a Village, and you still crawl on your belly," Lansa said defiantly.

Istaga rose from his chair. "Silence him!" He bellowed.

A guard stepped forward and kicked Lansa hard under his chin. Blood spewed from his mouth, and he fell, landing on his back.

"Father!" Moki cried.

Istaga glared at his prisoners. "I am going to enjoy cutting your hearts out on the altar of Tezcatlipoca," he said menacingly.

"You would kill your own grandson?" Kele asked softly.

"Kele, no," Lansa said.

Moki stared up at his mother with a shocked look in his eyes. She put her hand on his shoulder to comfort him.

"What are you saying, you wretched woman?" Istaga demanded.

"It is true," she said. "Moki is the son of Chuchip. I was carrying your grandson when I fled Chu'a Village. When I told Lansa, I thought he would leave me on the trail to die. By all the gods, I wanted to die on the trail. But Lansa stood by me and took Moki for his own. So I ask again, would you kill your own grandson?"

"Take them away and bind them to a tree. We will sacrifice them to Tezcatlipoca at sunrise. Leave the boy," Istaga commanded.

A guard held Moki tight, and a tear ran down his cheek as he watched his parents being dragged away. Kele looked back at him. "Be strong, my son," she said.

"Stop your crying, boy. Come sit by me," Istaga commanded Moki.

Moki hesitated. He was afraid. One of the guards grabbed him by the arm and guided him to Istaga, pushing him down at Istaga's feet. "Now that I see your face, you do resemble my son Chuchip," Istaga said. "Your true father, Chuchip, was a brave man and great Moiety. You would have been proud of him; he cared very much for his people. What do you know of Chu'a Village?"

"I know that my great-grandfather, the wise Kwahu, was a great Moiety and that he fell from a cliff and was killed," Moki replied.

"You poor boy, Kele and Lansa have filled you with nothing but lies. I knew Kwahu well. He was a weak man who cared only for himself. The day he died was a blessing for the village."

"You are the liar!" Moki shouted defiantly. "My great-grandfather was a noble man, loved by all. My mother told me!"

"Uh," Istaga grunted. "Let me tell you about your mother. When she was married to my Chuchip, she was sneaking around behind his back. She was having a dishonorable relationship with your false father, Lansa. She and Lansa wanted to be together. That was all that mattered to them, so Lansa murdered my son and they ran away together. That is the truth of it! Did they ever talk of Chuchip?" Istaga asked the confused boy.

"No," Moki answered.

"Do you know why?" Istaga snapped.

Istaga answered the question before Moki had a chance to respond. Raising his voice in anger, he roared. "Because they were ashamed of what they had done! They were trying to hide from the truth! They were hiding from their evil past, and now I find their evil has no bounds! They not only murdered my son, but they took my unborn grandson from me. They thought they had escaped when they ran from Chu'a Village, like cowards, but I have found them, and they will pay for their sins!"

Moki again started to cry. "I cannot believe the words you say. My parents are not evil. They could not have done all those horrible things."

"Stop crying. Crying is a sign of weakness. You must learn to be strong. You will live with me, and you will learn to be strong. You are not responsible for the sins of your mother and Lansa. I hold nothing against you. I will be your teacher now, and as you grow older, you will understand. You must sleep now. We will talk more when the sun rises."

◆❖◆

Kele and Lansa were hung by their wrists from the branch of a strong tree. The thongs that bound their hands were pulled up tight so that only their toes touched the ground. The deerskin thongs cut onto their hands, and before long, blood ran down their arms and dripped to the ground. There they were left for the night.

Even though Lansa's face was battered and his lips inflamed, he turned to Kele and muttered, "Why did you do it, Kele? Why, now, did you decide to tell Moki of his real father? He will think I betrayed him, and he will hate me."

"It was the only way I could think of to keep him alive. They will kill us in the morning, but now that Istaga knows that his blood also runs in Moki's veins, he might spare him. You need not worry, my husband, Moki could never hate you. You are the only father he has ever known."

"I wish we could speak to him. I wish we could explain, but at sunrise, we will be dead. Poor Moki will never understand," he said.

Lansa passed out and hung limply from the branch. The pain in Kele's foot and leg was excruciating, but she did not cry out. Her mouth was so dry she could not swallow, but she did not ask for water. The warriors stood around a fire talking and laughing and paid little attention to them. Before long, everyone in camp was asleep.

Kele watched the moonrise and the stars fill the night sky. The fire in camp glowed red. She could hear the sounds of sleeping men. "I have faith, Sun Father." She prayed. "I know you have not forsaken us, but if it is our time, we will come to you with gladness in our hearts. It will be a joy to dwell with you and all our beloved ancestors. I have but one request: Spare Moki, Sun Father. Let him grow to be a man like his father. Let him know the joys of life."

She laid her head against her arm and tried to rest. Suddenly, she felt a hand from behind cover her mouth. "Quiet," a man whispered. "I am a friend."

The man cut the thong holding her and gently lowered her to the ground. Kele's arms ached, but it was a relief to be free. The man went to Lansa and cut him free from the branch. He supported Lansa so that he would not fall to the ground. Lansa stirred awake and began to fight, but Kele gently held his head and quietly said, "It is all right, Lansa. He is a friend."

The man gestured for them to follow him into the woods away from the camp. When they had traveled a good distance from the camp, they stopped and hid behind a large rock.

"I do not know who you are, friend, but I thank you for your kindness," Kele said.

Lansa stared at the man and then said, "I know you. You were with Pavati."

"Yes," the man said. "I was one of Pavati's men. My name is Catori. I was with Pavati when Istaga and his men swept down on us. Three of us were spared, all the rest were slain. They kept the three of us alive to carry their stolen goods. We have no time to talk, we must run. It will be daylight soon, and we must be far away by then."

"No, Lansa! We cannot leave without Moki. I will not go without our son!" Kele cried.

"Your son sleeps next to Istaga," Catori said. "We will all be captured if we go for him. We must leave now."

"Where are we to go?" Lansa asked.

"If we walk quickly to the west, we can reach White House in two sunrises. We will be safe there," Catori said.

"Kele, I must get you to White House. When I know you are safe, I will come back for Moki. I do not know how I will free him, but I promise I will bring him back," Lansa said.

"Oh, Lansa, I am so afraid." Kele moaned.

"We must go now!" Catori insisted.

"Let us go," Lansa said.

"I cannot move quickly," Kele said. "I will slow you down. I will stay."

"You will not!" Lansa commanded. "I will carry you."

Catori lifted Kele onto Lansa's back, and they ran west to White House.

◆◈◆

With a full moon to light their way, they ran for the rest of that night and almost all of the following day, stopping only to drink the brackish water that stood in a few of the washes. Lansa's whole body ached and his lungs burned, but he did not stop. Catori stopped periodically and checked to see if Istaga's warriors followed them from the east. All through the day, he saw no sign of them. Finally as the sun was setting, Lansa could run no more. He needed to rest.

"I must rest for a while. How far to White House?" he asked Catori.

"We will rest here until the moon rises high in the sky, and then we will start again. If all goes well, we should reach White House by midmorning," Catori answered. "You and Kele sleep now. I will keep watch," he added.

Before long, Kele and Lansa were sleeping soundly. Catori climbed a small hill where he had a clear view to the east. He did not expect to see Istaga's warriors, but he watched just in case. He was very exhausted, though, and in time, his eyes grew heavy. He fought sleep with all his might, but he could not stay awake. He dropped off to sleep with his chin on his chest.

When he awoke, the sun was up and shining brightly. *Oh no,* he thought. *We have slept through the night!*

Frantically, he looked to the east, and in the distance, he saw men running. They were Istaga's men. Quickly Catori ran down the hill.

"Wake up!" he yelled to Lansa and Kele. "The warriors are coming! We must run for our lives!"

Lansa and Kele woke with a start. Catori lifted Kele onto Lansa's back, and they swiftly began to travel west. Again, Catori stopped to check to the east, and every time, he could see Istaga's men getting closer.

By midday, they were only a few miles from White House, but the warriors were now almost on top of them. Pointing to the northeast, Catori said, "The East Road leading to White House lies just beyond those low hills. Run with all your strength, Lansa. I will let them see me and turn them away from your path. They will follow me to the southwest."

"I cannot let you do that," Lansa said. "It will put you in danger. They could catch you."

"They will not catch me, my friend. I am much too fast for them," Catori replied.

"Please, Catori, stay with us," Kele pleaded.

Gently pushing them to go, Catori said, "We do not have time to argue. I will see you in White House." With that, he ran away to the south.

Lansa gathered all his strength and pushed hard for the East Road. Kele peered to the south in hopes of seeing Catori moving away. As they reached the top of a rise, she saw Catori running, but Istaga's men were close behind him. "Stop, Lansa!" she yelled. Pointing to southeast, she said, "Look! There is Catori. The warriors are almost on him!"

They watched in horror as one of the warriors notched an arrow in his bow and let fly. The arrow struck Catori in the back, knocking him forward and down a hill. Istaga's men gathered around him and struck him with clubs and axes.

Kele started to cry. "We barely knew the man, but yet he called us 'friend.' He gave his life for us, Lansa," she said through her tears.

"We will remember him in our prayers. He lives with the ancestors now; there he will receive his reward. We must not let his sacrifice be in vain. Look! There is the East Road. We are almost to White House."

◈◈◈

Honaw sat under the ramada outside his chambers with Alo and a group of children all around him. The children listened wide-eyed as he told them about Spider Grandmother and the Creation Story.

Suddenly, Choovio, Niman Moiety of House of the Sun, came running into the plaza. "Honaw, come quickly, visitors have arrived on the East Road, a man and woman! The woman says she is your sister!"

"My sister Kele?" he said to himself. Lenmana had come out of the chamber when she heard the shouting and stood next to Honaw.

"What is it, Honaw? What is going on?" she asked.

"Choovio says my sister is here," he said in a stunned voice.

He and Lenmana ran toward the steps that exited the plaza. Before they had covered half the distance, they saw Lansa enter the plaza, carrying Kele in his arms. They both rushed to him, and as Lansa handed Kele's limp body to Honaw, he said, "We have traveled far. Kele ..." Then he collapsed to his knees, too exhausted to utter another word.

Honaw carried Kele into his chamber in House of the Sun. Lenmana and Choovio helped Lansa to his feet and assisted him as they followed. They gently laid them both on bed mats. Kele was unconscious, and Lansa was too weak to talk. Lenmana went right to work cooling them with wet towels, giving them sips of water, and checking them for wounds.

Kele came to when Lenmana applied the towel to her forehead. She looked at Honaw. "Honaw, is that you? Oh, my little brother, it is so good to ..." Her voice trailed off.

"Do not speak now," Honaw said. "Just rest, we will have time later."

Lansa tried to lift his head as he struggled to speak. "Honaw, we need to warn you. White House is in danger." He had no more strength. His head fell back on the bed mat and he passed out.

"This is my sister Kele and her husband, Lansa," Honaw said to Lenmana. "I have spoken of them. It has been ten growing seasons since I saw them last. I was just a small boy. I did not even know if they still lived."

"They are both very weak from exhaustion," Lenmana said. "Let them rest and they will recover."

Honaw turned to Choovio. "You say they entered from the East Road?" he asked.

"Yes, the big man carried her in his arms. We could see that his strength was almost gone, and we tried to help by taking her, but he would not allow it. He insisted he carry her himself. He just told us that she was your sister, and that they must speak to you," Choovio answered.

"That sounds like the Lansa I remember," Honaw said.

Kele and Lansa slept all through the night, and Honaw and Lenmana sat by their side. Lenmana wiped Kele's and Lansa's faces with cool towels as Honaw told her stories of when they were children in Chu'a Village.

When Kele and Lansa awoke the next morning, they were still weak but feeling much better. Lenmana fixed them a hearty breakfast of deer meat stew and corn bread, and they ate as they talked of many things.

"Where are Mother and Father and Sihu?" Kele asked.

"I am sorry to tell you, Kele," Honaw said. "Father and Sihu were killed in a flood that destroyed Chu'a Village, and Mother died on the journey to White House. I did not understand what killed Mother until I met Lenmana. She explained to me that Mother died of a disease caused by an insect that burrows under the skin and forces its poison into the body. Mother had red spots all over her, and a terrible fever ravaged her body. The poison took two days to take her, so she did not suffer long."

Crying, Kele said, "I hoped I could see them all again, but I take comfort knowing they are all together with Grandfather and the ancestors. I am glad I still have you, Honaw."

"What of my mother, Honaw?" Lansa asked.

"Again, I am afraid I have bad news. Your mother died when she left the safety of her house during a terrible snowstorm. She ventured out to gather firewood and could not find her way back. She froze in the snow."

"Kele and I were also caught in a snowstorm. I almost lost her in the same way as Mother. It is strange, but in a dream, I saw Mother sitting in the snow. When I asked her why she was sitting in the snow, she smiled at me and thanked me for coming back to take care of her. Now I believe Sun Father was telling me she had gone to live with the ancestors."

"Many things have changed since we were young in Chu'a Village," Honaw said.

He then told Kele and Lansa how he came to be Tiyamunyi of White House and how thankful he was to Sun Father for bringing Lenmana into his life. Lenmana introduced Alo to them, and he repeated the Creation Story his father taught him. Alo impressed Kele and Lansa.

Lansa spoke of their farm along the river, and Kele told them about Moki and the fight with the wolves. She said her foot was painful and bothersome, but she had learned to live with it.

"Where is Moki now?" Lenmana asked.

"Moki is the prisoner of Istaga," Lansa answered.

"Istaga? You cannot mean the Istaga of Chu'a Village," Honaw exclaimed.

"Yes, he leads a band of the warriors who have come from the south, beyond the land of Sun Father. These warriors follow a horned serpent god they call Tezcatlipoca. They murder, pillage, and make human sacrifices to their god. White House is in danger. Istaga and his warriors are at your doorstep. He hates you, Honaw, and he means to kill you and enslave your people."

"Indeed, much has changed. We have heard that warriors from the south were raiding villages, but I had no idea they were coming here," Honaw said in a concerned voice.

"They are brutal, merciless warriors, Honaw. They killed Pavati and most of his men," Lansa added.

"We wondered why Pavati and his men had not returned. We were worried about them, and now I see we had good reason," Honaw responded.

Lansa related the tale. "We found the place where Pavati and his men were killed. It was an awful sight. That is where Istaga's warriors captured us. Istaga took Moki, and his men hung Kele and me by our wrists from a branch of a tree. They meant to sacrifice us to their god Tezcatlipoca, but Catori, one of Pavati's men, cut us free and we ran here to White House."

"We know Catori. He is a good man. Did he return to White House with you?" Lenmana asked.

"No, he was killed on the trail by Istaga's men. He gave his life to save Lansa and me," Kele sadly replied.

"You must prepare to defend White House, Honaw. Istaga and his warriors will be here soon. You must be ready to fight," Lansa exclaimed.

"We are not warriors, Lansa. We are peaceful farmers and masons. The men of White House do not know how to make war," Honaw replied.

"Honaw, you have but two choices. Either you prepare to defend White House or see your people be forced to denounce Sun Father and be enslaved," Lansa said harshly.

Kele chided Lansa for being disrespectful. "Lansa, you are talking to the Tiyamunyi of White House."

Lansa lowered his voice. "I am sorry I did not mean—"

"No, you are right, Lansa. Maybe you could prepare the men to fight," Honaw said.

"I will help, but it will have to wait until I return. I leave tonight to rescue our son," Lansa responded.

"How will you rescue him, one man against so many?" Honaw asked.

"I do not know, but I must try," Lansa answered. "I will assist you, but only you can lead the people, Honaw. You must lead them against this dark evil. White House has stood for generations. You cannot let it fall. You must find a way," Lansa said.

"I fear I do not have the knowledge," Honaw said.

"Your family has faith in you, and I know the people have faith in you. Together we will find a way," Lansa replied.

When Istaga learned that Kele and Lansa had escaped, he flew into a rage. He cursed the guards who were supposed to be guarding them. He ordered the guards killed, but Zaca stepped in and forbid it, saying that they needed every man for coming battles.

With eyes bulging and his body trembling with rage, Istaga stood before his men and bellowed, "Warriors of Tezcatlipoca, it is time we attack White House, kill my sworn enemy, Honaw, and make his people grovel at our feet. They are weak; their false god Sun Father is weak; they will fall before us like leaves falling from a tree!"

The warriors roared their approval until Zaca stepped forward. "Wait!" he commanded. The warriors quieted and Zaca continued. "Istaga, you gave us your word that when we had recovered our strength and attained more wealth than we had ever known, we would return to the land of Tonatiuh and crush our enemies there! Well, we are once again strong and we already have more wealth then we thought possible. It is time to return home and destroy our hated foes. The Tiyamunyi you speak of has done us no harm. He is not our enemy. Why should we care about him and his farmers?"

As if a man possessed, his face contorted with madness, Istaga screeched, "He has done me great harm! Have I not kept my word? Are you not once again strong? You just said that you have more wealth than you thought possible, but do you not want this wealth to continue into the future? There are untold amounts of food, copper, exquisite shells from distant seas, and precious stones in White House, enough to last a lifetime. When we conquer White House, we will control the land from here to Tonatiuh and beyond. We will be able to return each year and replenish our riches many times over. I promise after we conquer White House, we will return to Tonatiuh wealthy men, and we will be able to destroy our enemies just as we have destroyed all who have stood in our way! What say you, warriors of Tezcatlipoca?"

Again, a great roar came from the warriors, but once again, Zaca quieted them. "We will go with you, Istaga, but you remember what we told you when we started. If you lead us into defeat or break your word, you will suffer the consequences."

"It is impossible for the mighty warriors of Tezcatlipoca to be defeated by a mere rabble of farmers!" Istaga responded.

Kele and Lansa's escape did provide Istaga with an unexpected opportunity. With their escape, he thought he might have a way to drive a wedge between Moki and his parents. Istaga spoke to the scared and confused Moki. "Your parents are gone, Moki; they have abandoned you. They crawled away in the night like rats to save their own skins. I told you they were cowards. They cared more for themselves than they did their own son. It is a good thing you have me to take care of you and make you strong."

"I cannot believe my mother and father would leave me," Moki said dejectedly.

"Lansa is not your father!" Istaga snapped. "He lied to you all these years. It is important to know where you come from so that you can take your rightful place in the world. You are my grandson, the son of Chuchip, and all the lies in the world cannot change that. Your rightful place is at my right hand. I will teach you so that one day you will take my place and command the warriors of Tezcatlipoca!"

Istaga then stormed away, leaving Moki alone with his thoughts, *Why has my mother abandoned me? Why has she left me alone? Has the only father I have ever known lied to me, and did he actually murder my true father?* It was all too much for his young mind to comprehend. His head was spinning with fear and confusion. He buried his face in his hands and cried.

Kele walked with Lansa along the path leading to the east exit of White House. It was dark and only the moon lit their way. Lansa carried his bow and quiver of arrows; he had his knife and ax tucked into his belt. He packed lightly so that he could travel quickly.

"My dear husband, I am so afraid. What can you do against so many warriors?" she asked trembling.

Lansa held her close. "I will find a way, Kele. I promise you that I will bring our son back. Sun Father is watching over me; I feel his presence. I am confident I will not die this night."

Kele kissed him and said, "Come back to me, my love."

"I will be back, and I will have our son," he said. She watched as he slipped away into the darkness.

Kele's heart pounded in her chest and her hands trembled as she wrapped a rabbit skin blanket around her shoulders. She knew she would not sleep this night, so she sat down next to the path where Lansa left her and awaited his return. The night wore on and the moon rose high in the sky. The darkness turned the minutes to hours. Straining her ears and peering into the blackness, she waited.

She prayed. "Please, Sun Father, watch over Lansa. Keep him safe and help him to bring our son home."

Suddenly she heard movement along the path and then a faint voice. "Kele, help me. I am wounded." Jumping to her feet, she rushed down the path and found Lansa laying beside the trail with a spear protruding from his shoulder and blood covering his shirt. She knelt down, lifted his head, and rested it in her lap.

"Oh, my sweet Lansa," she cried. She reached to pull the spear from his shoulder.

"No, leave it," Lansa moaned. "I have tried. It will not move. Go for help. Get Honaw and Lenmana. They will help me to House of the Sun."

"I cannot leave you, Lansa!" she said as she cried.

"Go now," Lansa, said. "Do not worry. It is not yet time for me to live with the ancestors." Kele gently laid his head on the blanket, took up her crutch, and moved along the path as fast as she could.

Curse this worthless leg of mine. An old woman could move faster, she thought.

When she finally reached House of the Sun, she immediately went to where Honaw and Lenmana were sleeping. "Honaw!" she cried, trying to catch her breath. "Wake up, my brother, Lansa is hurt. He needs your help!"

Honaw and Lenmana woke in a fright. "What has happened, Kele?"

"Lansa is badly wounded. He has a spear lodged in his shoulder, and he is bleeding badly. He lies next to the path at the east entrance," she explained.

Lenmana grabbed her medicine pouch, and she and Honaw rushed for the door. Kele tried to follow, but her legs would not hold her. "Stay here, my sister, we will bring him back," Honaw said. Kele collapsed on a bed mat, exhausted.

As Honaw and Lenmana rushed across the plaza, Lenmana turned to Honaw. "Wake Choovio. We will need help carrying him," she said. Lenmana continued on ahead as Honaw went to Choovio's chamber. She found Lansa lying next to the path right where Kele said he would be. He was barely conscious. She inspected the wound. Lifting him slightly, she found that the spear had gone through his shoulder and that the spear point was protruding out the back. Honaw and Choovio soon arrived and knelt next to Lansa.

"Pull it out, pull it out," Lansa groaned.

"No, not here," Lenmana said. "Dirt will get into the wound. We must get him back to House of the Sun. Quickly, lift him and carry him back," she directed.

When they reached House of the Sun, they laid Lansa on a bed mat covered with a soft, clean sheepskin. Kele knelt by Lansa's side and wiped the sweat from his brow. Lansa opened his eyes and smiled at her. Again, Kele began to cry.

"The spear is tightly embedded in his shoulder. It will take all your strength to pull it out," Lenmana said to Honaw. She instructed Choovio to hold Lansa's torso down as she held his legs. "Try to pull it out with one swift jerk," she said. Honaw stood above Lansa and gripped the lance with both hands. With all his strength, he jerked the spear upward, dislodging it from Lansa's shoulder. Lansa screamed in pain and passed out.

Lenmana bathed the wound with warm water and applied a poultice to both the front and backsides. "It is a clean wound. With time, and Earth Mother's help, he should recover," she told Kele.

Lansa slept for a while with Kele by his side. When he woke up, he related what had happened. "I found Istaga's camp. It lies on the plain just east of South Mesa. Watching the camp from behind some rocks, I saw Moki. He was alive and unharmed, but Istaga kept him close to his side. I was waiting for the camp to sleep, when a night guard surprised me. I slashed him across his face with my blade as he drove his lance into my shoulder. He screamed in pain, alerting the camp. I had to run for my life."

Looking at Kele, tears welled up in Lansa's eyes. "I am sorry, Kele. I promised to bring our son back and I failed. Just let me rest awhile, and I will go out again, but this time I will keep my word."

Stroking his brow, she said, "You did all that you could, Lansa. I am proud of your courage. You do not have to apologize to me." She bent down and kissed his forehead.

"Do not worry, my friend," Honaw said. "We will get your son back. I think we have just begun to deal with Istaga and his warriors."

The next morning when Choovio entered Honaw's chamber, he had a worried look on his face. "What troubles you, Choovio?"

"Three strangers have arrived on the Great North Road. They are fierce-looking men. They wear feathered helmets and carry spears and shields. They demand an audience with you, Honaw. They wait for you on the plaza," Choovio replied.

"Oh, Honaw, they are the warriors of Tezcatlipoca," Kele said with fear in her voice.

"Let us go and see what they want," Honaw calmly replied.

Honaw stepped out onto the plaza and faced the three men. The men were very tall and wore feathered helmets, towering over Honaw. They wore breastplates adorned with a horned serpent. Honaw stood resolutely before them; he was determined to show no fear.

"I am Honaw, Tiyamunyi of White House. You wish to speak to me?" he asked.

"We bring you a message from the great Istaga, high priest of Tezcatlipoca and commander of his warriors," one of them proclaimed.

"The great Istaga, you say? I knew Istaga when I was a boy. There was nothing great about him then. He was a simple Moiety, and not a very good one at that," Honaw said .

"I would suggest you watch your tongue, farmer. Insulting Istaga will only make matters worse for you," the warrior said.

Choovio stepped forward, "No one talks to our Tiyamunyi in such a manner! I suggest—"

"Calm yourself, Choovio. His words do not harm me. I am proud to call myself a farmer. But enough of this banter, deliver your message," Honaw said.

"The great Istaga demands that you denounce your Sun Father god and surrender yourself to him before the sun rises tomorrow. Your people must also denounce your false god and recognize the mighty Tezcatlipoca as the only true god. If you abide by Istaga's wishes, your people will be spared. We will enslave them, but at least they will be alive," the man declared.

"If I refuse Istaga's wishes?" Honaw asked.

"Then we will attack White House at dawn and kill as many of your people as we wish; the rest will be our slaves for the duration of their lives. As for you, you will be sacrificed to Tezcatlipoca because that is what he demands to keep the sun crossing the sky. You will be dead either way. You have until sunrise to give us your answer," the man replied.

With that, the three men formed themselves into a triangle with spears and shields up. They worked their way off the plaza and disappeared up the North Road.

Honaw sent runners to all the great houses, with instructions to tell the people to come to House of the Sun as quickly as possible. Very quickly, the plaza filled with people. Honaw stood on the terrace overlooking the crowd. "Good people of White House, hear me," he said. "A great evil has come to destroy our home. The warriors of Tezcatlipoca, under the command of a wicked man called Istaga, plan to attack White House at sunrise tomorrow. These men are fierce and brutal warriors who understand the ways of war!"

Many in the crowd cried out in fear. Mothers picked up their children and held them tight to their breasts. "What can we do, Honaw? How can we be saved?"

Honaw raised his hand to quiet the crowd. "We have a decision to make. Istaga is an old enemy. I knew him as a boy, and now he has returned to have his revenge. If I give myself to him before Sun Father shows his face in the eastern sky tomorrow, he will spare your lives. You will be forced to renounce Sun Father and become followers of their god Tezcatlipoca and be enslaved. The life you have built here in White House will be no more!"

"What of you, Honaw? What will happen to you?" the crowd called out.

"I will be sacrificed to their god and Istaga will have his revenge," he answered.

At this, the crowd became angry. "No, no!" they cried. "Tell us what to do, Honaw! How do we save White House?"

"I told you we have a decision to make. I can give myself up and you become slaves to the warriors of Tezcatlipoca, or we can fight this evil!" Honaw answered.

A hush came over the crowd. One of the men stepped forward. "We are a peaceful people, Honaw. Sun Father tells us that to kill another is the gravest of sins. How do we fight them? We have no weapons."

"I know we are a peaceful people," Honaw began. "None of you has ever raised a hand to another. I know that Sun Father prohibits the taking of a human life, but I believe we must look at this differently. What do you do when rats get into your corn bins or ravens land in your crop fields? You kill the rats and ravens to protect your food, because without food there will be no life. These bloodthirsty men and their evil god care nothing for life. They spill blood just to show how powerful they are, and to frighten good people so that they will obey. These men are less than human! They have come to destroy our way of life. They must be killed like rats and ravens. I believe that Sun Father will stand with us. He loves his people and will not let them perish from this land! What say you, good people? Do we fight to protect our beloved White House and our way of life, or do we let our land be overrun by vermin?"

"We fight, we fight!" the crowd roared.

Again, Honaw raised his hands and the crowd grew silent. "Then we must prepare," he said. "You say you have no weapons, but how do you kill the ravens in your fields? When I was a boy, I used a sling and many of you use one now to protect your fields. A sling is a weapon, and you are skilled in its use. Hunters, get your bows and quivers. Make sure your arrowheads are sharp. We must work quickly! Sun Father will help in this battle, but we must be ready by the time he sets in the western sky. Women, gather your children and enough food for the evening meal and assemble at the path to the North Mesa. Lenmana and my sister Kele will lead you to the top of North Mesa. You will be safe there until our task is complete. Men, gather what you need and return to the plaza. Hurry, we do not have much time!"

Soon after, the women and children gathered at the base of the North Mesa, and the men assembled on the plaza of House of the Sun. Honaw stood with Lenmana and Alo, where the trail led up to the top of North Mesa. "Take them to the House of the Northern Sky," he told Lenmana. "I will send a runner to you when it is over. If no one comes by morning, keep moving north to the mountains."

"Oh, how I wish none of this had come to pass, my husband. Why has Sun Father allowed these evil men into our midst?" Lenmana asked.

"As I have grown older, I have come to better understand Sun Father," Honaw said. "I do believe he is all-knowing, but now I have come to believe that he is not all-controlling. Some things are out of his hands. Some things he leaves for man to decide. He has taught all people to live the right way and maintain the balance in the world, but just as in the Third World, some people do not always listen. I do know that Sun Father will never let evil triumph over good. Evil may triumph in this battle, but it will not win the war. In the end, only the good will survive. Even if we are defeated today, the spirit of White House will endure. Good will endure. Maybe not here in our beautiful canyon, but it will endure somewhere. Do not worry just yet; we still may prevail this day."

"Oh, how I love you, Honaw," Lenmana said.

"I love you also," Honaw replied. "I have from the very first night when you gave me deer meat stew. Sun Father was smiling on me when you came into my life." He kissed her and held her close in a long embrace. Then picking up Alo, he said, "I will see you soon, son. You take care of your mother and always remember, I love you." He handed him to Lenmana, and she and Alo started up the trail to the top of North Mesa.

Kele knelt next to Lansa and held his hand tightly. "I cannot leave you, Lansa," she said.

"You must," Lansa replied. "I cannot climb with my shoulder wounded this way, and Lenmana will need your help to care for the women and children. Do not give up hope. I still may find a way to bring Moki back to us. Honaw is a wise man; he will help me."

"Lansa, I have loved you more and more every day since the time when you first smiled at me in the mountains. I do not know what I would do without you," Kele said.

"You will not have to do without me," Lansa replied. "Have faith in Sun Father and Earth Mother as you always have. We will come through this and you, Moki, and I will be together again. You must believe that in your heart. I promised you I would love you until the end of my days, and I mean to keep that promise. The end of my days has not come yet. Now go, Lenmana will be waiting for you." Kele leaned down and kissed him and then started for the North Mesa.

When the men assembled on the plaza, Honaw outlined his plan to defeat Istaga and his horde of killers. He stood on the terrace and addressed the men. "Brave men of White House, today we have a task before us that we hoped and prayed would never come. Today we must fight and we must kill to save our home and way of life. We cannot defeat Istaga's warriors in hand-to-hand fighting. They are much too skilled and much too experienced in that type of fighting. We must use weapons in which we are skilled. If you stand with courage and follow my commands, we may carry this day. We must walk to the House of Southern Sky!" Honaw said.

Honaw and his men ascended the South Mesa, and when they reached House of the Southern Sky, they turned to the east. Honaw halted his men short of the eastern edge of the mesa and summoned Choovio to accompany him to the very edge of the plateau. When they reached the edge, they looked down into the plain, and there they saw the warrior's camp, just as Lansa had described. Honaw looked to see the position of Sun Father in the sky. "This is just what I wanted. Go quickly, bring the men to this point," he said to Choovio.

When the men came up, Honaw set about positioning them along the edge of the mesa. He told them to crouch down so that the men in the camp would not see them. He sent runners up and down the line to tell the men not to let fly with their slings and arrows until he dropped his arms. Honaw told his men they must make sure every stone and arrow struck its target. Istaga's warriors must not reach the top of the mesa. "If the warriors reach the top of the mesa, we will all be killed," Honaw reminded his little army of farmers.

When his men were in position, Honaw checked the position of Sun Father in the western sky. Sun Father was low on the horizon and shown directly behind his head. Honaw stood up and raised his hands above his head. "Istaga, you dog, Honaw is here to defy you. Come and do battle, you coward," he shouted in his loudest voice.

Istaga's warriors raised their eyes to the top of the mesa and looked directly into Sun Father's rays. Sun Father's brilliance blinded the warriors. "Climb the mesa and bring Honaw down to me!" Istaga bellowed to his men.

When Istaga's warriors started up the steep slope of the mesa, Honaw dropped his arms. Stones and arrows rained down on the warriors. Honaw's farmers and hunters were very skilled with their weapons. Great numbers of Istaga's warriors fell, mortally wounded, tumbling back down the steep embankment. Some of Istaga's archers tried to find targets, but when they looked up, Sun Father blinded them. Over one hundred warriors started up the slope to the top of the mesa, and when they were turned back, less than halfway to the top, only twenty-five bleeding and battered warriors remained. None of the farmers and hunters were killed or wounded. The men of White House stood, cheered, and gave thanks to Sun Father.

Suddenly, down in the plain a strong voice was heard. "Istaga, I have come for my son!" There, standing in the rays of the fading sun, stood Lansa, ax in hand.

Istaga had been sitting on his throne, holding Moki roughly by his side watching the debacle of the battle unfold before him. He pointed toward Lansa and screamed, "Kill him, kill him, I tell you!" The warriors who were left began to move reluctantly toward Lansa.

Zaca, with blood oozing from a wound on his forehead, commanded the warriors. "Stay where you are, men."

Istaga looked at Zaca with fear in his eyes. "I order you to kill him," Istaga repeated. Zaca just looked at his men and shook his head.

Lansa boldly walked into camp and stood before Istaga. He felt a presence beside him and looked over. There stood Honaw, shoulder-to-shoulder with him. The men of White House came down off the mesa and formed a circle around Zaca's men, slings loaded and arrows notched. "Step down from that chair," Lansa said. "I will not look up to the likes of you."

"I will not," Istaga said fearfully.

"Step down or I will have my warriors pull you down," Zaca said.

Istaga, still holding Moki tightly, stepped off the platform and stood facing Lansa and Honaw. "I have come for my son," Lansa said again.

"The boy wants to stay with me," Istaga said.

"Let him go!" Lansa demanded.

"He wants to stay with me, I tell you," Istaga said.

"Ask the boy what he wants. What say you boy, who will you go to?" Zaca asked.

Moki pulled away from Istaga and stood by Lansa. "You and I might have the same blood running in our veins, but you will never be my grandfather!" he said to Istaga defiantly. Reaching for Lansa's hand, he continued. "This is my father. He is the one who has taught me to live the right way. He is the one who loves me, and I love him." Even though it caused him pain, Lansa knelt and hugged his son. "I do love you, son," Lansa said.

"Moki, I command you—" Istaga started to say.

Zaca struck Istaga with his war club knocking him to his knees. Istaga groaned in pain, blood dripping from a wound on his head. "You have nothing more to say! Be silent!" Zaca said.

Looking toward Honaw, he continued. "You are the victor. We are your captives. We stand ready to be put to the knife."

"We are not like you," Honaw replied. "We have no desire to kill you. We are a peaceful people. We killed today because we were left no choice. We could not let White House and our way of life be destroyed, so we fought, and by the grace of Sun Father, we were victorious. Here are our only demands. You must leave your weapons of war. You will no longer be in need of them. You may take bows and quivers so you can hunt. You must also leave all that you pillaged and stole. Besides, there are so few of you now you could not possibly carry it all. We will redistribute it back to the people. You will not return home wealthy men, but you will be alive. Go, return to your land, and give thanks to the only true god, Sun Father."

Pointing to Istaga, Zaca asked, "What of this one?"

"We want nothing more to do with him. You can do with him what you wish," Honaw answered.

Looking about at his men, Honaw commanded them. "Men of White House, we are finished here. Let us go home!"

Honaw, Lenmana, Lansa, and Kele stood on the terrace watching Moki and Alo play on the plaza. There was great celebration and feasting in the days after the battle. Sun Father had delivered White House from a terrible evil, and the people rejoiced. "White House has seen many changes since Honovi's death," Honaw said. "Since the council honored me by appointing me Tiyamunyi, I have been acting as both Tiyamunyi and Soyala Moiety of the Spider Clan. I agree with wise Qaletaga that it is a heavy burden to carry."

Turning to Kele, he continued. "Lenmana and I were hoping that you and Lansa might stay here in White House with us. Your Moki will soon be of age to become the Soyala Moiety. The blood of Grandfather, the great Soyala Moiety of Chu'a Village, runs in his veins, so the lineage of the Spider Clan would continue. Until the time he comes of age, I will instruct him the way that Grandfather instructed me. He will make a fine Soyala Moiety.

"Before you make your decision. I need to speak with Lansa about another matter." He turned to Lansa. "With Pavati's death, House of the Sun is left without a cacique. I know that you are a very good farmer. You know much about crop fields and irrigation. You also learned much about food distribution from my father, Tocho. If you would remain here with us, I would like to appoint you cacique of House of the Sun. What say you, Kele? What say you, Lansa? Will you stay and live with us in House of the Sun?"

Lansa looked at Kele and asked, "What say you, my wife? Will you be happy here in White House, or do we go back to our farm by the river?"

"Belonging to the Spider Clan and being a granddaughter of the wise Kwahu is a great honor, but having my son be the Soyala Moiety of the Spider Clan at White House is a blessing I could not have imagined. Besides, because of my foot, it is becoming harder and harder to work in the fields. If Lansa is willing, we will stay," Kele answered.

"What say you, Lansa?" Honaw asked again.

"I do not deserve such words of praise, and I am just a simple farmer, but if you have that much confidence in me and are willing to honor my son in such a way, I will be pleased to stay in White House."

"You will live with us, here in House of the Sun!" Lenmana exclaimed. "I have never had a sister. I am glad that Sun Father has blessed me with one now. We will watch our sons grow into fine men and we will help our husbands build an even more magnificent White House for the glory of Sun Father." Joyous times had come to White House, and Sun Father was pleased.

After a few sunrises, Honaw and Lansa returned to the battlefield. They found many, many graves. They also found a chair with a staff driven through its seat. On the end of the staff, there was an impaled head. They removed the head from the staff and buried both it and the staff. Then they returned to White House.

EPILOGUE

Honaw ruled White House, with Lansa as his cacique, for another fifteen growing seasons. It was an era of peace and prosperity for White House. Under Honaw's rule and Lansa's supervision, White House grew to the height of its glory.

Kele's leg continued to get worse, and after only two growing seasons, an infection settled in the limb, and she finally lost her battle with the wolves. Regrettably, she did not live to see her son become Soyala Moiety of the Spider Clan in White House.

Lansa remarried and had a second son. Moki loved his new brother, and they were very close. Lansa went to live with the ancestors in the year 1081. He had seen forty-three growing seasons. He died peacefully on his bed mat and was buried next to Kele in the burial chamber of House of the Sun. Honaw saw forty-five growing seasons. He died in the year 1089. Lenmana went to live with him in the land of the ancestors the next year. The people said that Sun Father blessed Honaw with a long life because of his devotion and steadfast teaching of how to live the right way and keep balance in all things. Upon Honaw's death, his son, Alo, became Tiyamunyi of White House. He and Moki remained close and ruled White House together for many years.

Between the years 1090–1095, a severe drought struck the basin. Food was in very short supply and the people of White House suffered greatly. The people grew desperate in their hunger, and raiding parties crossed the land, pillaging villages for food. With great sadness, Alo decided it was time to abandon White House. He and Moki led their people north, but that is another story.

Author's Note

Light in the Darkness is a work of historical fiction. Character names and places are taken from the Hopi and Toltec languages. A pronunciation key and translation to English are located in the glossary. The great houses of Chaco Canyon did exist and their ruins still stand today, but the names of the great houses are imaginary. There were many outlier great houses, but there was no Chu'a Village. A volcano did erupt in northern Arizona sometime between 1060 and 1100, covering the Chaco Canyon area with a layer of ash. The remnant of the volcano is now Crater Lake, Arizona. In addition, archeologists did find two male bodies buried side by side in an inner chamber of Pueblo Bonito ruins in Chaco Canyon. These men were definitely elites because they were found with a large amount of turquoise, copper bells, and the bones of several macaws. The Toltec did have a sun god they called Tonatiuh, and there were battles fought between warrior-cults in northern Mexico. One of these cults did follow the horned serpent god, Tezcatlipoca, but there was no recorded battle between the Chacoan people and the warriors of Tezcatlipoca. The land of the San Juan Basin looked much like it does today, and the ancient farmers of Chaco depended heavily on rainfall and run-off water in the washes.

GLOSSARY

- Ahote (ah-HOE-tay) – in Hopi, means restless one
- Alo (AH-low) – in Hopi, means spiritual guide
- Birds on the plaza – parrots and macaws
- Black-and-red stones – obsidian
- Bluish-green stones – turquoise gemstones
- Cacique (kay-SEEK) – first assistant, a secular leader in charge of food distribution and construction
- Catori (cah-TORE-ee) – in Hopi, means spirit
- Cheveyo (cheh-VAY-yoe) – in Hopi, means spirit warrior
- Choovio (CHOE-vee-oh) – in Hopi, means antelope
- Chu'a (CHEW-ah) – in Hopi, means snake
- Chuchip (CHEW-cheep) – in Hopi, means deer spirit
- Hisatsinom (he-SAHT-see-nome) – Hopi name for the Ancient Puebloans
- Honani (hoe-NAH-nee) – in Hopi, means badger
- Honaw (HOE-nah) – in Hopi, means bear
- Honovi (hoe-NOE-vee) – in Hopi, means strong deer
- House of the Antelope – the ruins of Pueblo Arroyo in Chaco Canyon
- House of the Bow – the ruins of Chetro Ketl in Chaco Canyon

- House of the Northern Sky – the ruins of Pueblo Alto in Chaco Canyon
- House of the Rabbit – the ruins of Hungo Pavi in Chaco Canyon
- House of the Southern Sky – the ruins of Tsin Kletzin in Chaco Canyon
- House of the Sun – the ruins of Pueblo Bonito in Chaco Canyon
- House of the Western Sky – the ruins of Penasco Blanco in Chaco Canyon
- Istaga (EE-stah-gah) – in Hopi, means coyote man
- Kele (KEE-lee) – in Hopi, means sparrow
- Kokopelli (ko-ko-PELL-ee) – the little god who traveled through the villages playing his flute to change winter to spring and ensure successful crops
- Kwahu (QUAH-hoo) – in Hopi, means eagle
- Lansa (LAHN-sah) – in Hopi, means lance
- Lenmana (len-MAH-nah) – in Hopi, means flute girl
- Machakw (mah-CHAH-quah) – in Hopi, means horny toad
- Makya (MAHK-yah) – in Hopi, means eagle hunter
- Mansi (MAHN-see) – in Hopi, means plucked flower
- Mochni (MOCK-nee) – in Hopi, means talking bird
- Moiety (MOY-eh-tee) – two leaders designated by lineage and seasonal rotations
- Moki (MOE-kee) – in Hopi, means deer
- Mount of the Dagger of Light – Fajada Butte in Chaco Canyon
- Muna (MEW-nah) – the ruins of Guadalupe in eastern New Mexico
- Niman (NEE-man) – the summer solstice
- Nova (NOE-vah) – in Hopi, means clear water
- Qaletaga (kwah-leh-TAH-gah) – in Hopi, means guardian of the people
- Shiny yellow stones – gold nuggets

- Sihu (SEE-hoo) – in Hopi, means flower
- Sipapu (SEE-pah-poo) – passageway from the Third World to the Fourth World
- Soyala (soy-YAH-lah) – the winter solstice
- Takala (tah-KAH-lah) – the ruins of Gallina Towers in central New Mexico
- Tezcatlipoca (tes-CAHT-leh-poe-cah) – the horned serpent god of the Toltec who kept the sun moving across the sky
- Tiyamunyi (tee-yah-MUNE-yee) – a divinely appointed religious leader and supreme secular leader of the people
- Tocho (TOE-choe) – in Hopi, means mountain lion
- Tonatiuh (toe-nah-TEE-ah) – sun god of the Toltec and an area in northern Mexico in the time of the Toltec
- Tuwa (TOO-wah) – in Hopi, means earth
- White fiber plant – cotton
- White House – Chaco Canyon and the surrounding basin
- White trees with yellow leaves – aspen trees
- Yamka (YAHM-kah) – in Hopi, means blossom
- Zaca (ZAH-kah) – taken from the name of Moctezuma's brother in the time of the Aztecs

BIBLIOGRAPHY

Barnes, F. A., and Michaelene Pendelton. *Canyon Country Prehistoric Indians: Their Cultures, Ruins, Artifacts, and Rock Art.* Salt Lake City: Wasatch Mountain Publishing, 1979.

Childs, Craig. *House of Rain: Tracking a Vanished Civilization Across the American Southwest.* New York: Little, Brown, 2007.

Eidt, Jack. "Soyal Ceremony: Hopi Kachinas Dance at Winter Solstice." Last modified December 22, 2011. http://www .wilderutopia.com.

Fagan, Brian. *Chaco Canyon: Archaeologists Explore the Lives of an Ancient Society.* New York: Oxford University Press, 2005.

Fajada Butte: Solstice Marker. Oro Valley, AZ: Western National Parks Association, 2002.

Frazier, Kendrick. *People of Chaco: A Canyon and its Culture.* W. W. Norton, 2005.

"Hopi Cycle of the Year." Last modified December 20, 2013. http:// www.crossingworlds.com/articles/hopicycle.html.

"Hopi Prayer—Do not stand at my grave and weep ..." Last modified September 6, 2003. http://www.democraticunderground.com/discuss/duboard.

Kantner, John. *Ancient Puebloan Southwest*. Cambridge: Cambridge University Press, 2004.

LeBlanc, Steven A. *Prehistoric Warfare in the American Southwest* Salt Lake City, UT: University of Utah Press, 1999.

Lander, Debi. *Hopi Traditional Piki Bread*. Access date 2012. http://www.experiencehopi.com/piki-bread-making.html.

Lekson, Stephen. *A History of the Ancient Southwest*. Santa Fe, NM: School for Advanced Research Press, 2008.

Lekson, Stephen H. *The Chaco Meridian: Centers of Political Power in the Ancient Southwest*. New York: Alta Mira Press, 1999.

McNeley, James Kale. *Holy Wind in Navajo Philosophy*. Tucson, AZ: University of Arizona Press, 1981.

Nez, Chester, and Judith Schiess Avila. *Code Talker: The First and Only Memoir by One of the Original Navajo Code Talkers of WWII*. New York: Berkley, 2011.

Roberts, David. *In Search of the Old Ones*. New York: Simon & Schuster, 1996.

"Rocky Mountain Spotted Fever." Last modified April 30, 2014. http://www.onhealth.com/rocky_mountain_spotted_fever/article.htm.

Stuart, David E. *Anasazi America*. Albuquerque, NM: University of New Mexico Press, 2000.

Van Dyke, Ruth M. *The Chaco Experience: Landscape and Ideology at the Center Place*. Santa Fe, NM: School for Advanced Research Press, 2008.

Walker, Glenn. *Kokopelli Legends & Lore*. Last modified February 4, 2014. http://www.indigenouspeople.net/kokopelli.htm.